W9-BEJ-653

Praise for the previous novels of Jodi Thomas

"Compelling and beautifully written, it is exactly the kind of heart-wrenching, emotional story one has come to expect from Jodi Thomas." —DEBBIE MACOMBER, #1 *New York Times* bestselling author

"Will warm readers with its huge heart and gentle souls." —*Library Journal*

"Thomas's memorable, refreshingly candid characters are sure to resonate, especially the strong female protagonists. Series fans will be delighted." —*Publishers Weekly*

"A beautiful love letter to the power of female friendship, and when you read it, you'll feel like you've come home. Perfect for fans of Debbie Macomber and Nina George." —ROBYN CARR, #1 *New York Times* bestselling author

"Tender, heartfelt and wonderful. Jodi Thomas's beautiful writing and her compelling, vivid characters will work their way straight into your heart and stay there forever. I loved every word." —RAEANNE THAYNE, *New York Times* bestselling author

"You can count on Jodi Thomas to give you a satisfying and memorable read." —CATHERINE ANDERSON, *New York Times* bestselling author

"Highly recommended." —*Library Journal* (starred review)

Kensington books by Jodi Thomas

Someday Valley Novels
Strawberry Lane
The Wild Lavender Bookshop

Honey Creek Novels
Breakfast at the Honey Creek Café
Picnic in Someday Valley
Dinner on Primrose Hill
Sunday at the Sunflower Inn

Historical Romance
Beneath the Texas Sky

Anthologies:
The Wishing Quilt
A Texas Kind of Christmas
The Cowboy Who Saved Christmas
Be My Texas Valentine
Give Me a Cowboy
Give Me a Texan
Give Me a Texas Outlaw
Give Me a Texas Ranger
One Texas Night
A Texas Christmas

Strawberry Lane

JODI THOMAS

ZEBRA BOOKS
Kensington Publishing Corp.
www.kensingtonbooks.com

ZEBRA BOOKS are published by

Kensington Publishing Corp.
900 Third Avenue
New York, NY 10022

Copyright © 2023 by Jodi Thomas

This book is a work of fiction. Names, characters, businesses, organizations, places, events, and incidents either are the product of the author's imagination or are used fictitiously. Any resemblance to actual persons, living or dead, events, or locales is entirely coincidental.

All rights reserved. No part of this book may be reproduced in any form or by any means without the prior written consent of the Publisher, excepting brief quotes used in reviews.

To the extent that the image or images on the cover of this book depict a person or persons, such person or persons are merely models, and are not intended to portray any character or characters featured in the book.

If you purchased this book without a cover you should be aware that this book is stolen property. It was reported as "unsold and destroyed" to the Publisher and neither the Author nor the Publisher has received any payment for this "stripped book."

All Kensington titles, imprints, and distributed lines are available at special quantity discounts for bulk purchases for sales promotion, premiums, fund-raising, and educational or institutional use.

Special book excerpts or customized printings can also be created to fit specific needs. For details, write or phone the office of the Kensington Sales Manager: Kensington Publishing Corp., 900 Third Avenue, New York, NY 10022. Attn. Sales Department. Phone: 1-800-221-2647.

Zebra and the Z logo Reg. U.S. Pat. & TM Off.

First Zebra Books trade paperback printing: May 2023
First Zebra Books mass market printing: April 2024

ISBN-13: 978-1-4201-5508-2
ISBN-13: 978-1-4201-5509-9 (eBook}

10 9 8 7 6 5 4 3 2 1

Printed in the United States of America

For my family
who are always there to help

Prologue

The Will

A storm rattled the windows of the small Honey Creek Hospital, destroying any sense of calm within. Jackson Landry stood beside the bed, wishing he were anywhere but here. His tall, lanky frame didn't belong in the little square room any more than his new occupation fit him. Being called a lawyer made him feel like he was wearing another man's clothes.

"This mattress is too hard," Jamie Ray Morrell complained to his lawyer in a half-drunk whine. "I thought hospital beds were supposed to be comfortable. They cost enough. I ain't paying for the whole night. I didn't get here until after midnight."

"Mr. Morrell, I'm not involved in hospital furnishing or billing. I'm your attorney." Jackson lifted his briefcase as if showing proof of his new title. "Now, we need to get down to the topic of your will. You may not have much time left."

Jackson kept his voice low, hoping to sound older than twenty-nine.

The old guy reached for his cigarettes. Camels, no filter. "Didn't know they still made Camels. . . ." Jackson shook his head. "Never mind. Irrelevant. You can't smoke in here, Mr. Morrell. I don't think Dr. Henton would approve, and I saw the no-smoking sign when I ran through the emergency entrance."

"Jackson, you're no more fun than your dad was. The SOB up and died on me before I got my affairs organized." Jamie Ray gave a cough of a laugh. "I'd just finished listing my heirs from a few of those affairs I had years ago when they tossed me in the ambulance last night, and now I find out I've got a wet-behind-the-ears lawyer. From the looks of it I may have to delay my departure." Jamie Ray slapped one side of his rugged face as if trying to force sobriety on himself.

Jackson Landry shifted and repeated the order of tonight's happenings for the third time. "You were having a heart attack, Mr. Morrell. The bartender called 911. Then you told him to call me." Jackson noticed the drunk wasn't listening. If sins showed on a man's face, Jamie Ray Morrell was the bad side of Dorian Gray.

Jamie Ray coughed. "Every darling I slept with in my younger days cussed me out for not marrying her. I was fond of every one of 'em, but I just couldn't be bothered to do the paperwork. They all said I didn't have a heart, so that's proof I can't die of a heart attack. But you, being my lawyer, are going to make it right, Jackson, just in case? I'm keeping my word to your old man to sign a will. I plan to pay for my mistakes."

"I'll do my best to help you, sir." Jackson thought of cussing. He should have been an accountant, or a house painter, or the town dogcatcher. Anything but Morrell's lawyer. Accountants and painters probably went home at five every night and never had to get out in the season's worst weather to try to reason with a drunk.

His dad left him every crazy old goat in the valley to deal

with. Jamie Ray Morrell was as bad as the lady who came in every Monday to change her will. If one of her cats died or peed on the rug, the feline was disinherited.

"Good. Make it fast, boy. I'm feeling like death warmed over tonight." Morrell coughed again, then patted his chest. "About time to roll the dice on whether I walk out of this place one more time. The women I attract now'days are drunks, mean and ugly even with my glasses off. Might as well head down to Hell. The pickings couldn't be much worse."

Jackson leaned over the bed's railing. "That why you're refusing the heart surgery, Morrell? You want to leave it to chance?"

Jamie Ray smiled. "I may have done a hell of a lot of bad things, but I swear I'm not a liar. I've spent sixty years gambling and I ain't stopping now. I like women, but I wasn't born with enough heart to love even one. Strange little creatures, if you ask me. Nesters. And me, I was born to ride the open roads." He stopped long enough to push the call button again. "I've already cheated death three times. I got out of that hospital in New Orleans after I was left for dead in an alley for two days. Ten years ago, I was in a bad wreck they said no one could walk away from, and at twenty a medic took four bullets out of my chest. Jackson, it'll probably be another thirty years and another dozen women before I wear out, but I promised your daddy I'd make a will if I ever ended up in a hospital again. I got a few things I've collected and I want them passed out to my sons."

"Then, let's get started. How about we begin with your assets, Mr. Morrell? I know you have an old Camaro, a piece of land along the north rim, and an eighteen-wheeler truck. You never married. No living relatives that you've ever mentioned."

Waving Jackson away, Jamie Ray leaned back on a stack of pillows. "I'm tired, boy, and I'll miss the news if you stay any longer. I wrote down all you need to know while you was visiting with the doc." Jamie Ray handed him a folded piece of paper. "Draw my will up all legal like. Don't come back until after breakfast. The nurse said she has to spoon-feed me if I'm weak come morning." A wicked smile crossed his pasty face. "There ain't nothing nicer than a big-busted woman with short arms feeding a man."

Jackson had enough of Jamie Ray Morrell. The drunk was as worthless as Jackson's father used to say he was. "I'll take care of everything, Mr. Morrell." Just for spite, he added, "Anyone you want to notify to come to your funeral?"

"No. I'll go it alone. Cremate my body and spread my ashes out on Eagle's Peak."

Jackson put the folded paper in his empty briefcase and walked out of Jamie Ray's room. As he passed Dr. Ryan Henton, Jackson nodded once at his friend. "The old man thinks you're too young to be a doc, and I'm too dumb to be his lawyer."

Ryan took the time to look up from a chart. "He won't let me operate or move him to a big hospital for surgery. Claimed he'd chosen option number three: get over it. He told me he plans to be out of this place before happy hour tomorrow."

"What are his chances?" Jackson asked.

The man Jackson had played football with through high school was honest as always. "Not good. You might want to get that will done."

"I'm heading home before the rain gets worse to do just that. I'll work on it tonight and have it ready by dawn." Jackson hesitated. "Call if you need me."

"I will. Same to you, Jack."

Ryan turned toward the hallway. Jackson rushed for the door.

As the wind blasted him, Jackson turned his collar up and ran for his pickup, thinking if he ever made any money in this small town, he'd buy a proper car. Maybe a Lincoln or a BMW. Lawyers should drive something better than a twenty-year-old, handed-down, beat-up farm truck.

Half an hour later, Jackson was still holding the square of paper Jamie Ray had given him when the hospital called. As the nurse explained how Mr. Morrell died yelling for a drink, the lawyer read the note and four names with ages beside each. It read: *Give it all to my offspring.*

Morrell's signature was clear. Dated an hour ago. Witnessed by a nurse and some guy who wrote "janitor" under his name.

"Damn," Jackson said as he stared at the names. "The old guy knew he was dying. Probably didn't mention it just to irritate the hell out of me." Jackson growled low like his father used to do when he was frustrated.

Jamie Ray died leaving all he owned to four names on a piece of paper.

Four sons he'd probably never met. All with different last names and none of them Morrell.

ANDY DELANE—about 30—FORT SILL, OKLAHOMA

RUSTY O'SULLIVAN—32—SOMEDAY VALLEY, TEXAS

ZACHARY HOLMES—age unknown—AUSTIN, TEXAS (maybe twenty years ago)

GRIFFITH LAURENT—22—FRENCH QUARTER, NEW ORLEANS

Jamie Ray lived within a day's drive of three of his sons. O'Sullivan lived thirty miles away on the other side of the valley, but Jackson would bet not one of them had ever seen Jamie Ray. That could be a good thing. Jamie Ray hadn't been much of a man or a father. That not one carried his name was proof.

Jackson had taken over his father's practice in Honey Creek two months ago and his first client left this world without paying. He felt a bit guilty for thinking of the money. But, it was hard to believe he was a real lawyer, having never seen a check.

But Jackson Landry would do his duty and hope none of Jamie Ray's boys took after their sperm donor. He'd find the boys, now men, but he doubted they'd be glad to see him.

Chapter 1

Near Someday Valley

Saturday at Midnight

Rusty O'Sullivan gunned the old Ford's engine just before he swung onto the back road and headed up the hill toward Someday Valley. A storm was putting on a show. Rain pounded so hard he almost believed he was driving in an ocean. There was always a chance the car wouldn't make the incline in the muck, but he'd had a hell of a day and figured his bad luck had to run out sometime.

He'd made it over the last bridge but the rotted boards seemed to be crying out in protest. Half a mile later the road turned to mud. No one but Rusty lived beyond a rustic cabin. If someone gave his dirt road a name it would be "Nothing Beyond" or "Nothing Worth Seeing Up This Way."

The little cabin in daylight looked like a painting, but at night it was more a set-piece from a horror film. Except for one whimsical touch—someone had planted strawberries everywhere. There were dark green plants in the shade beneath the trees, along the edge of the porch, and lining every rock path. The strawberries would erupt in the summer, but tonight the plants were in winter's sleep, the leaves were almost black to match the sky.

The mud that was moving downhill like lava on his left drew his attention. A ten-foot drop was on his right. Bald tires didn't put up much of a fight to hold onto the two-lane road.

In the midnight rain, Rusty felt the Fairlane begin to slide sideways. Like a slow rerun of an old black-and-white movie, the Ford tilted right as the road disappeared and three thousand pounds of steel began to roll. Rusty tightened his grip on the steering wheel as if he still had some control of the car . . . or his life.

He didn't bother to scream or cuss. He simply braced for a crash. Bad luck had always ridden shotgun with trouble all his life.

The ground slammed into the passenger side, shattering windows and crunching metal. Then, as the roof hit the incline, he felt the cut of his seatbelt, and it seemed to be snowing glass.

The Ford rolled again and the driver's door pushed against Rusty's shoulder. He braced as it rotated once more and the inside of what had once been a car was now a coffin of flying glass and metal.

Something hit his head and the world went completely black, but for a moment, the sounds remained in his brain as if echoing since birth. *Unwanted. Nothing but a bother. Deserted.*

One last echo whispered through the bedlam. One word he'd heard for as long as he could remember.

Worthless.

Chapter 2

Starri Knight lay on the hardwood floor of her aunt's hundred-year-old cabin as she watched rain slide down the huge picture window. If she didn't move, maybe she'd feel closer to nature like she had when she was a child. Maybe the moon would play peekaboo with her through the storm clouds. She was almost positive the man in the moon had once seen her when she was small.

When she was a kid, stars winked at her and the moon smiled. She'd tell her Aunt Ona-May and they'd laugh together.

But tonight, all Starri saw were car lights making their way up the hill and lightning running across the sky like a tidal wave igniting.

All her life, pretty much everyone who took the back trail in rain got stuck. Aunt Ona-May would wait until morning to back the tractor out of the barn and go pull them out of the mud. For thirty bucks, of course.

No driver ever complained at the cost. A tow from town would have been fifty or more.

Starri watched the rain as she remembered the story of the night her aunt took her in as if she were kin. Ona-May said one rainy midnight a young couple, not out of their teens, took the road to Someday Valley way too fast. They collided with a pickup coming down hauling hay. The crash killed both the teenagers instantly, but the baby in the back didn't have a scratch.

Two farmers to the north heard the crash and came running to help the driver pinned inside his truck. Ona-May had crawled through a shattered window and pulled the baby out from the backseat. She said the minute she pushed the blanket away, the newborn reached up trying to touch the stars.

No one came to take the infant that night. Ona-May decided to call the tiny child Starri until kin came. But no one arrived. No one wanted the tiny baby.

Since Ona-May Jones was a nurse in her younger days, the county let her foster the child. That rainy night she became an aunt to a little girl who had no one.

Starri smiled, remembering the beginning of her story. She couldn't miss parents she'd never known, but she was thankful Aunt Ona-May had found her. Auntie might never have a family of her own, but she poured all her love on a child no one wanted to claim.

Tonight, watching as the car on the incline began to roll sideways down the hill, Starri froze. For a moment it seemed no more than an awkward falling star.

Then the sounds of glass and metal snapping blended with the rain.

Starri screamed.

Someone was dying in the same spot her parents had twenty years ago. She closed her eyes, reliving a memory that had formed before words.

As always, Auntie's arms surrounded her. "Starri, it's all right." As the old woman saw the car rolling, she added calmly, "Get on your boots. We've work to do. There is a soul in that car who may need our help."

Auntie's old body straightened into the nurse she'd been in Vietnam, fifty years ago.

While Ona-May collected supplies, Starri dialed 911 and was told the road between Honey Creek and Someday Valley was closed. One of the bridges was out. The only ambulance in the valley was on the other side of the bridge and would take an hour to circle around. "We'll take care of it, Starri. Don't worry," Ona-May whispered. "Doctoring humans is pretty much like doctoring the other animals around here."

Starri nodded, but this time she wasn't sure she believed her aunt.

As they trudged up the hill in mud that sucked at their boots, the lights on the car went out. The rattling continued as if the auto was dying a slow death. The engine was still sputtering when they reached the wreck. Their flashlights swept the ground like lightning bugs hopping in the night.

Her hand was too cold to hold the flashlight steady, and the whole world seemed to be crying while it rained. She circled closer to what had been a car but heard no cry for help. She feared that the soul her aunt had come to save might have already moved on. Tears blended with the rain running over her face.

"Here!" Ona-May yelled as she moved a few feet below the car. "I've found him!"

As she ventured closer, Starri saw the outline of a body. A tall man dressed all in black. Rain pounded on the stranger as if determined to push him into the ground.

Auntie pulled off her raincoat and covered him. "I can't see where he's hurt, but he's breathing. We'll wrap any wounds we see, then roll him on your coat and pull him to the cabin. If he makes the journey back to the house, I'd say he's got a chance."

Starri followed orders. She'd seen her aunt set a broken

leg and stitch up a cowboy who'd refused to go to the doctor. Auntie delivered babies when they had no time to make the drive to Honey Creek. The people in the valley were mostly poor and didn't go to a clinic unless they had to. They knew Ona-May would take care of what she could and often loaned them money if she recommended the doctor.

As they pulled the unconscious stranger over the wet grass, Starri thought of another talent her aunt had. She loved people. Not just the good ones or the righteous ones like the preacher counted. She loved them all, even the sinners and the drunks.

Starri figured Ona-May overlooked folks' shortcomings because she had a few herself. She wasn't beyond stealing the neighbors' apples or corn, and she cussed when she was frustrated. And every New Year's Eve she'd drink and tell stories of her days in the Army.

When they reached the cabin, her aunt started issuing orders as if she had troops and not just Starri.

"We'll put him on the floor by the fireplace. Get me towels and warm water. Start cleaning him up while I collect more supplies, then I'll call the doctor over in Honey Creek. Knowing those young doctors, they'll find a way to get to us. I can already see our patient has his right arm broke, so cut off his shirt. I'm guessing he's got internal injuries. Oh, add logs to the fire, girl. The way he's losing blood, he'll be shivering."

Staring down at the muddy man, Starri noticed hard times showing in worry lines on his young face. "You'll have to help me, mister. I can't even remember all the orders. Ona-May gets like that sometimes when she's excited, but my ears still listen slow. She was an emergency nurse for thirty years. You're in good hands."

"Starri, get moving!" Ona-May yelled as she came loaded down with bandages and antiseptic from the kitchen. "We got to keep him alive until the ambulance gets here."

She handed her aunt the phone as she ran for towels and a pan of hot water. When she returned, the stranger's eyes were open. She saw pain but not fear.

"You an angel?" he whispered.

"No," she answered. "I'm a star that fell out of the sky twenty years ago. Kids at school said I'm as strange as they come, but I'm not. I'm just different."

"Me too," he whispered through pain. "I'm Rusty O'Sullivan. Folks say I'm worthless. You're wasting your time fixing me up. I'll just scatter again."

He closed his eyes as she gently washed his face. She didn't know if he fell asleep or passed out, but the worry lines had faded. She barely heard him whisper, "Watch over me, little star."

"I will. You just rest. Don't worry about that windshield wiper sticking out of your side. My aunt can fix that."

Chapter 3

Jackson ran through his parents' rambling ranch house, stripping off his clothes as fast as he could with one hand while he held his cell in the other.

"Slow down, Ryan. I can meet you at the bridge with two mounts. I've got Mack saddling the horses and loading them in the trailer now. I can be there by the time you drive from the hospital to that old bridge heading into Someday Valley." Jackson hit speaker as he pulled on jeans. "Any idea who the injured man is?"

"Yeah," Dr. Ryan Henton answered in a clipped tone. "He's your departed client's son. He's Jamie Ray Morrell's oldest. One of the nurses said Jamie Ray talked about his boys when he asked her to be a witness to his will. Later, after she'd called you to notify you Jamie Ray was dead, a 911 call came in on a wreck. Rusty O'Sullivan rolled his car on the climb to Someday Valley. The nurse remembered the name."

Jackson shoved his feet into ten-year-old Justin boots he hadn't worn in a few years and ran toward the barn. "How bad is he hurt?"

"The caller was patched through to me. One vehicle roll-over on the dirt trail heading up the back side of the hill. The woman who called said she thought Rusty had a broken arm. Maybe a fractured leg. Internal bleeding and cuts all over his body. What sounded like a young girl said a retired nurse was with the guy."

Ryan hesitated and added, "With the bridge out it would take more than an hour to get to him by circling the north way. We can ride in on horseback in half that time. If we can get him stable, he might just survive the ambulance drive back to the hospital in Honey Creek. They'll have to take the long way out, but at least it's a good road."

"I'm en route." Jackson started running. "I'll meet you at the bridge."

As Jackson moved through the dark rooms of his child-hood home, he barely noticed dust covering everything or the mail piled up on the dining table. His boxes from college were still stacked in the hallway. He remembered kissing his folks goodbye and leaving for Austin to celebrate passing the bar. Four days later his uncle found him at a friend's house.

Jackson was hungover, but one look into his father's brother's eyes sobered him up.

Uncle Pete said simply, "You got to come home, Jack. Your folks crashed flying into Angel Fire, New Mexico, yester-day. I must have told him a dozen times to land at Santa Fe and drive over. I . . ."

Jackson had stopped listening to Uncle Pete. He picked up his duffel bag and went home, not to his folks' ranch, but to a room above the law office. He came by the ranch to col-lect clothes and check on Mack. The old foreman could run the ranch, but Jackson couldn't sleep here. Too many memories. An only child, the joy of his parents' lives. He couldn't let even good from the past in.

Home to Jackson was his dad's office—wrong, *his* office now. He slept in the bedroom apartment above the office after working until he was exhausted. That way he didn't have to think about how his life had changed in an instant.

He was living in his hometown, but Jackson never felt he was home. His dreams had been a big city. Dallas, maybe Houston. Starting off at the bottom of a big law firm. Not here, in a town where he could walk the length of it before he finished his morning coffee.

Ten minutes later, Jackson met Ryan at the bridge, or rather what was left of it. They'd been friends all their lives, from kids riding the ranch all summer to college roommates for the first four years at Tech. Ryan chose medicine and Jackson wanted law. More than once, they'd talked each other out of dropping out.

If this ride was dangerous tonight, they'd make it together.

The men swung into the saddles with medical packs on their backs full of supplies. The lawyer and the doctor, with generations of cowboy in their blood, morphed into midnight riders running full out into a hell of a rainstorm.

They didn't need to worry what direction. Down was the only option.

"Let's ride!" Jackson shouted as he raised one hand and turned his horse onto the rocky slope littered with pieces of wood and concrete from the shattered bridge. Both men had grown up on horseback, but neither had chosen that kind of life. Yet tonight, they were risking their lives to save a stranger.

Ryan's excitement blended with the thunder, but Jackson worried that if he didn't break his neck in a fall, he'd probably drown in the raging river below. He could almost hear his father yelling from the grave about wasting all that money for law school on a son determined to kill himself.

The race down was far more frightening than any roller coaster. They hit the water riding full out in what had been a stream a few hours ago. Now the water splashed almost to the saddles. Jackson laughed. "Geronimo!" he shouted and Ryan echoed back.

Their grandfathers had yelled the battle cry when they'd jumped as part of the 101st Airborne paratroopers in World War II. Both old men swore they were laughing when they dove out of the plane, and fighting fear when they hit the ground.

Tonight, their grandsons rode west with lightning blinking across the muddy road. Three miles from the broken bridge, they saw a cabin about halfway up the hill. Every light in the place was on and lanterns lined the porch.

They rode hard on horses born to run across unbroken land.

Fifty feet before they arrived, both men pulled up the mustangs.

Ryan jumped down, tossed his reins to Jackson, and ran for the woman waiting, with a lantern swinging on her arm, flashing bright light across her face one moment and leaving her in shadows the next. She didn't say a word. She simply held the door open.

Jackson took time to tie the horses before he slipped off his pack.

"I'm Jackson Landry, miss. That man who ran past you is Ryan Henton, the doctor. I'm not sure, but I think he came out of the birth canal running. We're here to help."

The young woman nodded. "Glad to see you both. I'm Starri. The ambulance called in and said they are still forty miles out and my aunt is doing all she can."

With worry in her eyes she added, "I'll take care of your

horses. The doctor may need your help. The man is half out of his mind with pain. I tried to keep him still, but I couldn't."

As Jackson ran inside, Ryan was already shouting orders. "Hold him down, Jack! We've no time to waste. I can see open wounds on his chest, but blood is also coming out from underneath him. He's going into shock."

Jackson met his friend's gaze and saw defeat. They might already be too late. A memory of their last high school football game flashed across Jackson's mind. Ryan had been the quarterback, always in control. Jackson, a lineman. One minute left in the game, two touchdowns from victory. A hopeless situation.

Jackson shouted now what he had yelled then on the football field: "What do we do?"

In a cabin, with blood covering the floor, Ryan gave the same answer he'd given over ten years ago: "We fight like hell!"

Nodding, Jackson echoed, "Win or lose, we fight like hell."

They'd lost that night years ago, but they hadn't lost yet tonight. And they weren't going to without a fight.

An old lady holding pressure on one leg straightened as if called to arms. "Damn right, men. We fight!"

About then, a bloody fist connected with Jackson's jaw and almost knocked him to the floor. Rusty was doing his own fighting, but it seemed to be against them.

"Hold him down, Jack!" Ryan commanded as if Jackson wasn't trying. "We've got to keep Jamie Ray's son from bleeding out."

In what might have been hours or minutes, the woman who'd met them on the porch reappeared. Her wet clothes were plastered to her body, but she joined in. It was obvious she wasn't trained, but she did have more skill than Jackson. Her low, soothing voice became the background melody as they all worked. She was petite, with an angel's face.

As the minutes passed, they all worked together. Jackson would have guessed Rusty O'Sullivan didn't have a chance, but by the time the ambulance arrived, the injured man had taken several swings at everyone trying to help. But they'd got him stable enough to transport.

Ryan climbed in with his patient and told the EMTs to help Ona-May in also. She'd been knocked over twice and, even with blood in her hair, she wouldn't let Ryan examine her wound.

"We stay with our patient, nurse," Ryan ordered the old woman. "Once we get him taken care of, I plan to have a look at that cut on the back of your head."

"All right, but it's just dripping, nothing serious," she answered as the ambulance door slammed shut.

Suddenly, Jackson was standing on the porch, alone with the woman who called herself Starri.

"They left us," she whispered.

"Do you have a car?"

"No. I've got a tractor but it has no lights. Aunt Ona-May loaned her car to the neighbor."

Jackson rocked back on his heels. "I got two horses. Can you ride? That seems our only way out."

"I've ridden a few times. I can stay in the saddle." She headed toward the barn and he followed.

Jackson watched as the ambulance lights turned onto the north road, the long way to Honey Creek. Then he looked at the climb to the south road by the broken bridge.

Starri seemed to read his mind. "We take the shortcut."

The rain had stopped, but the climb back to the downed bridge and his pickup wouldn't be easy. "If we ride up, then drive into town, we'll probably beat the ambulance to the hospital. If you don't want to try the climb, I can call you and tell you what's happening."

"No." She zipped her slicker. "I'm going with you. I need to be with my aunt."

Ten minutes later, Jackson was fighting to match her speed. Starri rode like she was born to ride rocky hills.

Jackson yelled the halfhearted battle cry, "Geronimo!" and tried to keep up.

By the time they made it to the pickup and loaded the horses, Jackson decided if the woman with the funny name had been with the 101st, jumping behind enemy lines, World War II would have been over six months earlier.

Chapter 4

Rusty O'Sullivan lay stone still, eyes closed, listening. He didn't want to see anything. He knew where he was. The mini-hospital in Honey Creek, thirty miles from his home.

The hospital was fairly new, but most of the docs were interns. The med schools sent them out to learn how to doctor. Rusty knew all about them because he'd been their guinea pig more than once. Bar fights he lost. Other wrecks. Accidents at work.

He remembered the smell of disinfectant. The stiff sheets. The background noise, almost music to the beeps and clicking beside his bed with braces on either side. A gurney with a loose wheel rolled by in the hallway. The tiny *ping* of the elevator sounded faintly. Someone crying a few rooms down. Doors opening and closing with a swishing noise that almost sounded like water brushing land.

Slowly, he opened one eye just enough to confirm his theory.

"Yep, Honey Creek Hospital." The rain and the wreck drifted back to him. Looking down at the bed, all he saw were bandages. For a moment he considered that he might have had a whole-body transplant. His head hurt like the worst hangover he'd ever had, so that part might be his, but from the neck down he felt nothing.

Maybe he was dead. It made sense that death had to start somewhere on a man. Maybe your toes died first, then your legs. Then the Grim Reaper slides along rotting skin, up your body. No pain once you passed, no worries. Only memories in the stillness.

Rusty would have yelled if he had the energy. It occurred to him that all his memories were bad. What a way to die. No kittens and lollipops. Just bar fights and work. Almost girlfriends saying goodbye without tears. Relatives echoing that they couldn't help him when he was a kid. One old cousin even whispered, "You do know you're illegitimate, don't you, kid?" Rusty hadn't figured out what that meant until he was ten.

When his mother left like a teenager running away, no one knew where she had gone, or cared. Later, when he was seven and she'd died, the few kin he had said they didn't have room to take him in.

His granddad and his third wife moved into Rusty's mom's shack of a house more for the free rent than to take care of him. No one cared if he ate or went to school. No one even had time to teach him anything. Once the sheriff visited and told Granddad that he had to send Rusty to school and feed him or it would mean jail time. It was the law.

After that, they fed him with the same care most people feed a stray dog and made him go to school a few times a week. Other than that, he was mostly invisible to them.

Now, panicked by the pain, Rusty tried to think of one good memory. He would hate to have to die without something happy or even just nice on his mind.

About the time he was considering giving up and just

dying, he remembered the young woman who'd washed his face after she and an old lady pulled him through the mud. He'd been in a warm cabin with her gently wiping away his blood. She'd smiled at him and told him her name was Starri.

Rusty tried to smile. She'd told him she was a star. What kind of grown woman thinks she's a star? "Maybe she is," he mumbled. "Maybe I'm a rock. No, that's not right. Maybe I'm a clod of dirt." He closed out all the sounds and smells and whispered, "How come some people get to be stars and some have to be clods?" Mentally scoffing, he wondered how he'd become a sage since he turned thirty. His mind passed into a midnight fog and he began mumbling into the wind.

"You talking to yourself, Mr. O'Sullivan?" a voice asked loud and clear . . . and about six inches from his ear.

Rusty jerked his head away and felt like he'd slammed into an anvil. He waited until the pain eased, then opened his one working eye. The unwanted visitor came into focus.

A masked intruder was staring at him. Blond hair cut short around her face, angry green eyes partially hidden behind glasses, and from the way she was leaning over him, she had to be at least six feet tall. Without asking, she forced his other eye full open and shined a bright light in it.

"Go away," Rusty said with as much anger as he could muster.

The woman lowered her mask and shrugged. "I would, but I'm an intern here, so I have to stay. I'm chained to this place for a year and I haven't slept for twenty hours thanks to having to put the stuffing back inside of you last night. You were one bloody mess when they wheeled you in."

Rusty managed a one-sided grin. "I guess that means we spent the night together."

"You wish, Humpty Dumpty." The lady grabbed his chart. "It took two doctors, one intern—me—and three nurses to put you together again."

"So does that mean I'm going to live?"

She finally pulled the mask completely off and smiled. "Don't ask questions, just answer a few. I'm in no mood to practice my bedside manner."

This intern was a beauty dressed in scrubs, but he wasn't sure he wanted to talk to her.

"You're going to live, Mr. O'Sullivan, barring any complication. A week in the hospital, a month in rehab, and maybe another few months on crutches, and you'll be able to run yourself off the road again."

He decided to blurt out what he was thinking. "You're a knockout, Doc. You know, like model beauty. Like a movie star." If Rusty could find his hand under the bandages, he'd slap himself. She didn't look like a woman who liked compliments. He was making a fool of himself. He liked women a bit shorter, hair long enough to curl around his hand, and some evidence of breasts. But if he admitted that to her, she'd pull out his staples with an ice pick.

To his surprise, she just shrugged at the compliment and gave him that same smile as if it had been issued with the name tag that read DR. A. ADAMS.

He needed to say something that made sense, fast. "I'll heal, Doc. Is there any chance we could go out dancing after I'm recovered?"

"I can't go for several reasons, Mr. O'Sullivan. One, I don't date patients. Two, you are obviously trouble. I've heard it from everyone here. You're a frequent patient around this place. Bar fights. A knife fight last summer. Two car wrecks and one motorbike totaled since last year. You've managed to fall out a second-story window and a plane trying to land. You broke your ankle playing touch football last fall and two fingers from punching the wall. I've read your history. If I ever did go out with you, I'd pack a bag."

He smiled for a second before she added, "My medical bag."

"I'm a little accident prone but we'd have a great time."

She shook her head. "No, Mr. O'Sullivan, you're a walking wreck. Oh, and the number three reason why I wouldn't go out with you: I'm engaged."

"I don't see a ring."

As she checked dressings, she replied without looking up. "I don't wear it at work."

Rusty leaned back and let her check all the wounds. In truth he had no idea why he'd asked her out. A woman like her would never, ever, ever go out with him. She was classy, educated, beautiful, probably rich, and engaged.

He didn't say another word to her and when she finished, she patted his arm.

Almost asleep, he heard her whisper, "Rest, Mr. O'Sullivan."

"I will. See you later, sweetheart."

She moved closer so fast he felt the wind blow even through the bandages. "It's *Doctor* to you, Mr. O'Sullivan." Her sexy voice lowered slightly and added, "If you call me 'sweetheart' again, I'll break your toes. From the looks of it, they're the only bones intact."

"You know, Doc, I may be banged up, but you've got anger issues."

"You're right. I hate men who see a woman and assume there is no brain beneath the blond hair."

"I know how you feel, Doc. I would never do that. When I see a pretty face and sunshine hair, I pray there's no brain." Rusty couldn't help himself. He had to say something to bug her.

She turned and stormed out. Just as she passed the foot of his bed, she bent one toe sticking out of his covers.

He had a feeling she meant it as a warning, but he took it as foreplay. The girl named Starri was too young for him and the intern was too mean. He might as well become a monk if he recovered.

Chapter 5

Starri Knight poked her head into Rusty O'Sullivan's hospital room. He was sound asleep, just like he had been the two other times she'd walked down the hall from Aunt Ona-May's room.

Only this time he looked better. He had a bit of color in his face, if she looked past the stitches and the bruises. His body had taken most of the hits during the crash, leaving his face almost handsome. Black hair covered his forehead and she thought she'd seen gray eyes with a "born to run" kind of steel flashing behind the pain.

She felt responsible for him since she found him. The admissions clerk said he'd been in the hospital before and had no next of kin listed to call.

Part of her knew she should just walk away from Rusty O'Sullivan, but another part of her wanted to shelter him, protect him from the hurt. When she'd been just a newborn, no one had wanted her but Ona-May. He was alone too.

The nurse said he was half wild and the other half crazy.

Starri was shy, sheltered, homegrown. If they ever talked for ten minutes, she'd probably discover they had nothing in common.

But he was hurt. Her heart wouldn't let her turn away. Even wild animals need care now and then.

As she approached, she started when he opened one eye. Gray. She'd almost said it aloud. Gray with just a hint of blue.

"Hi," he whispered. "That you, Starri?"

He remembered her name. "It's me. How are you feeling?"

"I'm fine. You mind telling that intern who keeps poking on me that I'm ready to leave? There is nothing more they can do for me. I'd just as soon exit."

"Sure, I'll tell her, but it won't help. It's Dr. Henton who has to sign the discharge papers, not the intern."

"Henton . . . wasn't he one of the men who came to help me?"

Starri sat on the corner of his bed. She told him about how Ryan Henton and his friend Jackson had ridden half-wild horses down from the broken bridge, and that he wouldn't be alive if they hadn't gotten to him when they did. "You would have just been a 'body pickup' for the ambulance."

"I guess I owe them one."

When she told him about how he had slugged Ona-May and made her head bleed, Rusty added one more person he owed.

When Starri ran out of things to tell him, she picked up a comb and asked if she could comb his hair.

"What for?" Rusty grumbled.

"You've got dried blood in it and probably leftover glass. With all the stitches and bandages you can't just step in a shower. I'll put a towel around you and try to clean it up. I'll be gentle."

She caught him whispering the word "gentle" under his

breath, as if he'd never heard it before. "I don't usually worry about my hair, but I could use some company."

As Starri worked on his hair, she told him that the lawyer, Jackson Landry, wanted to talk to him after his meds wore off a bit.

"He probably wants to sue me," Rusty guessed.

"No, I don't think so. He said something about your father."

Rusty closed his eyes. "I don't have a father. No kin, in fact. I'm the last of a thin line."

After a moment, Starri took his hand. "I'll be your kin if you like."

"Sure . . . I've always wanted to be related to a star."

When he fell asleep, she slipped out of his room. He probably wouldn't remember that she'd even visited.

He would be moved to rehab as soon as he was stable. It wasn't much of a move. Rehab in Honey Creek was the last two rooms of the nursing home across the street from the mini-hospital. His main exercise would probably be walking the hall, trying not to run into one of the walkers or sleeping residents in wheelchairs.

In big towns, rehab would have a gym and physical therapists to put the recovering patients through a routine of drills. The local nursing home, also rehab, had a guy named Eddie on staff who walked the halls, yelling at no one in particular. He carried huge rubber bands wrapped around his arms, pushed a shopping cart with barbells, a big ball, and a belt to strap on the patient so Eddie could hold on as he walked his charge.

Most of the injured claimed two days with Eddie would cure any handicap.

Starri had promised she'd visit Rusty if he moved tomorrow. Maybe bring him a book. He'd said he would look for her. Maybe they just might make it to a friendship level. After all, he'd slugged her aunt and she hadn't threatened to kill him, so Aunt Ona-May must like him too.

Chapter 6

Monday Morning

Jackson Landry opened his office, which still felt far more like his dad's space than his. Old law books lined the walls. His father's ashtray rested on the windowsill, even though the old guy would swear he only smoked one cigarette a day. A few of his hats were still on the rack by the door.

It had been almost three months since Jackson quit a job to bury his parents. He'd just been about to start his career in Dallas. Instead, he'd moved home to oversee his mom's horse breeding business and take over Landry & Son Law Firm. A dozen things had needed to be done as soon as the funerals were over, and Jackson had avoided all of them except the law office.

Mack, the ranch foreman and horse trainer, showed up every Monday with the ranch checkbook. Jackson signed a half dozen checks to keep his mother's breeding operation running.

To Jackson's surprise, the ranch made more in a week than the law office did in a month. He'd always thought that his dad funded his mother's hobby. Apparently, it was the other way around.

Even though he had chosen to live over the office, he didn't plan to sell his mother's horses or close the ranch house. He didn't change the sign on the door. There was no Landry *and* Son. There probably never would be at the rate he was going. It had been so long since he had a date, he couldn't remember the last one's name.

Grades came first in college, then studying for the bar, and now, somehow, he had to keep his dad's practice going.

As Jackson glanced around, he realized he'd grown up in this office overlooking the town square. He'd done his homework on the coffee table and taken naps on the worn leather couch. Honey Creek was the county seat so his dad was always busy.

His mother had stayed at the ranch, working with her thoroughbreds and the mustangs she'd rescued, so Jackson always walked the two blocks after school to his father's office and waited until they could go home together. His dad talked about his cases on the drive to their fourth-generation ranch and Jackson listened.

Even then his dad liked to introduce his only son as his partner. His dad had hung LANDRY & SON over the door when Jackson made it into law school, even though Jackson told him a dozen times he wanted to pursue corporate law. Dad would just smile at his son as if silently saying, "I'll wait."

Who knows, even if his parents hadn't died in an accident, Jackson might eventually have returned to Honey Creek anyway. It might be just a dot on the map of Texas to most people, but there was something welcoming about the quiet streets and friendly people.

Now with mourning weighing heavy on his shoulder, there was comfort surrounding him in the low sound of the creek and the church bells and even in the sorrow in the eyes of people he'd known all his life.

After all, this office was where Jackson fell in love with law. He belonged in this room even if the grief of losing his parents lingered here.

In the afternoon light slicing through half-open blinds, Jackson swore he saw the thin outline of his father leaning against the windowsill, staring at Main Street as he smoked and watched his people.

His dad seemed to think he was the guardian of Honey Creek. He'd handled everything from fighting parking tickets to criminal cases. He also handled divorces, though some claimed he talked more couples out of splitting than filed any papers for them.

"How am I going to help Jamie Ray's first son, Dad? He's wild as a coyote. If there's money involved, he'll go through it before the end of the year."

Jackson began to pace just like his dad used to do as he talked his problem out to the walls. "I know. That's not my job. Just hand him, and Jamie Ray's three other sons, the money or whatever their never-present father wanted to leave them and walk away. I'm just the lawyer, not their mother." He glanced over toward the window. "But you never made it that simple, did you, Dad? Doing what you have to and doing what is right aren't always the same."

A knock pulled him from his invisible conversation with a dead dad. "Yes!" Jackson shouted a bit louder than necessary, then he let out a low growl of irritation.

The door opened. A big man in khakis and a worn brown leather jacket, probably older than Jackson, filled the doorway. The silver-haired giant would have frightened Jackson if he hadn't known him all his life. Over six-feet-six tall, well over two hundred and fifty pounds, with a face chewed up by acne in his youth and never straightened out, Wind Culstee wore his Cherokee heritage proudly and demanded respect.

"Morning, kid. I got your message." Wind nodded once as if it were a silent salute. "I was already doing some background checks. Miss Heather told me you were visiting Rusty O'Sullivan in the hospital, so I thought I'd start snooping."

Jackson wasn't surprised. Between Wind and Miss Heather, they could run the office without Jackson most days. Wind did most of the records researching and Heather knew or was related to everyone in the valley. They were both in their forties and had worked together so long the odd pair communicated in nods or sounds. Once Jackson heard Wind huff and Heather snapped, "Don't you dare argue with me."

In his teens, Jackson had tried logging their strange way of communicating. Heather made a little sound when she didn't agree with Wind, and raised her eyebrows halfway to her hairline when she wanted him to express his opinion.

When Wind deepened his frown, Heather would go into more detail. If the big man looked away, she'd reel him back in by lowering her voice to a whisper.

He'd noticed that when she was angry with Wind, she'd point her pen at him and her lips would become invisible. Jackson wasn't sure exactly what that meant, but Wind usually started talking louder or shut up.

If he went silent, she'd nod once as if the discussion was settled.

Jackson sometimes wondered, if they were ever alone, would either speak to the other? Deep down he was convinced that Wind Culstee was a bit afraid of Miss Heather, even if she was a foot shorter and half his weight.

Jackson waved Miss Heather in now, wishing he had been able to crack the couple's code. The outer office had four desks but only Heather's was occupied. Wind never waited around unless he was called in, and if he needed to write something down, he used a notepad that fit into his pocket.

Now, the investigator spread out a folder on the coffee table. "This is what I've got so far, Mr. Landry."

Jackson smiled. "Mr. Landry? You've always called me 'kid.'"

Wind wrinkled up his face and, if possible, looked uglier. "You're still a kid, but you are also the lawyer in this office. I'll try to respect that, but I'll probably slip now and then."

"And if I mess up on being a good lawyer now and then?" Jackson thought the big man would say he'd quit or remind him of what his father would do.

But no. Wind puffed up and said calmly, "I'd beat the tar out of you and remind you who you are when you come to."

Jackson glanced over at the window, where he'd almost seen the outline of his father. "I don't think I'll forget my duty, but if I do, I'll take the beating and thank you for it."

Jackson pulled up a chair for Miss Heather and the investigator took up the center of the couch as he spread out papers.

"Rusty O'Sullivan's mother had him when she was seventeen," Wind began. "Jamie Ray, the presumed father, left town before his first son was born. The young mother lived with her parents until she turned eighteen. Then she left town, leaving Rusty with his grandparents. Both drunks. From what I heard, they weren't worth much sober either. They told the sheriff they passed Rusty to another relative down south, but neighbors said they'd seen the kid around the shack now and then. Some folks said the couple went to Las Vegas and left Rusty home to feed the chickens.

"No one ever saw the grandparents after that or Rusty's mother. Rusty must have moved into the grandparents' old house alone until he was fifteen. He dropped out of school and worked cleanup for a painter. By the time he was eighteen, he was running the small jobs for old Grady Brown. Everyone I talked to said he was a great carpenter.

"His boss claims he eats his lunch reading a book and stops in at one of the bars for supper, but always shows up to work early. He also mentioned Rusty O'Sullivan never complains. If something goes wrong on a site, he just straps on his gear and says, 'Let's fix this.'"

Wind scratched his thin hair. "Those three words are probably why his men are loyal. Every dang one of them interrogated me before he'd say a word about the man. They all seem to respect O'Sullivan, but don't know much about him outside of work. He likes to be alone. Can't blame him. His kin all left him. None of the men he works with have ever been in his house or even in any of his vehicles. They say he buys old cars, pays cash and fixes them up, then sells them for double what he paid." Wind hesitated a moment, glanced at Miss Heather, before adding in a low voice, "One painter said Rusty drinks, sometimes gets in fights, but he never goes home with any of the women from the bar."

Jackson smiled. "Maybe he is saving his money. Women are expensive."

The detective lifted his shoulders. "I don't know. The bartender commented that if Rusty had died out on Someday Valley Road, he doubted one person would bother to go to his funeral. A good painter, though. A fair foreman. And, from the looks of his driving record, the man doesn't care if he lives or dies."

Jackson straightened like a general facing his troops. "Well, let's get to work. We've got three more offspring of Jamie Ray's to find, and meanwhile we have to figure out what his estate is worth. A little or a lot, Rusty is about to come into some money."

Wind shrugged. "One other thing. He's worked for Grady Brown half his life, and Grady says the man never takes a vacation. Unless he's in the hospital, he shows up to work."

Chapter 7

Starri stuffed Ona-May's dirty clothes into a bag as she waited with her aunt for the neighbor to drive into town to pick them up.

Jackson, the lawyer, had driven her back to the cabin last night. He'd even stopped for hamburgers on the hour-long drive home. He'd waited while she'd changed clothes and packed her aunt's things in a grocery bag, and then driven her right back to the hospital.

She'd spent the night in her aunt's room, but it felt good to have on clothes that weren't spotted with blood.

As they waited out front of the hospital, Starri lifted her face to the sun so it could kiss her with a new freckle across her nose. "I'll be right back," she said. "I think I forgot something in the room."

Ona-May was half asleep in the wheelchair and didn't comment.

Starri ran back, not to Auntie's room but to Rusty's. She knew he'd be moving to rehab soon and she wanted to say goodbye. But when she got there, he was sound asleep. She softly kissed his cheek, then returned to her aunt.

Ona-May was tired and complaining to the aide who'd rolled her outside. She swore no human could sleep in a hospital unless they were in a coma. All she had was a slight concussion and four stitches. She maintained she'd be as good as ever once she got a good night's sleep in her own bed.

Starri couldn't help smiling as she sat down beside her aunt. She was twenty and she'd finally kissed her first man.

Of course, he'd never know it, but she would remember and that was what mattered. She knew he was a kind man. He said he'd be her kin.

Chapter 8

After half a day in rehab, Rusty O'Sullivan figured he'd had enough. Every part of his body hurt, but he'd quickly learned how to balance with one crutch. The trick was not to put too much weight on his bandaged leg. One wrong twist might pull at his cuts running from hip to knee. One sudden movement might open the deep gashes. The accident hadn't broken the bone, so if he was careful, the crabby doctor told him it would heal fast. It was time to leave. He could handle the pain and he figured he could handle rehab on his own.

Pain was nothing new. He'd ridden bulls on weekends for a few years in all the rodeos around. Since he wasn't very good at making the eight seconds, he was usually hurting by Monday. At work he'd fallen off more than a few ladders as he'd learned to paint. His boss, Grady Brown, had told him more than once in the early days that if he couldn't learn to balance, he'd better learn to bounce.

Rusty figured out when he was still in his teens that he might be short on brains, but he was hard to kill. One of the

EMTs had told him on the ambulance ride into town Friday night that it was impossible to find a place on him that didn't need doctoring or wasn't already scarred.

But Rusty knew he'd heal; he always did. So, why hang out at a rehab with Fat Eddie, the physical therapist, who hated his job?

Rusty's plan: sleep the afternoon away, then plot his escape. His first thought was simply to walk out the front door of the rehab/nursing home after most of the inmates at the place were in bed or asleep in their wheelchairs. Who would stop him? By dusk the guy named Eddie had gone home and the two caretakers had been having a coffee break at the main desk for over an hour.

But, if he walked past them, the younger one might look up and start yelling at him. She seemed to think he was hard of hearing. She yelled at him to eat his supper, then shouted at full volume when he didn't. She yelled for him to get in bed and stay there as if she'd just made a royal command.

He decided to leave unnoticed. He'd made up a few simple rules when he was fifteen. One was to never bother to talk to someone who was already mad. It just made that person yell louder. Another rule was that no one owned him.

So, long after dark, he flipped the lock on the back door of the silent insane asylum. The metal door was bolted but the key was left in it. His one friend in the world, Starri, had sent him a jogging suit a few sizes too big this morning, thinking he would need to walk out wearing something other than a hospital gown. Since she and her aunt had been the ones to find him, apparently they felt like they should be the ones to take care of him. He didn't mind that, but he'd make sure to pay them back one day.

The guy who'd delivered the clothes didn't bother introducing himself. He simply threatened to kill Rusty if he gave Ona-May or Starri any grief. Rusty might have only one eye functioning, but he could see that the deliveryman/neighbor wasn't kidding.

Rusty knew Starri's friendship wouldn't last long. No one hung around him. People in his life had the staying power of soap bubbles. The men he worked with respected him but didn't talk to him any more than necessary. He was the first on the job, the last to leave, and the fastest worker. They seemed to admire him and hate him at the same time. Even his boss's Christmas gift came in an envelope, no card, just a bonus.

As he pushed the back door open, Rusty choked back a groan. His right shoulder was bruised almost to his elbow, but at least it worked. The break near his wrist already felt like it was healing, and his leg was locked away beneath layers of bandages.

"Walk out," he ordered his body. "Then keep walking. No matter where I sleep tonight, it won't be here. I've had enough people around me." He had no doubt he'd have the smell of aging death following him for months no matter how many showers he took.

A block away was a little lodge with tiny cabins for rent scattered between trees. If he could make it there, he'd take a handful of the pills that bossy intern gave him and sleep for a few days. Then he'd find a way to get home and rehab all by himself.

Strange thing about being hurt, no matter how bad you feel or how often you are knocked to your knees, all you have to do is keep breathing and eventually you'll get better. He knew one day the plan wouldn't work and he'd die, the luck of the draw. He'd take it when it came. This life wasn't that great anyway.

The night air was cold but at least it wasn't raining. Slowly, with each step an effort, he moved into the midnight shadows. With one eye still almost swollen closed, he ambled toward the old lodge. He knew the owner of the place would have turned out the sign and gone to bed. All Rusty had to do was pop the lock of one of the empty cabins and he'd sleep.

His one boot hit a slick spot as he stepped onto the road just as a car turned the corner. He raised his arms trying to keep his balance, then tumbled with his good leg locked straight as he fought not to put weight on the other.

For a moment he lay spread-eagle in the mud. He heard the car trying to stop, but he took no action. Rusty didn't care—even if he got run over, he figured it couldn't cause much more damage.

The car stopped three feet away and a second later a screaming, angry woman bolted out of the driver's side.

She must have recognized him because she yelled his name in between calling him an idiot, a fool, a menace to health care, a brainless donor candidate.

When the lady in scrubs dropped to her knee an inch from his head, all he could think to say was, "Evening, sweetheart."

"What are you doing out of rehab, O'Sullivan?" the intern shouted at him.

"I'm running away from home. What are you doing out this time of night? I'm not your problem, so what do you care?"

She leaned low and looped his bandaged arm around her neck. "I'm taking you back to the nursing home and telling them to keep you until you're a senior citizen."

He tried to ignore his elbow, which was dripping blood. "I'm not going back. You cured me, Doc. I'm thinking if I could find some clothes, I might just go to work tomorrow."

She tried to stand him up, but he felt like a tripod missing a leg.

Finally, she managed to get him into her car, a rattling old Chevy that sounded like the engine needed an overhaul.

"I'm not going back." His words hung heavy in the air between them.

"Then I'll take you wherever you're headed. I swore an oath. I can't just leave you to freeze."

His brain seemed to have turned to water and was swashing back and forth from ear to ear. He wasn't about to tell her he was planning to break into the cabin, and he wouldn't let her know where he lived. Not even the mailman knew his address.

"The road to my place is out. Try to keep up, Doc. That's the reason I rolled down the hill a few nights ago."

She turned up the heater and calmed a bit. "I can take you to a friend's house or back to the hospital. I swear you're nothing but trouble. Of course, when I left, we had three women in labor and a teenager who'd overdosed and thought trolls were hunting her. One of the fathers-to-be was drunk and bellowing that his baby better come tonight because he had to work tomorrow. His wife heard him from the delivery room and started yelling back."

Rusty wasn't interested in her problems, but at least she was no longer screaming at him.

She looked up. "Full moon, I guess. They say the ER is always crazy on a full moon. You'd have to sleep in the lobby, but we wouldn't charge you."

Rusty had no idea if she was kidding. In truth, he didn't care. The heater was warming him and exhaustion had finally taken over. Leaning back, he whispered, "Just keep driving, Doc. I'll sleep here."

Fatigue rolled over every cell in his body and the pain vanished in his dream of floating on a raft down Honey Creek on a hot summer day. He loved the way the gentle current moved him along. Pills and no energy left to fight drew him into a deep sleep that he seldom felt.

Warm, calm, silent. The doctor, her problems, his pain all seemed to wash over him as he floated.

The first light of dawn woke him gently with laughter drifting on warm air. He liked this world and thought he'd stay for a while. His friend Starri had been gentle when she had cleaned the mud and blood off him. He'd liked that. He was a man no one touched. He'd had so little interaction with others, Rusty didn't even know to want it.

Laughter circled around him again.

He slowly opened his good eye and tried to decide if he was on-site of the filming of an R-rated movie or still dreaming. His whole body came awake one pain at a time, but Rusty barely noticed because half-dressed women were spinning past him and none seemed aware of him.

For a few minutes he just watched. One redheaded lady wore only a towel. Another woman had on only a bra and panties. Others had T-shirts that were so thin they were almost see-through. His doctor was wearing the top of a pair of pajamas that barely covered her bottom.

"I'm dead," Rusty mumbled. It was the only explanation. Somehow, he'd fallen into a Victoria's Secret heaven . . . or hell.

He just stared at the doc's long legs. They should be in a museum . . . a work of art . . . perfection.

It took him a while to figure out that there were seven women in a big warehouse kind of room. A few were eating breakfast as they walked around talking to the others. One was on the phone. Three were standing in front of a long mirror combing their hair, putting on makeup, and chattering so fast he couldn't make sense of it all.

"He's awake." One of the T-shirt girls passed by him as she ate from a cereal bowl.

All of them gathered around the couch he realized he was lying on.

When he met the doc's eyes, he said softly, "Where am I?"

She shrugged her shoulders. "You went to sleep in my car. I didn't know where you lived and I couldn't take you back to the hospital just because you were asleep. You said you would not go back to rehab, so I brought you here. This is kind of a dorm for interns, visiting nurses, and anyone else in training. Our rooms are the size of walk-in closets, our showers are communal, and this big room serves as kitchen, living room, and makeup counter because the light in our windowless bedrooms is dull."

The redheaded woman leaned close to him as if studying him. "It took four of us to carry you in, mister. Amber must have thought you were a lost pup."

"Who is Amber?" he murmured but no one answered.

The doc added, "I have to be on duty in fifteen minutes, so you can stay here until I get off my shift. I'll take you home when I get back. Be good." She actually patted his head. "The women coming in off their shift have worked all night. You make a sound, they'll kick you out in the rain, bandages or not. Most of them have worked double shifts."

Rusty looked around him. He did feel like a stray dog brought in from the cold. These weren't girls, all looked to be capable women. Even the shortest one could probably beat him up now, but she smiled and simply said, "You feel like breakfast? We got Wheaties or Froot Loops."

"Thanks," he said. "I'm not hungry but if you have water, I'll take some."

An hour later, after drinking his water and swallowing down a few pills, he lay back, his good eye almost closed, and watched the women. Several left, dressed for work, and more came in talking about their shift—the patients, the doctor, the wins and the losses.

The conversations seemed to be in a kind of code. "Be sure to check on five. His fever keeps spiking." "The new mother with twins can't get B to latch on." "The GI bleed after three units is finally stable."

One slender nurse stripped off her scrubs as she talked. She was down to skin before she noticed him lying on the couch.

Rusty figured his only defense was to fake sleep.

He felt like a human dropped inside a settlement of aliens. No matter how many women were in the big room, half of them were talking. They griped and complained one minute and then in a wink they were all laughing about something.

Rusty didn't say a word. In the center of the tribe, he tried to be invisible. Possum defense. But it didn't work. They were all caretakers. Now and then one would walk by and brush his forehead, or tuck him in, or stop long enough to re-bandage a spot on him that was still bleeding.

At one point they began to play a game of "What do we do with the bandaged guy?"

Should they rewrap all his wounds? Should they wake him up and feed him? Should they bathe him? Maybe they should move him to one of the bedrooms. That idea was ve-toed. No one wanted to give up her room.

Obviously, Rusty didn't get a vote. He didn't care.

In the end they just let him sleep. He wasn't yelling. He had no fever. Maybe he just needed rest. After all, a doctor had left him here. Dr. Adams should know if he was in dan-ger.

Late morning, he awoke. The room was silent. All the night shift must be asleep. Rusty rose slowly and hobbled to the bathroom. The narrow room seemed to be decorated in bras and panties that looked more like lace slingshots. Thin clotheslines crossed back and forth just above his head.

Note to self about a strange habit of women, he thought. *Men never hang their underwear, but it seems a common custom for women.*

He washed in the first of a line of sinks. Most of the places on his body that had been stitched up were just a dull ache now, but his side, where a windshield wiper had poked him, hurt with every breath. He pulled off a blanket he'd been using as a robe and began to clean around the bandage.

"Trying to wash away pain, Mr. Trouble?" A voice he recognized came from the doorway.

"Why not? If I could just get the hard-to-reach places I'd be healed."

His beautiful doctor moved into the narrow space between the wall and the sink. "It doesn't look that bad, O'Sullivan. You seem to be all muscle and bandages."

"You want to give it a try, sweetheart?" He expected her to yell at him, but she just moved close and went to work. She was almost as tall as he was and, as before, she seemed confident even though her touch was gentle.

"If you can lean down, I'll wash your face."

He followed her request, ignoring the pain. The feel of her so near almost made him forget to breathe.

Her body moved against his as she worked. "You must work out, Trouble."

"No," he answered. "I just work."

When she dried his hair with a towel, they were face-to-face. The doc was flawless and he just stared, thankful he could see her with two eyes now.

"Feel better?" She brushed off the thin line of dried blood over his black eye.

Then, as if she'd done it a hundred times, she slipped under his arm and guided him to the table that separated the kitchen wall from the living area. Just as he spotted a hospital tray, she lowered him into a chair.

"I brought you lunch. One of the mothers-to-be, who is now in her fourteenth hour of labor, didn't want to eat. You can have the meal, but I get the dessert."

Then, just as simple as that, they ate together as if they were friends. She told him about her morning and he tried to remember a few things the women talked about.

As she finished the pie, she mentioned that the lawyer who saved Rusty came by looking for him. "You remember him: sandy hair, blue eyes, looks confused most of the time. I swear the man thinks he's a wall ornament. Just hanging around. Yesterday I found him sleeping in the lobby. I asked him if he had a home and he answered, 'I guess so.'"

"I don't want to see him," Rusty said simply. "I have no need for a lawyer."

"Dr. Henton and Jackson Landry may have saved your

life. You can talk to the man. That's what normal people do when someone helps them. I may be wrong, O'Sullivan, but I have a feeling you were raised wild."

He laughed. "Nobody raised me, Doc. But you're right— I *am* wild. Stay away from me. I might bite."

As she stood up and reached for the tray in anger, her left breast brushed his cheek and he forgot what they were talking about.

"I told Jackson you'd talk to him. And you will . . ."

"All right, I'll see him." He knew what it was like to cuddle up to women on the dance floor or when he was too drunk to hold back, but no touch of a woman had ever affected him like that brush of her breast. Obviously, she hadn't even noticed it.

"Great," she said, sounding a little disappointed that he hadn't argued. "And don't you dare call me 'sweetheart' while he's here, or any other time for that matter."

His voice came low. "What is your name?"

Her eyebrows shot up in surprise and a bit of anger left her. "*Doctor* Amber Adams."

"Mind if I call you Amber since we're living together?"

For once she seemed to see his brand of humor. "Sure. Mind if I call you Rus?"

"Not at all, sweetheart."

She raised her hand to swing and then laughed. "Never mind. You've probably got brain damage. Tell me one thing, Rus: do you have a home?"

"I do, but the only road up to it is a river of mud right now. I'm in no shape to dig it out even if I had a car to drive. I was headed over to that little lodge a block behind the hospital when I fell. The old man who runs the place lets me have a cabin for half price if the weather's bad, but last Friday I must have been too drunk to check the weather."

Amber nodded as if she'd finally figured where he was going last night. "I saw a sign on that lodge that said 'closed for winter' last week, and you can't stay here. Maybe the lawyer will help you find a place."

"I got a better idea. I'm a contractor. It would take a few days to draw it up and check with the city ordinances, but, if you'll let me stay a week, I'll overhaul this place. High windows in the tiny bedrooms. Individual shower stalls. Whatever you want."

Doc smiled. "You know, O'Sullivan, you're starting to grow on me. We'd all die for some privacy around here but are you up to the work?"

"I know a few men who owe me favors. I'll draw up the plans and let them do the heavy lifting."

Chapter 9

Tuesday, Almost Midnight

A silence finally settled over the little hospital as Emma Sumers made her last rounds. Everything had to be right as rain before she left for the night. Honey Creek Hospital was her world. Her entire life since her father died. Before that, she'd worked as a night nurse and cared for him during the day for eight years.

Now she went home alone every night, so she was in no hurry to leave work no matter how tired she was. She'd drive the three miles to her little condo, eat, and sleep. Then when she woke, she'd make lists of what she needed to do when she got back to work.

All her patients were resting tonight, except for one new mother whose baby was having trouble nursing. In a hospital this small, she knew every patient, but she was checking on only one this late. The night staff would watch over the others.

She'd started work an hour before her shift and now the

huge clock near the elevator chimed midnight. A sixteen-hour day, and one more thing to do.

Heading to the last room on the second floor, she smiled. This wasn't a duty or a chore; this last check was a choice. Every night she stopped in to see Mr. Heath Allen Rogers. The patient who'd stayed the longest since this hospital opened. Sixty-three days and counting. He'd been a rancher for almost forty years and when he checked in one night having chest pains, everyone in town worried. He might be a loner, but he'd given the money to build the only real hospital in the valley.

Two specialists were called in to consult and operate if needed. Once he was stable, they flew back on a private plane.

After his surgery the local doctors waited, but Heath never woke up. When they finally took him off life support, every doctor and nurse waited for his death with sorrow, but he continued on in a coma.

He kept breathing. His heart kept beating. But he didn't wake up.

As she walked into his room, Emma spoke to the private aide who sat beside his bed. "Go take a break, Ruth. I'll watch him for a while."

Ruth nodded, closed her paperback book, and slipped out. "I'll be back in thirty, Miss Sumers."

Emma didn't take the aide's seat. She moved beside Heath's bed and brushed his warm hand.

"Evening, Heath."

He didn't move.

"I've had a busy day today. Three more new citizens of Honey Creek came into the world. Two were screaming and I swear the third one came out smiling." In a whispered tone she rarely used, Emma told him details. "You must have pulled thousands of calves and colts in your day, and me, I lost count of the babies I've helped come into the world."

She carefully sat her hip on his covers, the line of her leg almost touching the side of his chest.

At fifty-one, her hair was highlighted with gray, but his was still black as coal. She remembered he always wore it short, but after months in here, it was quite a bit longer. "If I don't get someone to cut your hair, people will think you're an old rock singer."

She laughed her shy little laugh.

Her fingers pushed a few strands off his forehead.

Her low voice seemed to circle around them, too soft for anyone from the doorway to hear, but drifting like music so light it sounded of a melody too faint to make out the tune.

Every night as the town slept, Emma poured out her thoughts, her dreams, and her wishes. Over the past two months she'd felt as if they were growing closer. He knew her fears and secrets. Though it made no sense, she believed he was listening.

She remembered him as a quiet boy in school, a few years older than she was. The few times she sat in on the hospital board meetings, he hadn't said a word, but if the hospital needed money, a check from Rogers would show up within a few days.

When their paths crossed, she felt he truly saw her. He'd smile and nod once as if paying his respects. She'd never noticed him doing the same to anyone else.

That one nod and his shy smile had always made her feel special.

She leaned close to his ear and whispered, "Did you notice that three women from the church came with flowers? They changed out the vase of roses they brought last week. I thought of telling them that you probably liked daisies better, but I guessed you might not want to hurt their feelings.

"The ladies didn't talk to you. Didn't even offer a prayer. I guess they thought you wouldn't hear them. One said you were pale as death."

Emma squeezed his hand. "I'll open the blinds in the morning so you'll get some sun."

For a while, she just watched him. He was a big man but over the months he'd grown thin.

A tear drifted down her cheek and dropped onto his chest. Emma followed it down, and just for a moment she rested her head near his heart as well. "I wish . . ." she whispered, unable to put her thoughts into words. "I wish we'd had time together. I know folks say you don't talk much, but I'd be happy if you just called me Emma once."

Emma straightened up as she heard the door open. Ruth had returned.

Their time was over.

"Good night. We'll talk again tomorrow," Emma whispered.

Ruth picked up her book and asked, "Did you know him well, Miss Sumers?"

Emma remembered watching him play baseball. Growing up, he always walked in long strides, making one step to her two. Even when he was just a boy he kept to himself. Both of them were too shy to talk to each other. She'd heard he went to A&M and she went to UT. When she graduated, she joined the call for nurses to go to South America. She'd signed on for two years, but it was ten years before she came back to the States. In her thirties, she'd drifted from one place to another, getting more training, getting a master's. Finally, she'd come home to care for her father. Her forties had passed working nights at a tiny clinic and helping him during the day. When Honey Creek began thinking of building a hospital, she volunteered to be on the planning committee.

She remembered dancing with Heath Rogers at the fundraiser for the hospital. When she'd stayed to help, she saw him more often, but they rarely talked with so many people around. When they'd stood side by side to break ground, he'd smiled at her as if the other dozen people were invisible.

After the grand opening they'd ridden down together in the elevator. They'd stood so close she thought he might kiss her. But the ride was short, and the chance was gone in a blink.

But now they talked every night. Or, more accurately, she talked. When he woke up, she would be happy to listen to him for hours, for days. It was only fair.

Emma turned back to the aide. "I knew him. We've been friends since childhood." She wasn't sure it was true, but if it wasn't, then surely everyone in life should be allowed one fantasy and Heath had always been hers.

"Good night, Miss Sumers," Ruth said as she settled into the recliner with her huge Coke, a book, snacks, and a blanket.

Emma was looking at Heath as she answered the aide. "Good night, dear."

Chapter 10

Wednesday

Jackson Landry figured at the rate he was going, he'd wear out the hardwood floor in the law office by Christmas. Nothing was working. The old woman with cats insisted on paying him in kittens. The couple he'd talked out of getting a divorce beat each other up on their way home from posting bail.

Sheriff Pecos Smith said Fred Patterson took the worst of the beating, but neither he nor his wife, Susie, seemed to mind going back to jail. Fred claimed she'd kill him if she got near him again, and she claimed she wasn't going home until he agreed to move out.

The sheriff hung sheets in the empty cell between them and shouted he was never letting them out. Crimes were piling up on them and the best sheriff Honey Creek ever had was forgetting every rule he'd learned in his criminal justice classes.

Then on top of all else, Jackson seemed to have lost his dead client's son. O'Sullivan had vanished. How hard could it be to find a broken man dressed up like a mummy? But then, how hard could giving away money be? Who wouldn't want to at least find out what the inheritance was?

When Jackson looked up, he saw Wind Culstee leaning against the office doorframe just watching his boss. The detective had reported that he'd found several acres of land up along the rim near Someday Valley that Jamie Ray Morrell had bought years ago. Jamie Ray's son, Rusty O'Sullivan, must have driven right by them a hundred times.

The full-blooded Cherokee investigator had found no sign of O'Sullivan. Wind commented that most folks he talked to in the little town didn't even know who Rusty O'Sullivan was. The man had lived in the valley all his life and was little more than a ghost.

Jackson would have thought the one-eyed painter with one working leg would be happy to know he'd inherited something. But no! The first son of Jamie Ray had broken out of rehab and vanished. He was running from good fortune as fast as he could.

"I'm not good at this job," Jackson complained to the window, and swore he saw a thin line of smoke drifting up from the empty ashtray. "None of my problems were in the law books. I can't find O'Sullivan to give him his share. The Pattersons are driving Sheriff Smith crazy making threats at each other from their cells, and now I've got kittens to support."

Wind Culstee showed little interest in Jackson's problems. "I've asked around. O'Sullivan isn't in the hospital, the rehab, or his home. He did call and tell his boss he was recovering. But where? Thanks to the rain, he would have to be a mountain goat to get up to his place. The guy doesn't have any kin who would claim him, and no friends as near as I can tell."

Jackson frowned. "Well, his car is in pieces at the bottom of a hill so he didn't drive out. He can't walk far. And last time I saw him he was wearing a hospital gown, although I understand that Starri sent him a jogging suit. Black with a red double-T logo on the back. He can't be that hard to find. After all, half the folks in town either went to Texas Tech or follow the teams."

"Maybe we should file a missing person on him?" Wind suggested.

"I tried. Sheriff Smith told me I'm not his mother. Rusty doesn't have to report in to anyone."

Wind shrugged. "That's it, then."

"What do you mean, that's it? I'm trying to give him something!" Jackson yelled.

Wind raised an eyebrow. "Did you tell him that?"

"I didn't have time. I'm dealing with Jamie Ray's death. I went by O'Sullivan's room twice, but he was asleep."

Wind's other eyebrow rose. "You could have left him a note."

"What would I say, 'Your dad, who you never met, is dead; he left you something, but I haven't figured out what it is yet'?" Jackson looked back at the window, but no help came. Maybe he should just forget Rusty O'Sullivan and worry about the kittens or the Pattersons. Come to think of it, he should make sure the quarreling couple had wills. With the threats flying, either one could be dead any minute.

"All right," Jackson said, "here's what we do. You go to the rehab and ask everyone breathing if they saw him leave or if anyone came to see him or checked him out. I'll go to the hospital and talk to everyone I can find to see if he mentioned going somewhere to recover. If we don't get any answers, we could try that cabin where I found him hurt. Maybe he mentioned something to Starri or Ona-May between moans and screams."

"I already tried talking to them and his boss. No one could think of anywhere he might have disappeared to." Wind turned back and nodded at Miss Heather. "He couldn't get far without a car."

Without saying goodbye, the big man walked out of

Jackson's doorway. As Wind passed Miss Heather's desk, Jackson heard him say, "I'm walking over to the nursing home. You want me to bring you back lunch?"

Jackson didn't hear a response from Miss Heather, but she probably answered in code.

The big man hadn't offered to pick up Jackson a lunch.

"I'm going . . ." Jackson told Miss Heather as he walked out of his office.

"I can see that." Miss Heather was straightening the bun on the top of her head and didn't even bother to look up. "Don't forget you've got a two o'clock call coming in."

"Who?"

"The county judge. He told me you'd better get the Pattersons out of the sheriff's jail. He's only got three cells and Pecos is promising to arrest you and put you in the open cell between the lovebirds if you don't solve this problem."

"Me?" Jackson complained. "What did I do? I didn't break any law."

"The sheriff said you are disturbing the peace. His peace at the office."

Jackson headed out growling again. Maybe he'd get a brain scan when he got to the hospital. He'd obviously lost his mind.

An hour later, Jackson was still getting nowhere. Not one of the nurses, aides, or even the intern on duty would say anything about O'Sullivan. They were all polite. They all smiled and offered him guesses to Rusty O'Sullivan's whereabouts. Most answered with "Isn't he in rehab?" Each one said they had to get back to work. And he would swear at least half of the staff was lying.

Jackson finally sat down beside a woman in the waiting room. She looked about ten months pregnant so he figured she didn't have anything contagious.

"You the new lawyer?" She grinned as if she'd figured out a puzzle.

"Yep." He straightened. "You want a kitten?"

"Nope."

That was the end of their conversation. She started a little whistle with each quick breath and he thought about moving down to the teenager blowing his nose every ten seconds.

When the pretty intern came out to the sunny lobby, Jackson jumped up like he'd been waiting for her. "Mind if I buy you a coffee, Dr. Adams?"

"Does it come with a sandwich? I'm on a lunch break."

"Sure." He mentally counted the few bills in his wallet. "It's a date."

"No, it's not."

"Yes, it is, Doc. I haven't had a date in this decade. If I'm paying, it's a date."

"All right, it's a date." She hooked her arm on his. "But, dates come with dessert. I've been living on hospital food for weeks. I've heard the café serves homemade pie."

"Any chance this date comes with a kiss?"

"Not a chance."

"Mind if I ask you a few questions about a patient, Doc?"

"Mind if I don't answer? Doctors do not talk about their patients for one, and two, if you're not wearing a badge, I don't have to tell you anything."

Jackson studied her. Dr. Adams was tall and pretty in an all-business kind of way.

She knew something, otherwise she wouldn't waste time telling him why she wasn't talking. He smiled his best smile and lied. "To tell the truth, Doc, I'd just like to talk to someone with a brain. You'd be surprised how many people in this town are walking around without one. Anyway, I don't care where O'Sullivan is. He'll show up eventually. If you don't mind, I'd like to talk about me. I've been in this job for two months and I think I'm cracking up. Everyone who walks through my door has a problem that was left out of the law books."

She opened the door to the café and waved him in. "Maybe you need to date a psychiatrist, Mr. Landry?"

"I should have opened the door for you. I *am* losing it. Maybe if you could not wear heels next time? I feel like a kid talking to his teacher."

"I'm not wearing heels. I'm six feet one in work shoes."

He frowned. "I've never dated a woman almost as tall as me." He pulled out her chair before she grabbed it. "Amber, right. Your name is Amber? Mind if I call you that?"

"No, I don't mind, Jack."

"It's Jackson."

She patted his hand. "Do we need to talk about you losing your mind, Jackson?"

"No, no, I just couldn't remember the last girl I dated and I don't want to forget you. So, I'll try to remember your name."

She raised one eyebrow and stared at him. "Okay, Jack."

"Ryan is the only person who ever calls me Jack. He never wastes words. Even shortened my name."

"Now you have two people who do." The smile on her full lips told him she was just messing with him.

Then she winked at him and he forgot what they were even talking about. Was she flirting or making fun of him? One wink and he was brain-dead. He might as well join the locals.

Hell, he thought, *now she thinks I'm a nut case*. This was the worst date in his life. If he said anything else it would trump throwing up at the prom on his date's pink dress, and then trying to make her feel better by pointing out that at least the throw-up was the same color as her dress.

Amber was looking at the menu on the wall. She made

no effort to talk to him as she ordered. Coffee, a sandwich, and pie.

He ordered coffee and the soup of the day. When it arrived, he almost smiled, thinking that if this date went bad, at least the soup was the same color as her scrubs. Pea green.

She finally asked where he went to school and how he knew Dr. Henton.

Jackson was happy to talk about his friend. As she ate, he told her of their adventures as boys running wild on his mother's ancestral home. By the time she finished eating he'd described when they'd played football and roomed together at Texas Tech.

"Wild parties in college?" she asked.

"Not really. We were focused on our goals: he wanted to be a doctor and I wanted to be a lawyer." He decided to be honest and hoped she would too. "But now, I'm not sure I was meant to be in law. I can't seem to find a man to give an inheritance to."

"Maybe O'Sullivan doesn't want it. I heard when he left the hospital, he wrote a check to cover the bill. Not many people do that."

Jackson straightened and leaned toward her. He was making progress. "What man wouldn't want something valuable? If it is a house or a truck, he could sell it and buy what he wanted. I doubt Rusty has much."

"Why don't you let the guy recover before you bombard him with something he might or might not want?"

"All right, you've got a point. But, Doc, tell me if he's safe."

She hesitated and then looked him straight in the eyes and said, "He's safe."

The look in her green eyes told him that this line of questioning was over. When her pie arrived, she pushed it to the middle of the table and they silently shared dessert.

They talked about the town as they walked back to the

hospital. She said goodbye, and then with a wave she headed to the building behind the hospital everyone called the nurses' quarters.

Jackson watched her. Tall, head up. Beautiful. The dorm kind of building she must live in was constructed to offer low rent for visiting nurses. In the three years it had been open, the town had never had a female intern. It made sense that Amber would stay there. His mother had told him that the place had a "no men allowed" policy. If anyone had a date they were picked up in the hospital lobby. He wondered what it would be like to have a date—a real one—with Amber.

He decided he'd better stop thinking about Amber, and head over to the sheriff's office to visit with the Pattersons locked in Smith's holding cells.

Chapter 11

Wednesday, Almost Midnight

"Evening, dear," Emma Sumers whispered to her cowboy, looking as if he were only sleeping. "You know, I've never called a man *dear*. My papa used to call me 'dear one' and I always thought it was sweet. He was a hard man in many ways, but he did love me."

She sat on the hospital bed. "I wish you could hear me. I've wished a hundred times I had taken a few minutes to just talk to you when we'd passed in the hallway all those times. Likely we would have had nothing in common. My life is the hospital and yours is the land. I can't remember you ever saying more than a few words to me, but the way you looked at me made me wonder if you might have liked to talk. Maybe you'd say something to me about the weather and I'd answer back. Who knows what might have happened?"

Emma held his hand. It was rough and scarred. "I wish I knew you. Maybe we would have been friends. I like talking to you now, so I pretend you hear me. You wouldn't believe the things I think we would do. You could show me your place. I hear it's pretty. We might tell each other our secrets. We might talk about why you never married after your wife died in childbirth. And me. I planned to marry but I never found the right man, or it wasn't the right time in my life."

Since he didn't interrupt, she continued, "I thought I was in love twice. Once in college when I was in love with love. The second time I would have staked my life that I'd met my soulmate. He was perfect. He spent hours telling me what our life would be like if we married. He was almost ten years older than me and he had everything lined out. We worked together, him an X-ray technician and me an emergency nurse. He loved talking about 'someday' but never seemed to set a date."

She leaned closer. "Turned out he was telling two other nurses and the admissions clerk the same story." Laughing now, she added, "I was easily fooled at thirty-four.

"After him, my life seemed to get busy. I didn't plan to never marry or never have children; it just happened that way."

On a whim she leaned down and kissed his cheek. "Crazy thing is, the first man I've really liked in Honey Creek is in a coma."

Tenderly, she put her hand over the scar from his surgery. "At least I know you have a heart. I saw it." She could feel it pounding away beneath her hand. "Wake up, Heath Allen Rogers. Come back. I don't want you dying before I know if I could have loved one more time. Who knows, it might be real for a change and not just in my mind."

As the door opened, she picked up the chart.

"Good night, dear." She brushed her fingers over his hand.

It was just a twitch, she knew, but his last finger caught

her little pinkie. His rough hand wrapped around hers in a caress for only a moment, then stilled.

Ruth said something, but Emma rushed out of Heath's room before her tears could drip onto her uniform.

Her make-believe love had touched her if only for a blink. Almost touch. Almost real.

Chapter 12

Rusty O'Sullivan couldn't decide if he was in heaven or hell. He felt like the dorm pet. The first morning, he was fed three breakfasts and no one was awake to feed him lunch. Except for Dr. Adams, everyone else just treated him as if he was no more than a patient dropped off for the ladies to practice on.

All the nurses were better looking than any woman he'd ever seen in the bar. They were all caring and he wanted to protect them even if he was wrapped up like a human pincushion. In their white uniforms, he thought angels were circling around him.

He liked watching the auburn-haired one the most. She always had her head up high and a regal walk when she crossed the room, as if she were on stage. Plus, her big, beautiful, creamy breasts looked about to pop out of the towel she wore. He tried not to stare because he had a feeling she'd knock him into tomorrow if she saw him watching her. But it wasn't easy.

One of the girls called her Paige, but Rusty decided a woman like her should have two names. Maybe Paige Marie.

The short nurse was Katie. She had a giggle that made him smile. Pure sunshine. She liked to sneak him sweets. As he ate them quickly, she'd laugh like they were partners in crime.

Then there was Molly, who was kind, and her midnight-black hair brushed across her hips as she walked. Her job seemed to be to worry about him. She was always waking him up to see if he needed painkillers or water.

Rusty refused all the painkillers. He was afraid they'd make him sleep and he'd miss something. These women were different from the girls he knew. None flirted with him. Not one of the nurses wanted anything from him.

The last one he could put a name to was Sloane. The fighter. She was chubby and bossy. When she talked to him, she spoke in threats: "You'd better eat or you'll wish you had." "Don't you dare throw up on the rug." "Stop picking at your bandages or I'll tape your fingers together." But, on the bright side, she smelled like lavender.

In truth, he was a bit afraid of Sloane. Right now she could probably beat him up. Once she saw him watching one of the girls and gave him the "evil eye" look. A chubby woman with an evil eye was not someone he wanted to mess with.

But the voice he waited to hear, the face he needed to see was Dr. Amber's. Even when she was checking his injuries, he wished he could touch her sunshine hair or look into her green eyes. She was so out of his league, he couldn't even put sentences together when she came close.

On his second morning, he was almost asleep after the night shift had passed through when he heard the door open one last time. The doc was always the last one to come in from her shift.

With his eyes almost closed he watched her. She looked

dead-tired. She filled a glass of water and stood at the sink as she drank it, then dunked her head under the faucet. When she straightened, she combed back her wet hair with her fingers and he was sure he saw tears running down her cheeks, mixing with the water.

He kept his eyes closed as she walked to him and knelt beside the couch and began checking him. Her touch was light. Opening his eyes, he watched as she worked. When she unwrapped the bloody wound at his side, he saw the worry in her gaze.

"I'll heal, Doc. Don't worry about me."

For once she didn't say something sharp. She just smiled. "I know. You told me you always do."

She pushed his hair off his forehead. "What am I going to do with you, O'Sullivan?"

"Anything you want, Doc. I don't much care. I learned there are lots of folks that no one worries about, and I'm one of them. Kick me out before you get into trouble, but let me renovate this place. You may not believe it, but I'm great at my job. You showed me your skills and I wouldn't mind showing you mine."

"None of us has any money and the hospital would never pay for an upgrade."

"I'll do it for free, if you'll dance with me someday. No cost." He couldn't resist brushing his hand over her wet hair. "I owe you one, Doc."

He wished he could look into those jade eyes and see what was wrong. "You all right, Amber?" Her name felt strange on his tongue.

"I'm just tired. In a small hospital you seem to see it all in a shift: birth, death, and everything in between. Last night I saw an old man smile as he held his wife's hand and passed. A minute later, I looked into his wife's eyes and saw them grow dark, dead, even though she was still alive. She whispered, 'He promised he'd never leave me.'

"After eight years of schooling, I still couldn't think of anything to say to her sorrow."

Rusty lifted his bandaged arm and pulled her close. For a while neither said a word. He'd never comforted anyone so he figured he'd talk about what he knew. "I could give this place a makeover. What color you want in the kitchen?" When she didn't answer he tried again. "What kind of music do you like to dance to?"

"Country?"

She looked up and in that instant, he sensed she'd just lied. She smiled a bit too bright and added, "I'll dance with you, O'Sullivan, but first you've got to talk to the lawyer. Every time I turn around, Jackson Landry is asking if you've shown up yet. He's just doing his job."

"All right, I'll talk to him, but I'm not buying anything he's selling." He pushed one curl of sunshine behind her ear. "As your hair dries it begins to curl."

"Doesn't yours?" she teased.

"Nope. When I was a kid, folks used to tease me about having weed hair. Even Doctor Ryan used to make fun of it, back in high school. I always laughed along with everyone. It was one of the few times I was noticed."

Amber laughed. "I'm surprised he noticed. Dr. Ryan Henton is all about work and himself. A Dallas reporter came by the hospital last night and interviewed him about him riding through a storm on horseback to save an injured man. He didn't mention Jackson at all and you were only mentioned as the 'poor patient.'"

She stood and retrieved a wheelchair she'd left by the door. "Speaking of the lawyer, he's camped out in the lobby. I'll roll you through the back door so he won't know you're staying here."

Rusty smiled. "So, that means you're letting me stay around?"

"Until the remodel is done. You can stay until you get the windows in our tiny rooms and individual showers. You can stay until the county gets the bridge to your place rebuilt. Until that time, O'Sullivan, you're mine. I'll be keeping an eye on you. I have a feeling you'll be trouble."

"Deal," he added.

She helped him into the chair, having no idea how dearly he loved being so close to her.

As they moved into the hospital, he wondered what Amber had against Ryan. The guy had always had it all—popular, rich parents, a job where he saved lives. He was even voted "most likely to save the world" in high school.

Everyone knew Ryan. The quarterback. Class favorite.

Since Rusty had dropped out of school, he wasn't the class anything.

Five minutes later, Rusty was staring at one of the men who had saved his life. Jackson had seemed a superhero the night of the crash, but now, in his wrinkled clothes and holding an old briefcase, he seemed ordinary enough. "Thanks for what you and Dr. Henton did. Several people told me I might not have made it to the hospital if you guys hadn't stabilized me."

"I just rode in with Ryan. He did all the heavy work."

Rusty shook his head. "The nurse told me you carried a fifty-pound pack and those were your horses who made the drive down on a rainy night. You both faced dangers to help a stranger. Take my thanks, Landry." Rusty offered his hand. "What can I do for you?"

They shook hands, then Jackson opened his case. "I have a bit of business with you, Mr. O'Sullivan. I'm sorry to say your father passed in this very hospital the night of your accident."

"I don't have a father." Rusty fought to keep the anger out of his voice. "My mother never said his name. She told me when she couldn't find him, her parents disowned her."

Jackson looked frustrated. "I understand, but the name on your birth certificate was Jamie Ray Morrell. He wasn't much of a father, but in his will, he named four men to inherit all his worldly belongings."

"I don't want anything from a man who wouldn't claim me." Rusty tried to not pass out. Part of him wished the pain of the crash would outweigh the memories of his childhood. "I don't want to hear about this Jamie Ray, but would you give me the other three names in his will? I'd like to know the other three men. Brothers."

Landry handed him an envelope. "I have their names and last location. I don't think Jamie Ray ever tried to contact any of you, so they don't know about you either."

Rusty opened it while the lawyer talked. "Captain Andy Delane is stationed at Fort Sill, Oklahoma, but is on a mission that the post is not giving any detailed information on."

Rusty leaned forward, not wanting to miss a word.

"We know Griffith Laurent, your second brother, was in New Orleans. He graduated from Tulane University in May and seems to have disappeared.

"Zachary Holmes, the youngest of your brothers, lived just outside of Austin. Jamie Ray didn't put down an age for him but he's young. We think his mother is in jail and there is no record of where Zachary lives. If he's a minor, he's maybe living with kin or friends because he's never been in the system."

"All of them sound like they could be related to me. No ties."

Rusty stared at the names. Brothers. No, half brothers. No matter how worthless they were, for the first time in years he felt like he had a dusting of family. "As soon as I'm recovered, I'd like to help you find them, but I don't want anything Jamie Ray Morrell left me."

"Well, there's one thing you have got to take now and

we'll talk about the rest later." Landry moved a few steps backward and picked up a box.

The lawyer set it on Rusty's good leg and he felt it shift. Then, before he could demand the lawyer take the box back, a puppy poked his head out. Big brown eyes, ears and paws too big for the pup, and a tail wagging so fast it shook the dog's whole body.

"My investigator found the dog at Jamie Ray's house. The mother drowned under the porch along with two other pups, probably on the stormy night you rolled down the hill, but somehow this one lived."

"I can't take care of a dog. I don't want him. This is my inheritance?"

Jackson shrugged. "This pup and about half of the land along the north rim of this valley are what we've turned up so far. Jamie Ray left town before you were born and returned about five years ago. He bought up most of the land thirty miles from you that wasn't worth farming or ranching. He was a trucker for the oil companies and my guess is he didn't know what to do with his money. Before that, he worked the oil fields in Oklahoma and West Texas. The few people who knew him said he came home to die. He'd told a few drinking buddies that his ticker wasn't working right."

Rusty interrupted. "I don't care what he did or where he lived. I'll find the dog a home, but I will not take anything from Jamie Ray Morrell, not even his name. From the looks of this list of brothers, they'll feel the same way."

Rusty felt Amber put her hand on his shoulder and somehow it calmed him.

Amber's words were professional. "I know you're just doing your job, Jack, but my patient needs rest."

"I understand." Landry held out another paper. "You mind signing this authorization for my office to look into Jamie Ray's assets?"

"I'll sign. I don't care what you do. Not interested, but

one of my brothers might be." The word "brother" felt heavy on his tongue. Somewhere in this world he had three half brothers. If he could meet them, he would be able to talk about them when everyone talked about their families. He had a brother who graduated from college and another who might still be a minor. The one closest to his age was in the army. Rusty didn't even know them and he was already proud of them. They were his little brothers.

He straightened just a bit as he silently took on the title Big Brother.

As the doc moved him out the back door of the hospital and down the little walk to the dorm, Rusty patted the dog. By the time they rolled into the big room, the pup was asleep.

For the first time, Rusty tried to sit up on the couch. He lifted the ball of fur up beside him. "You know, pup, if we shaved all that hair off, you'd be about rat size."

"You need anything before I crash?" Amber asked as she sat down on the other side of the pup. "I've had a hard night."

"You want to tell me about it?" He'd never said that to anyone. Usually, the less he talked to people the better. But he didn't want her to leave.

She leaned against the back of the couch. "I need to unwind. How about we talk about anything *but* the hospital?"

"Sounds good."

He couldn't stop smiling. The doc was like a toy that had been wound up too tight. Sometimes she asked him a question, like "Where'd you grow up?" and then answered her own question.

After half an hour he knew where she grew up and all her sisters' names. She told him why she wanted to be a doctor and how hard she'd had to work in school. She even told him about her first love, who turned out to be a jerk. "I pretty much always date jerks. It seems to be my habit. One guy sold my car to pay his tuition. Another kept calling me by his old girlfriend's name. The last guy I dated sent me an invitation to his wedding inside his Valentine's card."

As she wound down, her speech slowed and she leaned closer. Finally, she laid her head on his unbandaged shoulder and fell asleep.

He just smiled as she wrapped her arms around his arm, as if the limb was her nighttime toy. As he brushed his stubbly chin against her soft hair, he closed his eyes and slept.

Chapter 13

Thursday Afternoon

Jackson Landry didn't go back to the office after he talked to Jamie Ray's son. He needed to think, and the best way was to climb on a horse and ride.

He drove out to his family ranch. Correction, *his* ranch now. He was the last Landry in the valley.

In truth, he'd always thought of the land as his mother's ranch. Her great-grandparents homesteaded here. His grandfather lived here all his life and his only child inherited it. Granddad had told Jackson once that he loved road trips as long as he could be home before dark.

Jackson always smiled when he remembered Granddad's sayings. Once when Jackson was complaining about law school, the old man said, "Nothing in this world that comes easy is worth having."

The old guy loved his only grandson as much as he loved waking up on his land.

His mother was the same way. Jackson always thought his father must have loved his mother dearly. Even when they'd lived in the apartment over his dad's office as newly-weds, she'd still driven out to the ranch to work with her horses. Once Jackson was born, his grandparents moved to a cabin they'd loved near the river. They didn't even have a TV, but they watched a thousand sunsets and sunrises.

All of his mother's people liked to say they had the dirt of this land in their blood. Jackson felt it, too, but he longed to explore the world before settling down. How can you say you live in the best place in the world if you haven't traveled? As he passed under the gate and turned toward the house he said, "Still doesn't feel like my land . . . not mine alone . . . not yet . . . maybe not ever."

Mack, the foreman, had one of Jackson's mother's best mares saddled by the time he pulled up between the house and the barn. Jackson took a minute to pull on an old pair of jeans and his boots. But this time, for the first time, he opened the drapes in his parents' home as he walked out. It was time to stop acting like his folks were coming back. They were gone forever and leaving all their things around would not ease the grief.

When he stepped into the barn, the smells of his child-hood surrounded him. His mother might have kept a spotless house, but the barn was his playground. He and Ryan had played *Star Wars*, building forts out of hay bales, and they'd been outlaws burying treasure then drawing maps. Ryan even made a secret code to find anything hidden on Landry land.

Jackson swung into the saddle and thanked Mack for having the horse ready, then he remembered when he and Ryan had found Mack's magazines under the tack. They weren't very racy compared to the internet dating sites today, but to two thirteen-year-old boys, the magazines were hours of entertainment.

Mack touched the brim of his hat. "It's good to see you ride, Jackson. I'm guessing your mother is smiling right now. Anything else I can do for you?"

For a moment, Jackson silently hoped his mom couldn't read his mind. The skimpy pictures were still floating in his brain. "Yes, Mack, you could help. Call that cleaning service Mom always used." He couldn't bring himself to order his mother's things packed away. "Have them clean the house and pull all the drapes down. The place needs some light."

"Will do," Mack said as Jackson turned out. "How about I have them put all your mother's things in her closet?"

Jackson didn't look back at Mack. "Good idea, but leave my dad's desk untouched. I'll clear it myself." As he rode out of the barn, Jackson didn't bother to wipe the tear off his cheek. He hadn't cried over his parents, but he'd thought about it a hundred times over the last few months. Somehow, he figured if he cried, he'd have to face the fact they were both dead.

Within minutes, Jackson was riding full out over land that had never known a plow. The day was cool with the last rain still in the air. He might not love horses as his mother had, but he loved the freedom of racing the wind.

When he finally slowed, he found himself riding near the bridge that led to Someday Valley. He thought it strange that Jamie Ray had lived on the north rim of the valley and his son lived maybe forty miles away on the south rim. Three small towns were scattered in this natural bowl. Father and son were not that far apart.

According to the county map, Jamie Ray Morrell had lived alone about as far away from folks as he could, and Rusty had another location just as isolated.

Without much thought or direction, he rode toward the cabin of Ona-May and her adopted niece, who'd faced the storm to help Rusty when his old Ford rolled.

Adrenaline had been flowing wild that night. The stormy darkness, the pounding rain, the accident made it all seem untamed. The only calm of that night had been Starri. She was a woman, but there was something about her that made her seem childlike one minute and a sage the next.

He had no doubt that her name, Starri Knight, had been given to her by her adopted aunt.

Jackson told himself he wanted to see if she was real. He'd seen her once at the hospital but they hadn't talked. As he rode toward the cabin, he wondered if there was a chance they might be friends.

The ride down the hill wasn't nearly as frightening in daylight, with the land drying in the sun. He gazed into the distance, taking in the view. Most of the time he didn't think about how beautiful this valley was. The memories of his home were mostly of the town. The city hall. His dad's office. The football field. The main streets. Charming shops and old inns that dotted Honey Creek. The small college in Clifton. The loneliness of Someday Valley with its scattered homes looking as if none of the people wanted to live too close. All the settlements laced together by a river and miles of farms and small ranches.

If you weren't born here, you'd always be "that guy from somewhere else."

As he neared the cabin, Starri stepped out on the porch. Her hair was up in a ponytail and her feet were bare. "I knew you'd come, lawyer."

Her grin told him she was happy to see him.

"How did you know I'd come?"

She smiled. A woman's smile, not a girl's. "I feel things about people."

He tied his horse to the porch railing and sat down on the top step. "What do you feel about me?"

"You're wandering, Jackson. Looking for something." As she stared at him, she lowered her voice and added, "You're also grieving. When they leave loving you, they leave a part of them in your heart. It hurts for a while, then slowly it's a comfort."

Everyone in the valley knew about his parents. The news of their deaths was all over the local news. "I understand what you mean," was all he could answer.

He stared out at the land. The signs of the Friday night wreck were still there. Scars in the rolling hill where grass grew as tall as his knee. There was something comforting about her aunt's little place, or maybe it was the kind woman behind him.

When he turned, the porch was deserted and, strangely, he felt the loss.

The screen door creaked as she came out with two Coke bottles laced between her fingers and a plate of cookies in the other hand.

After half a dozen Oreos, he finally asked, "You think cookies cure sorrow?"

She smiled. "It works as well as anything, I guess. Except riding a horse full out."

There it was, Jackson thought. She'd read his mind.

Without saying a word, they sat on the porch steps and he finished off the cookies.

When the snacks were gone, she stood and started toward the barn. "I'll race you to the bridge. Give me time to saddle up."

He followed her and watched. Maybe it was the barn and his recent memories of Mack's magazines. Or maybe Starri was just sexy in her worn jeans and tight sweater. He reminded himself that she was just a kid. The seven or eight years between them seemed almost a generation.

But then he'd thought the doctor was sexy in her scrubs when they had lunch. That seemed more normal since they were almost the same age.

Hell, he thought, maybe something was wrong with him. It had been so long since he had a date, he'd gone mad. It would be just a matter of time before he started buying magazines of half-naked women and hiding them in the tack room.

Starri swung up on her horse and looked down at him.

He followed her lead. Instead of going straight up the hill, she rode on a trail that circled upward. Suddenly he was enjoying the ride. The beauty of the valley was like riding into a life-size painting by a master.

When they reached the ridge, she stopped and slid to the ground. He did the same. They walked up to a clearing and turned to look over the valley below. Honey Creek was too far away to see even the top of the courthouse, but the houses and trailer park of Someday Valley looked like toys scattered across the brown grassland.

Starri turned to face him. "You all right? I can almost see you aging, Jackson."

"Yeah, I'm surviving. And you're right, these past few months *are* aging me."

She took his hand and swung it as if they were kids holding on to each other as they climbed. "Grow backward, Jackson," she whispered. "There are too many people in this world who age beyond their years."

He wasn't sure what she was talking about, but being here felt right. Without thinking about it, he circled her waist and dropped onto his back. She landed on top of him and they rolled down the incline they had just climbed.

Her laughter echoed through the valley and he joined her.

When they finally rolled to a stop, their arms and legs were tangled up in each other. As he helped her up, he thanked her for rattling the old man out of him.

She took his hand again and they finished the climb to the rim. Both silent. Both smiling. The view took his breath away as she pointed out her aunt's cabin below, which now seemed toy size.

As they relaxed and talked, Jackson took her hand once more as if it was the most natural thing to do in the world.

"I've been feeling like I'm unraveling lately. I studied for what seemed like years to pass the bar, then all I could think about was starting my career in Dallas. Then my parents crashed and everything changed. I haven't even unpacked my new big-city suits. Look at me. It's the middle of a work-day and I'm in jeans and boots. I haven't shaved in two days and no one noticed."

Jackson figured he was on a roll and couldn't stop now. "It's been almost three months and the ranch house still looks like Mom and Dad could walk in any minute. Every man I pass in town says he's sorry for my loss. Every old lady hugs me."

He raised his head and the wind caught his words. "I'm cracking up and no one notices. They don't even see that Honey Creek has the worst lawyer in Texas. I got a piece of paper on the wall that says I'm a lawyer, but I don't feel like one."

She leaned her body against him in comfort.

In a low whisper he added, "They left together in the crash. Sometimes, deep in the night, I get mad at my dad and mom. Not that they died. I'm angry they didn't take me with them. They were my family. I have a couple of relatives I see a few times a year, but no one who'll love me no matter what."

Finally, it was all out. Jackson took a deep breath. Telling the world all his problems so far from anywhere or anyone to hear him made Jackson grin. He'd always wondered if in-sanity taps on your shoulder or slams full force into your brain all at once, no time to see it coming.

Right now he'd go for the slamming theory.

Starri remained silent for a while, then she said in a whis-pered tone as if hoping he wouldn't hear her, "You want me to hug you?"

He turned around and studied her. In truth, he'd forgotten she was even there. To his surprise, she didn't look fright-ened. Likely more confused at his ranting. Like he wasn't nuts but just baffling.

"I might like a hug from someone under eighty. Only if you're offering, of course."

She moved to him as he froze. Her arms wrapped around him and she stood on her tiptoes and hugged him.

Slowly, like a man thawing from a block of ice, he held her close as if she was all that connected him to the earth. He didn't try to kiss her and she didn't pull away. Maybe she needed a hug just as badly as he did.

When Starri moved her head and bumped into his chin, she smiled and whispered, "You do need a shave, Jackson, and you smell more like your horse than a lawyer."

He kissed her forehead. "Thanks for noticing. Mind telling me what lawyers smell like?"

She took his hand. "File cabinets and dusty suits and sometimes pipes."

"And what do farm girls smell like?"

She giggled and said, "Chickens, hay, and peach cobbler."

They sat in the clearing as he talked about how he was going nowhere. He told her they were probably near Rusty O'Sullivan's land, and she said she'd adopted him as a brother.

"He's a hard man to keep up with. I seem to lose him again and again."

Starri laughed. "Maybe he's keeping up with himself."

Jackson liked the way she thought. There was something different about Starri. It was as if she was born out of her time.

He asked questions and she answered, weaving the story of her life together. When he asked about her education, he wasn't surprised that she'd been homeschooled by her aunt. What did surprise him was that she graduated from high school at sixteen and planned to finish her degree in the spring.

They rode back, slowly talking as they watched the sunset. There was a calmness about Starri. He wished he could freeze this moment so she'd never change.

When he said good night, he asked if she'd take a ride with him again sometime.

"Of course. When sorrow eases your heart."

He rode home thinking of what she'd said. All he'd been doing was concentrating on what was wrong with his life. Starri made him believe in something good happening.

He was relearning the town and finding himself. Wherever that led him couldn't be as bad as where he'd come from.

Chapter 14

Friday

Rusty O'Sullivan sat at the kitchen table with his stitched leg sticking out as he drew up the design for the windows in the tiny bedrooms. They'd be high, frosted so no one could see in, but light would pass through. He'd already called in the supply list and asked half a dozen men to show up at eight Saturday morning. It would be a long day, but he hoped to get the job done over the weekend.

To his surprise, not one man turned him down and a few even volunteered their kin or friends. They all had asked for his help several times, and this was his first ask. The nurses planned to leave for Dallas for the weekend, so this might be the only chance. His doc said she'd find an empty bed at the hospital to stay out of the way. She was on call all weekend.

Rusty promised he'd be fine alone. He was planning to camp out at the construction site. If all went well, he'd only be without water and electricity for one night. Besides, he had the dog for company.

He barely noticed the nurses rushing around him after

their shifts were over. They were getting ready for a rare weekend off. It was only when the pup barked at one that he noticed the women were jumping over his cast when they passed.

Somehow, he'd melted into their tribe. Sloane stopped by to give him an extra blanket and threaten him with death if he tried to work with the men. Paige bounced over to remind him she'd packed him sandwiches and left them in the cooler with Cokes and water.

Even as they loaded their cars, Molly stopped by to check his wounds one last time. Then the whole band of them lined up and kissed him goodbye. On the head, on the cheek, even on the nose. Not one hit his mouth.

The moment they left, the silence of the place surrounded him. He'd lived most of his life alone and had never noticed it, but now it seemed like such a void.

He kept working on tomorrow's plan. Making sure all details were covered. He hobbled around, checking the materials. His boss, Grady Brown, had sold him the supplies at cost. He even said he was proud of Rusty for helping the girls out.

The old guy probably had no idea how much money Rusty had in the bank. When you grow up with nothing, you hold on to what you earn.

The doc didn't show up with a hospital tray by seven, so he knew they must be busy tonight. Friday was usually hopping but Saturday would be worse. He didn't feel like eating alone so he fed the pup, who followed him everywhere. They passed the empty rooms one last time to make sure everything was ready.

By dark he started to worry about the doc. The wind was up and his phone told him the temperature was dropping rapidly. He could still turn on the heat, or even the oven, but he waited. She might not make it over to check on him tonight, but he wanted to be awake in case she did make it in.

It didn't matter, he told himself. He could take care of himself and the pup. She had a job to do. He wasn't her problem.

By eleven, he turned out the lights and covered up on the couch. By twelve, he knew she wasn't coming. He told himself she probably collapsed in an empty bed at the hospital or in her office. He didn't want to think about her rushing around in the emergency room with blood all over her scrubs.

He could see the lights of the hospital. All seemed calm, but still he didn't sleep.

Sometime after three he heard the door open.

"Amber?" he whispered.

"I'm sorry. I didn't mean to wake you. I just needed to check on you." She moved toward him. "It's been a terrible battle in the emergency room. When all calmed down, I just wanted to be somewhere quiet for a while. I forgot all the beds in our tiny rooms were folded up this morning."

He lifted his blankets. "Climb in. We'll share the couch. I can hear you shivering."

She slipped carefully in beside him. He took the shock of her freezing body, the smell of hospital disinfectants, her shaking so hard it was painful against his chest.

But he didn't back away. He lifted the sleeping pup to rest between his bandaged leg and good leg and pulled Amber against the length of him. "Just warm up, Doc. I'll tell you about my plans tomorrow. That'll put you to sleep."

She shivered for a while. He thought she cried a little and then she warmed and melted against him. In a whisper so low he barely heard her, Amber said, "I'm around people all day, but I always feel so alone. Sometimes I feel like I'm freezing from the inside out."

"I got you. You're not alone. You can be a warrior tomorrow, but tonight you might need to step down, and just be human. No one will see, and I won't tell a soul. Rest, sweetheart."

She poked him slightly, then he thought he heard her laugh. "I'll kill you later."

"I'm looking forward to it. Sleep."

He held her until dawn. Listening to her slow, steady breathing. He'd never held a woman like this. As she slept, he brushed his cheek against her curls. He knew he wasn't right for this kind of woman. Intelligent, driven, a crusader, but tonight, only one night, he could be what she needed.

Someone to hold her.

Icy rain pinged against the roof, but she was warm and protected. For a few hours, she was almost his.

Chapter 15

Emma Sumers rarely took shifts on weekends. She had her routines. She cleaned her house and did laundry every Saturday while her weekly soup cooked. Then she divided the servings up and put them, all but one, in the freezer. The last one would be her dinner as she watched her weekly movie. Sunday was for church and visiting her aunts at the nursing home.

But this Saturday she didn't want to clean or cook. She was restless. By ten, she couldn't get Heath Rogers off her mind. He'd moved his fingers. No. He'd reached for her hand three days ago. She swore she hadn't been mistaken.

Maybe she should run up to the hospital. She could say she left something in her locker and just decided to drop by his room.

Three evening visits had passed since he'd moved his finger over her hand as if reaching for her. She circled by his room several times yesterday, not counting when she relieved Ruth for a break. Some of that time he could have been asleep, but surely once again he could have tightened his fingers around hers.

Emma didn't know the rancher well, but somehow, she couldn't bear watching him die. As a nurse for over thirty years, she knew watching people die was part of the job, but she wasn't ready this time.

She dressed in her jeans and a sweater, then went back to the hospital. She wasn't going to work. She was going to visit someone she cared about.

Five minutes later, she entered his room. She was surprised to find no nurse or even an aide sitting with him. She'd read his doctor's directions. Heath was to have someone with him at all times.

For a while, she stood just inside the door, trying to control her temper. Maybe the nurse was in the restroom or maybe she went after a medicine.

Five minutes.

Ten minutes.

Emma moved closer. He was breathing normally. Nothing seemed to be wrong. She would not leave him. Not alone.

Fifteen minutes.

Thirty minutes.

She held his hand and the warmth of it calmed her. "I'm here, Heath. It's Emma. I will not leave you." She leaned closer and lowered her voice. "Don't you dare die on me, cowboy. One dance two years ago wasn't enough. When you wake up, I'm going to ask you out, bold as can be. Or maybe I'll invite you over and cook you a meal. We'll have a real date. We may be in our fifties, but that's still young these days."

She brushed her fingers over his hand. "Somehow, in this crazy world, I thought we might be friends. I saw kindness and intelligence in your eyes. I wish we'd made time to have a cup of coffee when you visited the hospital. I heard someone say once in a board meeting one of the members mentioned, 'Nurse Emma Sumers insisted they needed extra crash carts on every floor.'

"And you said, 'If Emma needs it, we'll find the money.'

"I wish I'd thanked you for that." She placed her first two fingers in the palm of his open hand. "If you hear me, Heath, squeeze my fingers."

Nothing.

"Hold my fingers." Her tears fell on his chest. "I need to know that you're still there."

Slowly, she felt his hand twitch. Then, without moving any other part of his body, he circled his big, rough hand around her fingers.

For a moment, it was almost painful to hope, then he squeezed again. It hadn't been a twitch; he had heard her demand and he'd answered.

She looked up at his face, nothing, but his grip was solid around her fingers.

"You're in there. You can hear me."

His hand closed again.

"Are you in pain?" Emma was so excited she almost forgot the protocol. "One squeeze for yes, two for no."

Two times his hand slightly tightened.

"You're in there," she almost shouted. "Fight your way back, Heath. I'm waiting for another dance."

The aide finally returned from her break. She looked frightened to see the head nurse waiting for her, but Emma only listened as she explained they needed help in the emergency room and she got blood all over her and had to shower and change before coming back. The two doctors on call rushed in but it was still hectic down there and the aide knew this room was her duty even if nothing ever happened. "I got back as fast as I could, I swear."

Emma really didn't care why she left. "Go back to emergency if you're so needed. I'll finish your shift. Don't leave this room when you're on duty, ever again, or you will not have a job."

The aide almost ran from the room.

Emma took a deep breath. Ruth, the night nurse watching over Heath, might read a book a night, but she sat close to Heath's bed and didn't step out. Emma tried to relieve her on weeknights, and she'd heard Ruth brought her own dinner on weekends.

"I'm staying with you for a while if you don't mind." She pulled off her jacket, then touched his hand. No response. "It's Emma, Heath. Looks like you're my date this Saturday night. Maybe we'll have dinner, then we can drive out to your place and have a look at the moon.

"Squeeze my hand," she whispered. "Let me know you can hear me."

He didn't move.

"Try opening an eye, or both. I'd like to see at least one of your brown eyes."

She moved her fingers over the stubble of his cheek and laughed. "I'm flirting with my date in a coma."

To her surprise his hand closed over her finger for a moment.

She repeated the drill two more times before Ruth, the night nurse, came in.

Heath didn't respond.

"Evening, Emma." Ruth seemed surprised to see the head nurse on her day off. "I thought I was the only one who came every night. I told them I'd take the overtime until they hire a few more people."

"I got a response last week, and hoped he might be coming out of the coma." Emma straightened to her head nurse stance. "Try every few hours to get him to hear you. Watch his eyes. Even if he blinks, I'd like you to call me."

"Will do." She wrinkled her forehead. "He means something to you, doesn't he?"

"He does. All my patients do."

Ruth nodded. "I understand. I'll call you. He's lucky to have someone as skilled as you checking on him."

Emma picked up her coat. She didn't want to leave Heath, but there would be talk if she stayed any longer. When she walked out into the dark parking lot, she took a deep breath and called herself a fool for caring so deeply for a man she barely knew.

Chapter 16

Rusty O'Sullivan scrubbed the sawdust out of his hair. He'd had one hell of a day.

First, just after dawn, he woke with Amber gone. She'd slipped away as silently as a dream. For a moment, he didn't move. He wanted to feel her next to him one last breath. They weren't lovers, or even friends for that matter, but he still felt the loss of her body against his.

The pup moaned as if offering sympathy, then jumped off the couch and padded to the door and whined. He wasn't trained, but the dog seemed to think he had to stay close to Rusty. The nurses were always taking him outside, but the minute the door opened the pup ran back in and settled beside the couch.

Rusty groaned and forced his muscles to wake one at a time. Using a crutch, he made it to the door and let the pup out. Two minutes later, the dog was scratching to get in.

When he opened the door, Rusty noticed the first spark of

dawn and realized he had maybe an hour to get ready for his men.

Feed the dog. Wash and get dressed the best he could. Go over his plans and the orders for each job. Remeasure everything one last time. They didn't have time to build anything twice. He'd had one of the men he worked with bring over the change of clothes he always kept in his locker. It felt so good to be in his own clothes, even if he did have to cut the jeans leg to accommodate the bandages.

Half an hour later, one of the women from the hospital kitchen brought him a gallon thermos of coffee and said the doctor had told her to keep it coming. The cook also had a basket of doughnuts. As she walked toward the door, she added, "I'll be delivering sandwiches at eleven thirty."

The cook looked around at the huge room. "Where are the nurses?"

"They took off to Dallas. They'll be back tomorrow night. I hope to have a few things around here in better shape once my help gets here. I've got ten guys coming to help."

"Who? You sure they are coming? It's a cloudy, cold day."

Two men stepped through the door she'd left open. They wore tool belts and layered clothing for outside. One was cussing at the weather and didn't notice the cook at first. The moment he did, he froze.

The well-rounded cook put her fists on her hips. "What are you two doing busting in this place? You could have knocked like you were taught manners. And, Wade, I'm telling your mother how you cuss at the good Lord's weather."

The big bricklayer whined, "Auntie, that's how we talk on the job. Don't mean nothing. I'm working today. Ten of us are volunteering to make this shack livable for them nurses you brag about all the time."

She turned to the other man. "And you, Donny, you help-ing?"

"I am."

Rusty watched three other men slip in. Apparently, the cook wasn't kin to them. They didn't say a word; they sim-ply followed the smell of coffee to the kitchen area.

"Warm up, boys!" Rusty yelled. "Wade and Donny's aunt brought us doughnuts and promised to keep the coffee com-ing."

Each man ate one doughnut while she poured the coffee, then took a few more to have with his drink.

The cook took their thanks, then turned to Rusty. "Ten men, you say. I need to double the lunch order and it ain't gonna be just sandwiches. I'll have soup and cookies."

Two more men, loaded down with power tools, stepped inside.

An army of men, ready to do their jobs.

The cook welcomed them as if she were the hostess. "You men are doing a good thing for the ladies. Now, drink your coffee and get to work."

Rusty watched her waddle between more men arriving. The cook reminded him of a fat mouse weaving between restless horses.

At the door she stopped and pointed at Wade. "And there will be no cussing today. This is a place where sweet angels sleep."

Fifteen minutes later, everyone had their jobs. Men were mounting lights that ran from a generator and measuring windows and shower stalls. Wade started knocking out bricks. Two carpenters were measuring where the bathroom shelves and hooks would go. All the others started on their own tasks.

Rusty grinned. If everything was organized, they worked like ants. Only this morning they were laughing, stopping to help one another, and even stepping out of each other's way without complaining.

To his surprise, not one man cussed but they did comment that maybe the nurses would want to invite them in for a group shower.

Rusty hadn't invited the married men—he figured they'd want to be home on the weekend—but by midafternoon several dropped by to help for a few hours. It was like no one wanted to miss the party. A few patched the roof and put in extra insulation. Even old Mr. Brown, who hadn't worked a site in years, stopped by twice and made two trips to pick up extra supplies.

Rusty tried to help with everything, but he was more in the way than helpful with his leg hurting every time he put any weight on it and the crutch tripping everyone up. Every time someone would yell, "Get out of the way, boss!" the others would echo him, and everyone but Rusty would laugh.

It was a great day when they got to yell at the boss.

Since Rusty couldn't cuss or yell at men doing him a favor, he took the abuse with a forced smile.

By six, the job was done. When a few ran out of anything to do, they painted the kitchen wall, and even Rusty's boss, who never did anything but the books, spent half an hour cleaning up.

As the men headed to the bar for free beers and nachos on Rusty's tab, he was too tired to join them.

After they left, dragging tools and trash with them, Rusty collapsed on the couch. His plan to remodel had worked. He patted the pup, who'd been asleep on Rusty's blanket for a few hours.

When the men had first started, the pup was in the way. They tried tying him outside, but the handful of a dog chewed his rope. Rusty tried locking him in one of the trucks, but he howled unless Rusty was with him. Finally, they brought the pup in and sat him beside Rusty. One man even gave the dog a command to bite Rusty if he got off the couch again.

For some crazy reason the pup must have understood. All afternoon he didn't move from Rusty's side.

It wasn't even dark and both man and dog were asleep before the last helper pulled away from the dorm.

Hours later, Rusty felt Amber slide in next to him as she floated a blanket over them both. It was too dark to see her, but he knew the feel of her.

He circled her waist, tugged her against him, and went back to sleep. It made no sense that two people so different would fit together so perfectly. He thought about asking her if she'd agree that they would not talk to each other in daylight. Then, at night, they'd sleep together. Just sleep.

Before he dozed off again, he wondered how it was possible to pack so much into one day. The cold and the aches didn't matter. He'd liked working with the men, though he couldn't pull his weight; the men seemed to take up the slack. He'd seen their kindness, their humor, and, strangely, Wade's fear of his auntie. They'd worked hard and fast, not for money but just to help out.

Rusty spent the night with his cheek against Amber's curls. He was too tired to even dream, but each time he almost came awake, he smiled.

At dawn, he woke to find her gone as always. She was on call all weekend. He probably wouldn't see her until nightfall. By then the nurses would be back and logic told him she wouldn't be cuddling with him again.

He felt all the way to his core that he'd miss the feel of her beside him for the rest of his life.

The pup curled back to sleep with a whine.

"I know how you feel, pup," Rusty whispered. "I miss her too."

Chapter 17

Sunday, 1:03 a.m.

Emma had fallen asleep in the recliner even before she'd finished watching her weekend movie. When the phone rang, she had to fight her way out of her blankets.

She grabbed her cell phone before she realized the house phone was ringing. No one but scam calls came in on that line, but she always answered anyway. She straightened and walked to the old phone that had been on the wall since she'd moved into her tiny one-bedroom townhouse.

"Hello," she said calmly, even though she was angry that someone was bothering her this late.

"It's Ruth, Miss Sumers. Heath Rogers opened his eyes fifteen minutes ago and all he keeps saying is 'Emma.' He's thrashing, trying to get out of bed. Dr. Henton is on duty tonight and told me to call you. If you don't get here fast, we're going to have to sedate him."

"Put your phone to his ear." She could hear another voice saying, "Easy now, sir. Your lady is on the line."

Emma started talking before she heard anything else.

"Heath. Heath! It is Emma. Relax, Heath, I'm coming. I'll be there soon!"

"Emma. Emma." The second time seemed lower.

"It will take me a few minutes before I'll be there. Now, you relax. Take a deep breath. I've got to find my coat." She moved around, putting on her raincoat, looking for her purse. "I'm on my way. Stop giving the doctor a hard time. Hand the phone to Ruth and tell her to call my cell." Emma knew Ruth's cell was on speaker. Ruth would have heard every word.

She ran outside without turning off a single light. Her phone rang as she started her car. "Heath. I'm on my way. I'll be there in five minutes."

"Emma," he said calmer than before. "Emma."

As Emma put the phone on speaker, Ruth was saying, "She's headed to the hospital, Mr. Rogers. I can hear the sound of her little car. Your Emma is on her way."

A tear ran down Emma's cheek. She wasn't his. She'd never been anyone's, really.

Ruth sounded nervous as she kept talking. "Miss Sumers is driving toward us right now in that little car that looks like it should belong on a bumper car track. It has been raining but don't you worry, sir. It's not cold enough to freeze."

There was a long pause and Ruth added, "Miss Sumers, you still there?"

"Yes."

Ruth let out a sigh. "He seems to be resting easy. Drive safe."

"Thank you, Ruth. Stay with him."

"I will. I'll count the minutes out loud and let him know you're getting closer."

Emma pushed the accelerator. She planned to be at Heath's side when he opened his eyes again.

Chapter 18

Dr. Ryan Henton waved Jackson into his office. "I've only got a minute, Jack. You do know you can't have your morning coffee break in my office."

"That's all I need, one minute. Just want to check to see if you've seen Jamie Ray Morrell's son. I seem to have lost Rusty—again. How hard could it be to keep up with a guy with a sliced-up leg, a messed-up arm, and cuts all over his body?"

Since Ryan didn't look up from the file on his desk, Jackson figured he'd have to repeat the question.

Jackson used his briefcase for a table as he sat across the desk from Ryan and waited for the new doc to remember he was in the room. Jackson tried to relax. He didn't want to put his doughnut, even wrapped in a napkin, on the furniture. Not one speck of dust was on the polished mahogany so he guessed a chocolate doughnut with chocolate icing wouldn't be welcome.

Ryan was probably figuring out how to save a patient's

life and Jackson was worried about crumbs. Sounded about right.

The whole office looked like it was staged. Which meant one of two things: his college roommate never spent any time here, or he'd become a neat freak after years of picking up his clothes off the floor as he ran to class. All through college Jackson had watched Ryan decide what needed laundering by smell. He went around sniffing until the basket was full.

Jackson frowned at his own wrinkled shirt. His law office looked like the play table in kindergarten. His car hadn't been washed in months, and the ranch truck he drove was so dirty he didn't remember what the color was.

When he'd come home that fateful day, after getting the worst news in the world from his uncle, the ranch phone was ringing as he walked in.

An official voice introduced himself.

Jackson was tired and only half listening. "Are you Jackson Landry?"

The voice came again, lower, slower as if Jackson might not understand the stranger's words.

Jackson nodded then realized he had to talk. "I am."

"I'm sorry to be the one to tell you this . . ."

Jackson had put the phone down. He'd already heard it once. He wasn't sure he'd ever answer an unknown caller again. The voice just continued, "Your parents have died in a plane crash in Oldham County. We believe strong winds were the cause. I'm sorry for your loss."

Jackson hadn't packed or called anyone. He'd simply walked to his car and driven home, as if he could get back to Honey Creek and fix everything. But there was no fixing anything. People, friends, neighbors he'd always known but rarely talked to had surrounded him and helped him through the worst days of his life.

A friend packed his things at his new apartment in Dallas and sent everything to Jackson's parents' ranch. But Jackson didn't wear any of his new suits. He only wore what was in his closet at home. Almost three months later and the boxes were still there.

He'd become the bum and Ryan, even in his scrubs, out-shined him.

Even an office no one probably saw was kept neat. It was as if Ryan was growing, shining, and he was stuck in the mud. Jackson couldn't unpack. Couldn't sleep at the ranch. Couldn't get on with living. All he could do was try to work. He could be a lawyer—maybe not a good one, but he could function.

Jackson closed off the sorrow in his brain and focused on his best friend's sudden change of habits.

Of course, the only real answer was Ryan probably didn't work in his office. In fact, Jackson silently noted, no one really knows what a doctor does in his office.

It wouldn't be a "doc goes wild" thing like Jackson had seen once in a B-movie. None of the staff could pass the casting call. Except for the nurses at the dorm, most of the nurses were middle-aged, married and no makeup kind of women. One big nurse in the emergency room looked like she could handle half a dozen truckers at the same time. And Jackson had no memory of a nurse wearing heels. They all got their shoes at the Ugly White Shoe Store . . .

"What do you need, Jack?" Ryan asked as if he was in a hurry.

Jackson started. He'd gotten a little too caught up in his woolgathering.

Ryan looked up from the chart he'd been reading. "Look, Jack, you're the lawyer, not me, but I don't think you or I can make Rusty O'Sullivan take his inheritance, if that's what you're trying to talk me into.

"I can't blame him. From what I heard, Rusty raised him-self. He was passed around as a kid. I heard the staff talking. They said he lives alone, never talks, eats his dinner at the local bar. The guy is more of a loner than a koala."

When Jackson didn't say something fast, Ryan added one of his worthless facts. "Did you know koalas sleep sometimes twenty hours a day? Then, when they wake up, all they do is eat, and mate now and then."

Jackson finally grinned. "I had a great-aunt who was like that."

Ryan didn't laugh. "If you're looking for O'Sullivan, you might walk out the back of the hospital. I saw Amber rolling him into the nurses' dorm. Maybe they're practicing on him, or they've adopted him as a pet."

Jackson dropped the last of his doughnut, his lunch, in the trash. He had to go talk to his lovebirds, the Pattersons, still locked away in jail. Then he'd come back over and check out the nurses' dorm. It would be all right, he told himself. After all, he was on official business.

Ten minutes later, Jackson was sitting in the middle cell of the county jail. Fred and Susie Patterson were not speaking to each other today.

For the third time, Jackson tried to start a conversation. "You two ready to go home? I could get you out and you could go your separate ways. I'll even draw up the divorce papers for half price. Susie, you could go visit your grandmother in Someday Valley, and, Fred, you've got four brothers. Surely one would take you in. You two don't have to even see each other again."

Silence. After yelling for days, they must have run out of words.

Five minutes passed before Fred said, "Any one of my brothers would take me in, but I can't stand any of my sisters-in-law. Susie is a saint compared to them. She's double prettier than any one of them too."

Jackson waited for him to say more, but he didn't. Five more minutes passed before Susie said in a whisper, "I'd rather go back with Fred than go live with my grandmother.

She's got chickens, dogs, a duck, and two skunks. None of them know where the outhouse is. The last time I slept over after cleaning her house, I woke with a momma cat who'd had three kittens on my bed during the night."

Fred laughed. "I guess I'm not so bad to sleep with. Right, baby?" Then he whispered, "You know, honey, I didn't mean to fall out of bed on top of you. I swear I didn't try to hurt you."

"And I didn't mean to hit you four times with the broom."

"Five times," Fred corrected.

"No, four. The first hit I meant to do. I was mad. The other hits were just because I was on a roll and it's hard for me to stop."

Fred whispered, "I know, honey. And I'm just saying that trait ain't all bad at times. When you get on a loving roll, I just decide dying in bed ain't a bad way to go, sugar pie."

The lawyer walked out of the open cell door. Jackson couldn't take any more sweet talk from Fred. All the loving names Fred was using were making him sick. If he had Susie's broom, he might take a swing at the man.

But they were finally talking, and from the sound of it there would be no divorce.

As he passed Pecos's office, Jackson nodded at the young sheriff.

Pecos smiled. "Maybe I'll make it home for supper tonight. How much longer should I leave them alone? They've been whispering all morning and I have a feeling I'm too young to hear what they're saying."

Jackson shrugged. "If you don't hear any yelling by five, let them out. Did you ever figure out what they were arguing about?"

"Everything and nothing, I guess. It seems they had to dig through every disagreement they had in the ten years they've been married." Pecos laughed. "I'm happy to be married to a woman with a short memory."

"You are a lucky man, Pecos." Jackson waved goodbye and thought about finding Amber at the hospital. It was almost five; maybe he'd get lucky and catch her on a dinner break.

As he turned to leave, Pecos stood. "Mr. Landry, I need a bit of your advice. We've got a runaway in our back office. Grocer caught him stealing food. I don't want to charge him, but he won't tell me anything—not where he's from, his name, who to call. He's tall, but he can't be more than fourteen or fifteen."

"How can I be of any help?"

"He keeps telling me to let him go or get him a lawyer. I thought you might be able to talk to him. I don't think he's from around here and I hate to call Child Protective Services in on a kid that will just run."

They walked to the interrogation room, which Jackson knew had been painted black, for some reason or other. Pecos continued, "He's got a mouth on him. He looks so thin I let him eat the evidence *and* my lunch an hour ago. He pushed them down so fast I don't even think he chewed."

As the sheriff opened the door, Jackson saw a bone-thin kid leaning back in an old office chair with his long legs propped on the table. He looked sound asleep. His right wrist was cuffed to the chair.

"Wake up, kid, your lawyer is here." Pecos tapped on his boots. Army boots. Not cowboy boots. Pecos backed out and closed the door.

The kid cussed for a while, then opened one eye and looked at Jackson. "You don't look like a lawyer. How long you been one?"

Jackson sat down across the table from the boy. "You don't look much like eighteen. I'm guessing fourteen."

"What do you care, Mr. Lawyer?"

"I don't. I was tricked to come in and talk to you."

"Great, I got a dumb lawyer." The kid scratched a scar into the table with his dirty fingernail.

Jackson leaned back and stared at the boy. Something about him seemed familiar. Black hair, thin, gray eyes. Maybe he'd seen him somewhere else.

"You don't have a lawyer yet. I just agreed to answer a few questions. You have to pay me before I'm your lawyer."

For a second, Jackson felt like he was mimicking his father. The slow, low way he talked to people. Kind, but factual. "Look, kid, if you convince the sheriff you're eighteen, he'll lock you up in the real jail while they figure out who you are. If he thinks you're still underage, he'll call Welfare, and I'm guessing you've already been down that road."

The kid rattled his cuffs down the arm of the chair until he could reach the top of his boot. With two fingers he pulled out a folded ten-dollar bill. His words came out more frightened than angry now. "If you'll help me, I can pay."

Jackson looked at the bill in the center of the table. Another case he had no idea how to handle, but at least he was getting paid.

He grinned, knowing it wasn't about the money. It never would be for him. "I'll do my best to help you. This case shouldn't be hard; you ate the evidence. But, before I take you on as a client, I have to know your name and where you're from."

The kid stared at his hands for a while and finally said, "I'm Zach Holmes and I'm from nowhere."

Jackson felt as if a ghost slapped him. He didn't hear or feel the blow, but he reacted deep inside. Zachary Holmes.

The kid raised his head and stared. "That's all I know. I'm not even sure when I was born. Some clerk behind a big desk filled out the blanks on my file when I was too young to be in school. She wrote July fourth as my birthday. She said that would be a fun birthday and the government didn't like blanks on forms."

The lawyer stared into the boy's gray eyes. Zachary Holmes. The same name on Jamie Ray Morrell's handwritten will. Jamie Ray said he didn't know how old this son was so he just guessed. He'd guessed wrong.

Jackson pushed the ten back to the kid. "I'll try to help you out, Zach. You pay me when the job's finished. Promise you'll stay here until I get back. If you leave, they'll find you, but if you stay there's a chance I can help."

The kid shook the handcuffs as he shrugged.

Jackson knew he had to hurry. In the hallway, he almost knocked Fred and Susie over. They were making out like sophomores between lockers. "Why don't you two go home—you're married, you know?"

They ignored him.

As Jackson walked away, he yelled, "I'll send you a bill for my time! Three hundred an hour!"

Fred pulled his mouth off Susie. "*What?*"

"That's the going rate, but I'm considering double for the ear damage." Jackson ran away from the cussing. His first paying client would probably file a complaint against him.

When he passed the sheriff, Jackson ordered, "Keep the kid in the black room cuffed. I'm sending Wind to watch him. I'll be right back."

Pecos yelled back, "Tell Wind to bring food! Kid is probably still hungry. I know I am."

Walking toward the hospital, Jackson called his staff. Surprisingly, Wind, his investigator, and Miss Heather, his secretary, were both in the office. He relayed everything he'd learned. Wind said he'd go sit on the boy before Jackson asked, and Miss Heather said she didn't mind doing some digging. Now they knew he was a child everything changed.

As he clicked off all the details he knew, Jackson said aloud to himself, "All I have to do now is find O'Sullivan, and the only person who might know where he is seems to be Dr. Amber Adams."

Ryan had said he'd seen her rolling Rusty toward the

nurses' dorm, and right now it seemed to be the only place he hadn't looked in the entire valley.

When he didn't find Amber at the hospital, he walked out back where the nurses' dorm was. Like everyone in town, he knew no men were allowed. But then he was here on official business.

Halfway up the walk, two men stepped into Jackson's path as if their bodies were a locking gate. They were both older than Jackson, one by ten years, the other maybe twenty. He might not know who they were, but he knew what they were. Anyone born in Texas could recognize them. Tan slacks, white shirt, tie, and cowboy boots. Texas Rangers. Real Texas Rangers, not the ones who play ball.

Jackson straightened. "Evening, gentlemen. You're a long way from Waco or Austin."

The older of the two smiled. "You're Jackson Landry. Right?"

Jackson tried to hide his surprise. "Right. I didn't know I was on the Texas Rangers' radar."

"You're not. I'm Ranger Daily. I knew your father. You favor him. Sorry to hear about the accident. Your folks were good people. I enjoyed working with your dad a few times and I counted him as a friend."

Jackson shook the Ranger's hand. "Thank you, sir. If you ever need my help I'd be honored to be at your service. I took over my dad's practice."

"I'm glad. Your parents were always so proud of you. When I pass this way again, I'll stop in for coffee and tell you about a few cases we worked on. Your dad might not have been a detective, but he loved lining up the facts."

"I'd like that. Would you mind telling why you're here tonight?"

"This time we're just checking something out for a friend. Nothing official. We were in the county and thought we'd check how one of our buddy's relatives was recovering from an accident."

Jackson tried not to let curiosity show. "I thought you might be guarding the nurses' dorm. No men allowed, you know."

"What nurses?" the younger Ranger said, then stared at Jackson as if he'd guessed Jackson was really a criminal. "And, Mr. Landry, if it's no men allowed, what are you doing walking toward the building?"

"Guilty as charged," Jackson said. He considered making a run for it. He'd never be able to fight these guys but he might be able to outrun them.

The friendly older man, Ranger Daily, said simply, "Carl is just messing with you. If we were after you, we'd already have you cuffed and in the car."

Jackson summoned up his best lawyer voice. "What would you be charging me with, Ranger?"

One side of Carl's mouth lifted. "Talking too much. All lawyers are guilty of that."

Both lawmen laughed and Jackson smiled.

As they said goodbye, Jackson added as he walked toward the dorm, "Carl, you should stop by for coffee next time you're in the neighborhood. You're a funny guy."

Now the only man who laughed was Daily.

Chapter 19

Rusty watched the lawyer slowly slide around the front door as if no one would notice a six-foot man with a briefcase coming into the dorm.

Katie, the shortest and youngest of the nurses, squealed and jumped up from the table when she saw Jackson. "Men are not allowed in here."

Rusty guessed since she had twisty sticks poking out of her hair, she was embarrassed. What bothered Rusty more was Katie didn't seem to notice that he was a man. He'd been lying on the couch for days. He had to get out of this patient/pet zone.

Sloane, the warrior, stood ready to fight. "Are you lost, lawyer?" Her question echoed through the large room.

Rusty glanced over to make sure Paige was wearing more than a towel. She was like a biscuit can left out of the fridge. Those nicely rounded breasts might pop out any minute.

Then all the ladies stood and moved toward the couch as if protecting him from an invader. Rusty decided to just smile.

If Jackson was sharp with any one of them, he vowed he'd beat the lawyer later even if he had saved his life.

To his credit, Jackson looked at no one but Rusty and held his briefcase against his chest like armor.

Rusty laughed. He cared about every one of these ladies, but they didn't need him to protect them. Every one of them was a warrior.

Then he remembered that Jackson had ridden through a hell of a storm to help him. It would be hard to beat up a man who saved his life, but he'd do it for the ladies.

Rusty had to act fast. Sloane was already demanding Jackson leave, and tiny little Katie had reentered the room with her curling iron, which could be classified as a weapon. All the ladies who spent their lives putting people back together looked like they were about to tear one lawyer apart.

"Jackson! You came!" Rusty shouted. "I have a legal question. Roll that wheelchair over here. I'll climb in and we can talk outside." He glanced over at the women. "You're not supposed to be in here. So, if I'm going to talk to you, it'll have to be somewhere else."

Jackson looked at the women and quickly apologized as he followed Rusty's orders. As he rolled Rusty out, he whispered, "I've seen lynch mobs in old Westerns that looked more friendly."

When they were in the clear by twenty feet, Jackson added, "Thanks. You saved my life in there."

"No problem. Just paying you back. This was nothing. Last night they decided to get into a tickle fight. Me against all of them. I thought I might laugh myself into an early grave. I'm not ticklish but I laughed. I haven't been around many women. It's a whole different world." He couldn't stop smiling. "One minute they were tickling me and making me duck and dodge, and the next they were telling me to be careful of my stitches."

"I wouldn't know about many women," Jackson said as he kept rolling the chair down the sidewalk. "The nearest

I've come to a date in years is sharing pie over lunch a few days ago."

"You must have gone out with the doc. Every day, when she brings me a tray from the hospital, she eats most of my dessert. She thinks shared pie has no calories."

"Seems we're dating the same woman."

Rusty shook his head. "Nope. I think it's the pie, not a date. One day I was asleep and she just ate my dessert and left. I woke to a cold lunch and a tiny plate dusted with crumbs."

They both laughed as Jackson kept pushing him along. "Mr. Attorney, mind telling where you're taking me? I really don't have anything to talk to you about. I was just saving your life from a mob."

"We're going to the county sheriff's office. There is someone you've got to see."

"No. Take me back." Rusty couldn't see any way this could be good. "Take me back right now. I'm in rehab. I can't have visitors."

"It will only take a few minutes, Rusty, and you might learn something."

"No. I don't want to meet anyone in the sheriff's office. This is some kind of trick. The sheriff can't arrest me for rolling down a hill in my car. That's not illegal, is it?"

"I can't say. I'm not your lawyer, remember? You fired me when I tried to give you your inheritance."

A deputy stepped out of the sheriff's office, noticed Jackson pushing a wheelchair, and held the door open. He moved back inside so he could make room for the chair.

"Officer!" Rusty shouted. "I'm being kidnapped!"

The tired deputy didn't even blink. "That happens sometimes. Never trust a lawyer who wear spurs on his boots."

Rusty decided the deputy and the crazy lawyer were just two examples as to why he never had anything to do with people. People didn't make sense. They never had. Live alone. Eat in a crowd so no one notices you. Don't talk to people unless it's necessary.

"Thanks, Deputy," Jackson said politely. "Mind opening the interrogation room's door?"

"Not at all, if you can get that mountain of a detective out of the way. He was in with the kid, but he stepped out to give his ears some relief." The deputy grinned. "I wouldn't be surprised if that kid didn't gnaw off his hand to get out of the handcuffs."

Rusty had heard enough. "Take me back, Landry, or I swear I'll file charges on you. I'm not talking to some kid. I don't even like kids." It crossed his mind that the lawyer might be using him as a bad example for driving too fast on a muddy road in a rainstorm.

"Take me back! I'm not—" was all he got out before Jackson pushed him inside a little room and a big guy in black slammed the door.

A beanpole of a kid started yelling that he wasn't some kind of freak on display.

As Rusty heard the lock click, the boy tossed a can at the door. "And I want a Dr Pepper, not a Coke!"

It only took a few minutes before Rusty stopped listening to the kid and looked around. This was the most nothing room he'd ever seen. Everything in the room was painted black, making even the one light swinging above seem in shadow. One black table. One black chair and the kid was cuffed to it. No posters. Not even paper on the floor. This seemed the perfect place to line the walls with wanted posters, but Rusty had no intention on advising the sheriff's office on decorating.

He rolled close to the door and shouted a few death threats to Jackson, but got no response. He had no idea why he'd been brought in. Or why he'd been locked up with a kid who looked like he wasn't old enough to shave.

He glared at the boy. The kid glared back.

Finally, the kid said, "What you in for?"

"I don't know. How about you?"

"I caught a ride out of Austin a few days ago. Figured I'd have a look at California before I got any older. This trucker said he had to drive north, then he'd catch Interstate 40 and head west, so I thought I'd sit back and see the world."

Rusty didn't want to listen but at least the kid wasn't yelling.

"The guy played show tunes so loud my brain cells were committing suicide and my ears mutinied completely. After a while I couldn't take it. So, when he stopped at a truck stop, I hopped out, walked across the street, and picked up lunch. I noticed this place was named Honey Creek. My mom told me once that I had a relative here, but I decided any kin wouldn't welcome someone like me.

"The trucker was gone when I walked out. A lawman grabbed me and said I forgot to pay. I tried to tell him I was brain dead from hearing 'Mamma Mia' a hundred times, but he just said he never heard of it."

"Too much information, kid. I don't care." Rusty grabbed the doorknob. It was still locked. "How about we forget any idea of being friends? I don't need anyone, including you." He slammed his good arm at the door. The door didn't move, but the reaction sent Rusty rolling toward the table.

"Yeah, I can see that. You're a man in control. Who beat you up? Looks like maybe half the town got in a hit."

Before Rusty could tell him to worry about his own problems, Landry opened the door enough to poke in his head. "You figure it out, O'Sullivan?"

"Of course—we've solved world hunger. How about letting me go back to the nurses? It's time for my nap."

Jackson closed the door with a bow like he thought he was a greeter at Disneyland.

The kid asked again, "What you in for?"

"Unlawful imprisonment. What about you?"

The kid leaned closer and whispered, "I was just mind-ing my own business. Looking for kin. I told the deputy I was so excited I forgot to pay, but he didn't believe it. Apparently, it's illegal to ask questions about any resident in this county. You wouldn't happen to know—"

"Nope," Rusty said.

Anger flared in the kid's eyes. "Look, mister, I saw the name of the town and remembered my mom talking about Honey Creek, Texas. Maybe it was just something she thought she remembered. Drugs had dulled her brain. This place was no more real than my birthday. Some clerk at city hall had filled in the blank when I was four or five."

Rusty tried to act like he wasn't even listening, but it was hard. He knew how the kid felt. He had so many potholes in his past sometimes he felt like half his insides were missing.

The boy didn't know when to stop. "Might be a kick if I found my father here. Everywhere I go, I watch people. Looking for one trait they've got that I have. I'm pretty ordinary but I got gray eyes. Less than one in a hundred people have my color. Maybe that's my pop's tell. Maybe that's how I'll recognize him."

Rusty laughed the raw kind of laugh people make when nothing is funny. "Look, kid, I got gray eyes and I can guarantee I'm not your father. Far as I know I've never met another gray-eyed person in this town, but I tend to avoid most people. You might as well move on. The lady behind the desk when you were four probably filled in 'Honey Creek' the way she filled in your birthday. Just a name. Just a date."

"Probably so."

Rusty looked directly at the kid for the first time. Gray eyes with a hint of blue tint—exactly like his. Same black hair, straight, in need of a cut. Same widow's peak Rusty had when he pulled his hair back. Lean body. Tall, or he would be in a few years.

Jackson opened the door again and slowly moved two steps closer to his captives. "*Now* have you figured it out, O'Sullivan?"

Rusty didn't take his gaze off the boy. "Yes, I think I have." His stare didn't waver as he asked one question. "What's your name, kid?"

"I thought you didn't care."

"I'm asking now."

"Zachary Holmes. Do *you* know your father's or mother's names, mister? My mom is Frances. Goes by Fran but you can't call her. She's two years into serving ten to fifteen years for selling drugs. She told me once that she wrote my dad to ask for money, but he either never answered or never got the news." Zachary folded his arms.

His voice shook a bit and Rusty knew exactly how he felt. "I'm Rusty O'Sullivan. I grew up in this valley and I think I may be your brother. Half brother. Same father, different mothers. And I'll bet you a Dr Pepper our father had gray eyes."

The kid looked as if Rusty was trying to trick him. "You ain't got no proof of that."

Jackson moved closer as though he thought Rusty needed help. "Zachary, I'm your father's lawyer. I have a handwritten will naming you as his son. He wrote it the night he died. He missed your age, but he knew your name."

Rusty watched a tear roll down the boy's cheek. Then, like the child he still was, Zach lowered his head in his folded arms and cried.

Chapter 20

Monday Afternoon

Emma had been by Heath's bed for almost twenty-four hours. She'd taken the day off from her duties, gone home once to shower and dress, but other than that she'd been at his side.

Sometimes Heath whispered her name in his sleep and didn't settle until she held his hand.

The big, powerful rancher, who had always seemed so strong, now looked frail. He needed her for some reason.

She reminded herself that they really didn't know each other well. They'd passed in the hallway at the hospital when he came to board meetings and they'd danced once at a fundraiser. After his heart surgery, he'd slipped into a coma, and she'd dropped by every night to talk even though he never answered. She'd told him her whole life story—all her fears, all her dreams—as he slept.

Now, the only word he'd said was her name. As if she were the only one he cared about.

Heath drifted back into sleep and his hand relaxed over her fingers.

Emma took the time to settle in the chair a foot away. At sunset, Ruth brought her a dinner tray and they talked low.

"Dr. Henton called Mr. Rogers's daughter a few hours ago," the night nurse whispered as if Heath might be listening.

"I knew he had a daughter but no one has seen her for years." Emma smiled, realizing Heath had lived a whole life she knew nothing about. A wife who loved him once, maybe. A daughter he raised after his wife died in her twenties.

Ruth leaned closer. "I heard his wife's two sisters insisted on helping raise the girl. Jasmine is her name. I think she goes by Jas. I heard he was too broken up after his wife died, so he let the aunts take over. The best private schools, and trips with one of the aunts on her breaks. People said by ten Mr. Rogers's daughter refused to ride a horse, and by twelve she declined to spend school holidays with her 'boring' father.

"Apparently, she became a brat and he became a workaholic. She married well a few years ago. Wedding in Paris. Mr. Rogers paid for the wedding, but his housekeeper told me one of her aunts' husbands walked Jasmine down the aisle. Jasmine is into her thirties now and probably no one in town would recognize her."

Emma felt she'd been alone all her life, even with family around. She wondered if he'd felt that way too.

The thought struck her. Heath had been in the hospital for months, and no relative had ever visited—to her knowledge—just the ladies from the church and a few cowboys. She'd heard one of the men say he'd keep the ranch running until Heath was in the saddle again.

Emma felt like she was gossiping, but she had to ask, "Where does his daughter live? It must be far away if she never visits."

Ruth shook her head. "She lives in Fort Worth. Dr. Henton said he left four messages before she called him back, then she said she was busy and would come when she could.

"I almost feel sorry for her. Her mother died in childbirth. Mr. Rogers tried to raise her here, but his wife's two sisters insisted on helping. I heard Jasmine say she hated even visiting a small town. No one has seen Jasmine in town for over twenty years. Folks say Mr. Rogers never mentions her and people quit asking. My grandmother said the aunts blamed Heath for his wife's death. Back then, there was just a tiny clinic in Honey Creek. They weren't able to handle a difficult birth."

Emma couldn't believe she'd never heard the story. It must have happened when she was away at school, and she hadn't really known many of the Rogers family growing up. If it happened thirty years ago, he must have been in his early twenties when he became a father. It would have been hard trying to raise a baby girl and run a ranch while grieving.

By the time Emma had moved in to take care of her own father, the story was long forgotten.

"Emma," Heath whispered. "Emma."

She leaned close. "I'm here, Heath."

His grip was strong now. He was coming out of the coma. Now and then he'd open his brown eyes, but didn't seem to focus on anything.

"Emma, don't leave me. Promise me. You're my Emma."

"I'll stay right here." She almost added that she had nowhere else to go.

Chapter 21

Monday Night

All was silent in the dorm, but Rusty couldn't sleep. The day nurses were asleep in their rooms with milkglass windows letting in just enough moonlight. The night shift was probably staggering their midnight dinner breaks. To him it seemed staff was always short in the hospital and the hours were long. Now and then one of the girls came in to pick up something or nap for thirty minutes before going back on, but all was still tonight.

Dr. Adams rarely came this late, but he usually stayed awake just in case. She'd had one of the staff deliver him a tray and hadn't even taken a bite out of the dessert. She'd only cuddled beside him three times to sleep, yet he felt a hollowness at his side because she wasn't there now. In a primal way, he'd found a part of himself that should have been there all along.

Rusty wasn't hungry for anything but her tonight. If he could hold her one more time. One more memory to take with him when he left.

He couldn't get the kid out of his mind either. Zachary Holmes had been all spit and vinegar at first, but in the end, he'd cried like the boy he was when he thought no one was looking. Rusty knew without asking that the boy was alone, no one to turn to, no one to trust.

Rusty had finally put his hand on the kid's shoulder and slowly told all he knew of Jamie Ray Morrell, which wasn't much. Somehow, talking about a father neither knew bonded them. They both knew they'd been throwaway children, but on his last day of his life their father had listed them as his.

The brothers had talked for a while when Jackson stepped out to take a call. They'd agreed they'd stand together to see this through. Like Rusty, Zach didn't want the old man's money, but for some odd reason he wanted to stay close to Rusty. He'd asked three times if Rusty was really his kin. And three times Rusty said yes, then promised the kid they'd find the other two brothers together.

Jackson must have been leaning against the open door, listening for a while, before either noticed him. He suggested that if Zach had kin on his mother's side, they might hold Jamie Ray Morrell's money in a trust for him. The kid could make up his mind to keep it or toss it away when he was eighteen.

Zach said he wouldn't trust a relative on his mom's side, including his mother.

After a silence, Rusty asked, "Is there anyone we need to call to let them know you're safe?"

"No. My mom's uncle took me in when my mother was arrested, but all he does is gripe about me eating up his food. A couple of days a week he keeps me out of school so I can work his farm. My teacher just thinks I'm poorly, but I'm not. He works me from dawn to dark."

Rusty felt like he was looking in a mirror of his past at that moment. He turned to Jackson and asked, "Can the sheriff keep Zach for the night?"

"He can," Jackson answered.

Rusty straightened. "I'm going home tomorrow and I'll take my brother with me, if he's willing to come along. I'm guessing he'll want to hear the final facts about our father as much as I do. We might even plan a road trip and try to find our two other brothers."

The kid lit up with excitement as Rusty continued, "Once we know about the inheritance, he can take off for California or stay with me until he's eighteen. I'm his brother and that will not change no matter what we discover."

Rusty met the boy's stare. "If you come to stay with me for a while, you come as a man. You make your own decisions. We stand equal. We help each other out."

The kid looked at the wheelchair. "You look like you need help. And, since we are brothers, I guess I could stay if you've got room. But if you ever hit—"

"I won't." Rusty grinned as Zach seemed to grow an inch before him. "I promised I'd never act in anger when I was about ten."

The kid was tired and overwhelmed, but he cleared his throat and answered, "I'll stay to see what happens, but if I don't like your place, I won't promise anything."

"Fair enough. Can you drive?"

"I can drive a tractor."

"Close enough. Jackson will come get you from here tomorrow. We'll go get my old pickup at the shop. You'll have to drive us home and yourself to school."

Jackson interrupted. "Wait a minute, Rusty. The kid isn't old enough to drive. That's a law too."

"Get him an emergency license. The doc said it would be a few weeks before I can drive without hurting. Amber will check the wounds and put on fresh bandages in a few days. Until then, I see Zach driving being more like bending the law, not breaking it."

The kid didn't say another word, but he couldn't stop smiling.

Jackson whispered, "You're going to keep me busy with that kind of attitude."

Rusty stared at his new brother. "We never break our word to each other, or to our lawyer. While you live with me, you remember that. But when we have to, we bend just a bit. The church ladies might call them little white lies, but I consider them convenient lies."

The kid nodded but he looked a bit confused.

The deputy came in and asked Zach politely if he'd follow him to a cell for the night. Then he'd get Zach an extra blanket and takeout from the diner. As the pair left the room, the last thing Rusty and Jackson heard the deputy say to the kid was, "You're our guest. Understand? You're not in jail."

Rusty heard his little brother answer, "That mean I can have a Dr Pepper and a bag of M&Ms from the machines down the hall? I prefer the M&Ms without the nuts."

"Sure. Your big brother remodeled my mother's house so she could get around easier. I owe him a favor. If it stays slow around here tonight, I'll teach you to play poker and the M&Ms can be the chips."

The bone-thin Zach put his arm around the beefy deputy like they were friends.

Rusty and Jackson talked as the lawyer rolled him back to the dorm, laughing about the kid claiming he knew how to play poker so the deputy would be broke and hungry within an hour.

The lawyer mentioned that Zach would need to be enrolled in school next and he'd need clothes.

Rusty was sure the kid was old enough to enroll himself and admitted he was more worried about feeding the kid than dressing him.

When Rusty finally fell into his bed on the couch, he could feel his life changing. For the first time, he was responsible for another person, if only for a while.

* * *

The next morning Rusty showered as best he could with his arm and leg tied up in trash bags. One of the nurses had washed his work clothes and they felt so much better than his horrible jogging suit. The morning shift was leaving when Jackson and Zach came to pick him up.

Zach was quiet. He seemed unsure what to do. He gave a quick smile when Rusty introduced him to the nurses as his little brother.

The boy seemed to be walking on another planet, trying to find his footing. When his big brother told him to take the pup along, Zach wrapped the dog up in a towel as if he were a baby. Jackson showed him a pet carrier in the back of his pickup, but Zach held him tight. "I'll just hold him. He's unsure of where we're going."

The pup licked Zach's hand.

Zach laughed. "He's a good dog. He just doesn't know it yet."

With one nod, Rusty agreed and added, "He was the only pup who survived after a rainstorm. Maybe he's part duck."

Zach held the bundled pup up. "How about we call him Duck?"

"Sounds as good as any name." Rusty reached over and touched the dog's head. "You'll have to take care of him until I heal. That okay?"

"Sure."

A few minutes later, Rusty was trying to climb into Jackson's pickup when Amber caught up with them.

"You cutting out on me, Trouble?"

He grinned. "I figured you'd be glad to get rid of me."

"I am." She moved closer and held the wheelchair as he stood. With only an inch between them, she whispered, "I'll miss cuddling with you on cold nights."

Rusty blushed, possibly for the first time in his life. "Me too," was all he could answer.

Then she kissed him on his cheek.

"You missed," he said without moving.

To his surprise she kissed him full out on the mouth. He was so shocked he didn't even react.

As she helped him put on his seatbelt, he wanted a do-over of the kiss, but he knew it wouldn't happen.

By the time he could form words, she was ordering Zach around. "Now you take care of your brother, do you hear me? Bring him back in a week. And if he starts dripping blood, call me."

"Yes, I hear you, Doc." Zach backed away, out of range in case she swung at him. "Half the town probably heard you." He jumped into the back with a wheelchair, crutches, and a walker before she could yell again.

A block later, he leaned forward and said through the back window, "Rusty, that doc is pretty, but I don't think she'd be easy to live with. Promise you won't bring her home for a sleepover."

Rusty didn't say a word but Jackson answered, "I think you're right. She's not pretty; she's beautiful, but she steals pie. Never could stand a woman who did that. And another thing: I think she needs glasses. I'm the good-looking one and yet she kisses Rusty."

Zach nodded as if the lawyer made sense as they climbed out of the lawyer's vehicle at a huge building called The Shop.

Rusty was silent for a minute, then finally said, "She was just thanking me for some carpentry work I did." He knew they didn't hear him but he had to tell himself that.

Jackson backed Rusty's pickup out of the storage barn, then climbed out.

The beat-up pickup looked worse than Jackson's piece of junk, but Zach couldn't stop grinning as he climbed behind the wheel. He had wheels.

"I'll take the lead to the stops we need to make," Jackson said as he made sure everything in the back was tied down.

Rusty leaned back and fought sleep. "Just follow the lawyer and tell him to charge me for anything you need. Be sure to get a phone, clothes, boots, and all the junk food you want."

While Jackson and Zach made a few stops, Rusty closed his eyes and pretended to be asleep. If he didn't move, or talk, or even think, he could still feel Amber's lips touching his. It had been so long since he'd kissed a woman, he'd forgotten how it felt.

She was way out of his league. She had twice the education. Probably made double what he made in income, or would as soon as she finished her internship. But there was something that drew her to him, and deep down he knew if she came to him, he'd never turn her away.

He must have dozed off because when Jackson and the kid came back to the pickup, they threw clothes on top of groceries packed in the back.

Jackson stood by Rusty's window. "You think you can make it home okay?"

"Sure. Thanks, Jackson."

"Don't worry, I'll be out to see you in a few days."

"You don't know where I live." Rusty had never brought anyone to his house.

Jackson laughed. "I'll head down the road where you wrecked that Ford and watch for this old pickup. You want to tell me what color your house is?"

"Nope." He patted the dog now sleeping between Rusty and Zach. "Remember, I've got a guard dog. You might want to call before you come."

"I'll remember that." Jackson stepped away and waved as Zach slowly backed up. They drove off so slow Jackson could have walked beside the driver's window.

While the brothers drove past the city limit sign, Zach told him how Jackson made him tell the manager of the grocery store he was sorry for accidentally walking out without paying, and it wouldn't happen again.

"The manager actually shook my hand. Can you believe that, bro?"

Rusty smiled despite watching Zach hit every pothole in the road between town and the south rim of the valley where his place was. "From now on, if you need something from the grocery, tell them to put it on my account. You pick what we're eating for meals and I'll do my best to do at least half of the cooking."

"How do you like sandwiches and canned soup? That's about my limit."

"Whatever we need, just say, 'Charge it.'"

"That sounds too easy."

"Sure. You'll be the one cooking for the next few days. Buy what you plan to cook or buy off the 'Grab and Run' cart on your way home from school. The barbecue is good, but stay away from the fish. By the way, how'd you pay for those groceries?" Rusty pointed to the back.

"The lawyer did. He told me to tell you the groceries will be on his bill."

Thirty minutes later, all the bags, hospital leftover junk they make you carry out, and the crutch were in Rusty's house.

Zach had been so nervous he dropped a few bags. When he pulled the pup out of the cab of the pickup, the dog ran around his legs as if he were trying to trip Zach. The kid's laughter seemed to echo across the valley.

Rusty finally swooped the ball of hair up, set him on his good leg, and rolled inside. In a few weeks the dog would jump down, but now he was too small to risk the fall. "Come on, Duck. We're home."

"Your pickup drives great!" Zach laughed as he set his bags just inside and ran back to hold the door. "Looks like crap, though. What did you see that made you think it was worth fixing up? Where's your bathroom?"

Rusty rolled over the threshold, smiling. "One question at a time."

The kid moved to the center of the room and looked like he was trying to make his head turn completely around.

To Rusty's surprise, the pup was doing the same thing.

Rusty tried to keep from laughing as he started answering questions. "I like buying old cars and pickups. Always overhaul the engine first. You got something you can use, then. If you paint it up first, all you got is a yard ornament."

The kid nodded as if to remember important advice.

Zach yelled as he unloaded the bags and his big brother sat down, "This place is great! You know, forget what I said before: you and that doctor should get married and move her out here. Then no one in town would have ear damage. Can she cook? I might not mind her yelling orders if she can make spaghetti."

"I'll consider that," Rusty answered as he remembered moving into the run-down shack no one had wanted. His always-drunk grandparents didn't even try to sell it when they left. Rusty had lived in it until he was eighteen, then bought the farm for back taxes. By then he'd known how to swing a hammer and set to turning the shack into a house. The first thing he'd built had been steps, replacing the boxes his mother had used.

For a moment, Rusty just stared trying to see what the kid saw. The big main room was painted in bright colors, the shelves and cabinets were hand carved; even the TV stand was designed with skill.

The kid brought in the last load, a paper bag that he'd used as a suitcase when he'd run away from his uncle. Slowly, he stood in the center of the huge room and turned around. "Wow. Wow. This place is a work of art. It's like a treehouse on the ground. I love the big windows, and that fireplace must have taken you months to build."

Rusty straightened a little with pride. "I started with a two-room shack and every summer I built on another room. One winter I brought up rocks from the creek and made the fireplace. I didn't do it right the first time so I took it down, read up on how to do it right, then built it all over again. Since the house was built against the rise to the rim, I decided I'd just build up the slope when I expanded."

"You ever think of painting the additions the same color, bro?"

"Nope." He looked at the rambling house, which seemed to be stair-stepping up to the rim. "It might have been a good idea, but I didn't want to start over again."

"You got any animals around this place?" Zach was running in and out the back door as if he had too much to see to take it all in standing still.

"I've got a dozen or so guineas. They all look alike so I call them all Larry. They're half wild. I feed them every night in winter, but they prefer bugs from spring to fall. They nest up in the low tree branches and are the best alarm I could have. Any man or animal that steps on my property, the birds let me know. They squawk around on parade."

Zach watched the gang of Larrys run across the corner of the yard. "They're about the ugliest birds I've ever seen, and they sound terrible."

"You'll get used to them." Rusty turned to slowly make it to the center of the room as the kid examined his new school clothes.

Zach held up shirts, jeans, a jacket, tennis shoes, socks, and a pair of boots—cowboy, not biker. The next bag had underwear and school supplies. "I don't think I've ever had clothes with the tags on. The lawyer collected what I needed for school. Claimed he was an expert."

When the kid folded each piece of clothing up and put everything back in bags, he stood tall and said, "Thanks."

"We're brothers. We help one another out. I'm guessing you'll be helping me out until I recover." Rusty had to change the subject. "This first room is mostly where I live. The space is large and open. Thanks to the windows I can enjoy both the sunrise and the sunset. I built the kitchen with a long bar separating it from the living room, but I never got around to buying chairs or stools.

"A couch, a desk, a TV that only played DVDs was all I needed. Now that you are living here, we probably should buy some more furniture. A couple of recliners might be nice—one for you and one for me."

He let out a long sigh. "Home," Rusty whispered as if it had been a long journey back to his place.

Zach bumped into his wheelchair as the kid began digging through groceries. "Real nice house, bro. It's a home. But when company comes they wouldn't have anywhere to sit. I have a feeling the lawyer will show up."

"Maybe you could help me pick stuff out. Before you arrived, I thought I had all I needed. I can't believe there will be company."

Zach set the milk and butter on the bar and opened the refrigerator. "Lucky that lawyer thought of food or we'd have to fry up one of the Larrys for dinner."

Rusty lowered to the couch and leaned back. It took him a minute to build up enough energy to talk. "I live alone. I eat out most of the time. No one has ever visited me. I've got canned soup in the cabinet, health bars, and cereal. There is change on top of the refrigerator in a coffee can. When you need lunch money for school, take what you need."

"I've decided I'm not going to school. I need to stay home and take care of you."

"No, you're going. Jackson says it's the law." Rusty turned his head to see the kid's reaction. No one was there. A moment later, Zach bumped through the door with a folding camp chair.

"If I'm going to school, I'd better get settled and go to bed. You want to point the direction to my room? Jackson said I'd probably need a chair for my room and a clock."

"Good idea. I'll get you up in time to eat breakfast. I promised Jackson I'd make sure you made it on time."

Zach nodded once.

Rusty was too tired to even care what else the kid and Jackson had bought.

"Before you drift off, mind telling where I sleep?"

"The hallway on the left. My bedroom is the first one, then the bedrooms kind of climb up. Best view is the top bedroom. There's a cot and blankets up there, somewhere. Big windows to see the valley. I built two rooms on every level and a bathroom on every other floor."

Zach had already started climbing so Rusty yelled, "The hallway on the right of the kitchen has a laundry room and a bathroom! There's blankets, sheets, and towels in there. Take what you need. The third door opens out to the garage that's full of tools."

Zach shouted from probably the third floor, "You rent this place out on Halloween? It's a maze up here. Hope I find my room before dark."

"Just keep climbing."

Leaning back, Rusty closed his eyes. "Home," he whispered again. The thought occurred to him that he built so many bedrooms because he'd never had one growing up.

Rusty was almost asleep when someone knocked on the door. For a moment, he thought it might be one of the Larrys come to welcome him back. Then he heard the soft voice of Starri Knight. Her name was as strange and pretty as she was beautiful.

Zach rattled down the stairs and ran to open the screen door. "I saw you drive up from my window. Come on in. You must be a ghost because my brother says no one ever comes to see him. You sure are pretty, miss."

Starri laughed. "Thank you." She nodded at Rusty on the couch, then turned back to the kid. "Jackson called and said Rusty was coming home today. I brought a potpie. I just followed the tracks in the road to find you men. No one has driven up this way since the rain last week."

She set the iron pot down and pulled a cell phone from her pocket before she faced Rusty. "I found your phone when I walked the hill near where you rolled that night. Jackson said he'd bought you a new one. Told me to search the bags and give it to your brother."

She looked at the counter covered with white bags. "Got any idea which bag?"

Zach almost shouted, "I'll help. I'm his brother, but he didn't know me until yesterday. Did I say you're a real pretty lady? I'm almost fifteen. I'm moving in with Rusty. I guess that makes us neighbors."

Rusty grinned at his new brother. "I think I'll go sleep in my own bed. Maybe Starri can help you figure where the groceries belong." Rusty tried to get up, but it took both of them to pull him to his feet. He used a crutch to make it to his bedroom and then crumpled into bed.

As Starri pulled off his one shoe and covered him, he said, "Thanks for coming. Would you mind settling the kid in and giving him the phone Jackson bought? Show him how to use it. I'm guessing he's never had one."

"Will do," she whispered as she kissed Rusty on the cheek. "I'll put in your number, Jackson's number, and mine."

He closed his eyes, already half asleep, but he smiled. Apparently, after almost dying, he'd become downright irresistible to women.

Chapter 22

Emma had her uniform on when Heath's daughter walked into her father's hospital room. Like many people do, she ignored the nurse standing by the bed just like patrons ignore the waiter in a restaurant.

Dr. Ryan Henton followed Heath Rogers's tall daughter, who was dressed in white down to her boots. In his usual fast pace, he explained the facts of Heath's condition. Dr. Henton was a good doctor, but he didn't waste time visiting or consoling family. Jasmine Rogers Armstrong asked questions rapid-fire, as if she'd memorized them and wanted this over as fast as possible.

Emma watched the young lady out of the corner of her eye as she logged the facts of Heath's condition. Jasmine must favor her mother. Except for her height, she seemed to have nothing in common with her father. No gentle smile. No kind eyes. No slow, polite way of entering a room.

Jasmine was a young-looking thirtysomething. She had "rich socialite" written all over her. Tan. Fit. Permanent boredom lines cut into her forehead that she'd have removed in a few years.

She didn't address her father. She didn't even touch his hand. She wasn't interested in the man, only his diagnosis.

Emma fought back tears. Heath had lived a quiet life. She'd never heard a person in town say a bad word about him. Emma picked up her blanket and asked the daughter if she'd like to sit down beside her father.

Jasmine shook her head. "I haven't got time."

High heels tapped on the tiled floor as the only daughter of probably the richest man in town walked out. She hadn't bothered to thank the doctor for his time. She didn't even look at Heath as she left. Her father was dying and Jasmine was in a hurry.

Emma moved close to the bed. In the silent room, she leaned and kissed Heath lightly. "Come back to the world again. I'm waiting to talk to you." She giggled almost as if they were young. "Someday I'll give you no Monday morning kisses. Someday I'll give you a Friday night kiss."

As was his habit now, when she laid her hand on his, he closed his fingers and held on tight.

"Someday, when you're fully awake, maybe you'll hold more than just my hand." She pushed a tear away. "I've had way too few hugs in this life and I have an idea so have you." She blushed as she brushed his black hair off his forehead with her free hand. "I'm being too bold, but sometimes I think of you holding me when I sleep."

To her surprise, his hand closed tighter over her fingers. "Emma," he whispered. "My Emma."

Chapter 23

"Look, Jackson, just because you saved my life doesn't mean you have to call me every day to see if I'm still breathing."

The lawyer heard Rusty fighting down laughter on the other end of the line. "Shut up, O'Sullivan. I'm not worried about you. I got a call from Zach. I'm worried about *him*."

"This is his third day in school. How much trouble can he be in?"

"You dressed, Rusty?"

"I am. I sleep in my clothes. It's too hard to pull my jeans on and off." Rusty laughed. "You dressed, Jackson?"

"Shut up and listen!" Jackson was near panic. "I told the kid if he was in trouble to text me one word: GERONIMO. His text came in three minutes ago. Your little brother is in trouble. When I tried to call him back, it went straight to voice mail."

"I'm sure—"

"Rusty, shut up—"

"Stop saying that or I'll tear off my cast and beat you with it."

There was a pause, then the lawyer said calmly, "He put the one word in all caps. Wind, my detective, and I are headed to the school now. Something is wrong, really wrong. I can feel it. Is there any way you can meet us there?"

"Starri just pulled up with our daily meal. She can drive me in. We'll be headed that way as soon as I get my one shoe on."

Jackson dropped his cell in the cup holder with the speaker still on as he looked over at the huge Cherokee investigator he'd known all his life. "What do you know, Wind? Rusty and I both want to hear what you dug up. I'll drive. You report."

Wind's answer came slow and direct. "I got a call from Austin half an hour ago from a friend who happens to be sheriff of a little town just north of Austin. He said he heard I was asking around about Zachary Holmes's uncle so he did a bit of digging. I was waiting for the rap sheet to be faxed before I filled you in. But Zach's text came in first."

Wind huffed as if irritated that the order of things had been altered but he continued, "The uncle filed a missing person on the kid yesterday and some clerk said there was a lawyer in Honey Creek requesting the boy's school records and birth certificate. I don't know if he wants to use the kid as free labor or he smells money. Either way, it won't look good for Zach if the uncle finds him before Rusty gets custody.

"Miss Heather called the high school and was told she was the second person asking about Zach today. Which is a strong hint that the uncle is on his way to pick up Zach."

Rusty's voice came through the phone. "Since you got the text from the kid, that means he knows he's in danger.

And since he called you and not me, he knew you'd get to him faster than me."

"Agreed," Jackson answered.

"We're on our way, but it will be half an hour. Call me with any update. Starri's driving like she rides—fast and wild."

Chapter 24

Zachary Holmes stood just inside the big doors of his new school. Fourth school in less than a year. Not that it mattered, he'd been lucky to attend three out of five days most weeks. Most kids had reasons for missing school. The flu. Snow days. Death in the family. Zach had reasons, like Mom too drunk to drive him. No clothes clean enough to even wear out. Then, when Mom went to jail, his uncle said he needed Zach to work the farm. Or sometimes, Zach was hurting too bad from a beating.

Most kids couldn't wait to get out of school for vacation. For Zach, he dreamed of making it to school all week. As he looked out the front door of Honey Creek High at the parking lot, he realized he wasn't going to make a week in Honey Creek.

Chaos was waiting on the gravel parking lot not fifty feet away. Vern Bonney, who thought he was descended from Billy the Kid, was Zach's uncle by common-law marriage.

Zach would bet there was a two-inch-wide belt lying on his uncle's old Corvette's passenger seat and a pistol under the driver's seat. He could see what was going to happen. Vern would hit him a few times when Zach got in the car. Then, as soon as they were on a back road, Vern would make him lie over the hood of the car and whip him. Once, when Zach screamed, Vern shoved the barrel of the pistol in his mouth.

Zach figured Billy wouldn't claim Vern as kin any more than he did. The worst thing that haunted Zach was that Vern laughed as he whipped him.

Pushing against the school's brick wall, he wished he could just vanish. For a moment, he'd thought he might have a chance to not be afraid all the time, but that wasn't going to happen.

He had been in math class when he'd glanced out the window and saw his uncle pull up. Vern parked in front of the school's five-foot-tall initials in a loading zone. When he got out and began to pace, Zach could feel a storm coming even though the sky was clear.

Vern's car was one of a kind and there was no mistaking the beat-up old 1967 Corvette Stingray. Zach's mom told him once that Vern stole it in the seventies and hid it in the barn for ten years before he drove it on the back roads for fun. He never had the money to fix it up, so it was rusting away and rattled like a washing machine full of rocks, but Vern seemed to think he was someone big when he drove it.

When math was over, Zach skipped his last class so he could keep watch. Vern was now standing in the school's parking lot with his arms folded. He'd never been a patient man and Zach knew trouble was about to break out. He pushed two on his new phone and typed in "GERONIMO."

The lawyer had said he'd come, and he was thirty minutes closer than Rusty. But it was Zach's guess that Jackson wouldn't show up. No one ever did. People always said things like "call me if you need me," but they didn't mean it.

When his mother had gone to jail, she'd told him to go live with his uncle. Her exact words were, "He ain't worth much, but at least I'll know where you'll be when I get out."

Zach had been twelve then. Mostly his uncle ignored him the first few months. Once he'd found him crying in the barn. His uncle had pulled off his belt and gave him something to cry about. After that, Zach never cried again.

As he grew, more and more chores came his way. First it was just Saturday chores. Then weekday chores before he could go to school on Monday. By the time he turned fourteen, the chores lasted until dark and Monday had become the day to finish his weekend chores. If he didn't finish by dark, there would be no supper.

Now, Zach knew exactly what his uncle was doing in the parking lot: He was figuring out how he was going to get his free farm worker back. He was cussing and making plans to make sure Zach never ran again.

Zach thought of hiding somewhere inside the school, but that wouldn't last long. His uncle would say he was Zach's legal guardian even though there had never been any papers filed. If that didn't work, he'd throw a fit. He'd turn mean, cussing, threatening everyone. Once he got mad, people tended to give in or run. But once he got angry, eventually he'd have to take it out on someone and Zach was usually his target. If he tried to run or fight back, it would only be worse.

Zach liked it here with Rusty. He liked this school. In new clothes, he fit in with the others. The other kids talked to him. One said his dad worked for Rusty O'Sullivan. He even added that his dad said Rusty was a good boss. If they worked overtime, Rusty was right there working double time.

A couple of guys in his gym class asked him if he'd be interested in trying out for track.

A short girl in his history class smiled at him. "I'm Lou-Ann," she'd said as if he cared.

Zach didn't say anything, but he did smile at her. If he ever saw her again, he'd say, "I'm Zachary." He liked using his whole name. It made him feel like someone.

He couldn't let them see his uncle knock him down and call him names. His only choice was to meet his uncle in the parking lot and tell him he wasn't going back, and he had to do it before the last bell rang.

But he hesitated one moment too long. The bell rang and Zach was washed outside in the river of kids.

His uncle was leaning against the hood of his car, waiting. He was smiling like he could smell Zach's fear.

Zach stopped ten feet away from him and waited for him to recognize his nephew in new clothes.

When he did, anger fired in the big man's eyes. "Get in the car, boy. I've already wasted a day driving up here to get you."

"I'm not going back." Zach's entire body was shaking.

"Yes, you are! You're coming if I have to drag you. All your new friends will see you get the beating you deserve."

Zach's nightmare was coming true. Kids were stopping to watch.

"I'm living with my brother now. I want to go to school every day and not have to miss two or three days a week because you need me to work. I'm tired of being hurt." Now a crowd was circling them, but Zach couldn't stop. This time he had to make a stand. His uncle was going to beat him no matter what he did.

Uncle Vern uncrossed his beefy arms and rolled his big hands into fists. "I'm going to beat the ornery out of you, boy. I'm going to hurt you so bad you'll never talk to me like this again and you'll never try to run away. I made up my mind on the way here. There ain't no reason for you to go back to school at all. You've learned enough. It's time you earned your keep."

Zach heard movement behind him, but he didn't dare

take his gaze off his uncle. His brother was too broken to fight his fight and the lawyer hadn't gotten here in time.

There was no one around to help. All the kids would see him beaten and dragged off. They didn't care about him. Nobody did.

His uncle took one step, as anger seemed to boil inside him. Then another step toward Zach. He was a bull of a man and he was proving it.

Zach didn't back down. He just stared into his uncle's angry eyes and swore he saw insanity there.

Something brushed his shoulder. The arm of a leather jacket. The football player was big, almost as big as his uncle. Zach couldn't remember him, but he looked like a senior. The school was so small he'd seen everybody by noon the first day, but he had no idea what the kid's name was.

Another guy stepped up and bumped Zach's other shoulder. Then, like a roll call, a dozen boys stepped forward. Most were older than Zach. A few he'd seen in his classes. Some were jocks, others dressed in Western clothes. They stood shoulder to shoulder, fists ready to fight.

"Get in the car, boy!" his uncle growled at the dozen boys beside Zach. "Or you'll be sorry and so will your new friends. You wet-nosed kids don't know what you're dealing with. Don't you dare try to stop me. I can topple you all with three blows."

For a moment, silence blanketed the whole parking lot. Then the shattering of glass cut through the air.

Zach looked past his uncle and saw a short little redhead with a rock almost the size of her head in her hands. There was a crack in the Corvette's windshield.

"Oops," she said. "I must have dropped my rock on your car, mister."

The tiny girl's gaze focused on the man as a crowd circled. She was ten feet away and didn't seem to realize she was in real danger.

Vern huffed like a bull again as his head went back and forth from the girl to Zach.

She shifted and let the big rock fall on the windshield. The glass didn't break, but the crack spread. "Oh, no, I dropped it again."

A few kids watching began to laugh.

The boy next to Zach yelled, "You better get out of here, mister! You don't want to mess with LouAnn. We got rock storms out here in this part of Texas and she can predict them."

Several kids in the crowd knelt, picked up a handful of rocks, and stood ready to throw them.

"You nosy little bastards can't stop me from taking my kin. I'll call the police on you all."

A voice from the back of the crowd yelled as the kids stepped aside. "They may not be able to do anything legal, but I can! I'm Jackson Landry, attorney at law, and I have proof you're unfit to keep a minor. Now we have Zach's brother to act as guardian; you'll have no part of this boy's life."

"His mother gave him to me. I can do anything I want." Vern seemed to fill with air, but Jackson didn't even blink.

"As Zach's lawyer, I disagree. Within an hour you'll have a restraining order against you. I suggest you leave the county fast. I can think of a few reasons to have you arrested, and if you've got a weapon on school property, you'll be locked away for decades."

Fear replaced anger as two sheriff cars pulled up.

"Don't set foot in this valley again or I'll see you go to jail. And I'm a damn good lawyer. Don't mess with me!" Jackson yelled with an anger he'd never felt.

Vern opened his mouth to say one last threat as he backed toward his car.

The deputies were weaving their way toward him, so he reconsidered. As he turned to run, the sound of glass shattering filled the air.

"Oops!" LouAnn didn't sound sorry. "I dropped my rock again."

Zach saw his uncle run for his car, but one deputy was younger and in shape. He tackled Vern, knocking him down so hard cuss words dripped out his mouth along with blood. Cuffed and being pushed toward the nearest cruiser, the big, mean bully didn't seem so big.

Zach barely felt the football player put his hand on his shoulder and say, "We got your back, Holmes." All Zach saw was a tiny little redhead heading his way.

As Vern was driven off in the back of one sheriff's car, everyone started talking while the deputies took statements. Zach just stood next to LouAnn, who was still holding her rock. His mind kept seesawing between her or Uncle Vern as to who he was more scared of.

Finally, when most of the kids had left, the deputies decided to make sure Vern Bonney left the county by calling in the highway patrol and suggesting they stop any old Corvette Stingray. Zach looked down at the redhead. "I'll be fifteen in June."

"I will turn sixteen in September." She giggled. "You like older women?"

He thought for a few moments and asked, "You think if I hang around by then that you'd be my girlfriend? I ain't ever had one."

She smiled. "I might. You'll have to ask me when I'm sixteen. My parents say I can't date until then. But no matter what I decide about you, I'm keeping my rock."

"Fair enough."

As he turned, he noticed Rusty limping his way across the parking lot. For a moment, all he saw was worry in his brother's gray eyes.

The boy in the almost-man surfaced and Zach ran full out to safety.

He ran straight toward Rusty.

Chapter 25

Everyone around Jackson was talking, but Jackson just stood there smiling.

"I'm a lawyer," he almost said aloud. "A real lawyer." All the years of college. All the nights of studying were worth it. Words had been his weapon and he'd used them. He'd won.

Starri walked up beside him and whispered, "Feels good, doesn't it?"

He didn't care if she read his mind. "It does. We saved someone from being hurt. Well, us and a few dozen kids."

"No, you saved him. You made Uncle Vern run."

Jackson laughed. "He wouldn't have gone far. The highway patrol was on the lookout for him. If he had a taillight out, he would have been stopped. And thanks to a rather large rock, Vern has a cracked windshield to replace. That little girl with the rock is one fireball. A bit strange that she accidentally dropped it on Vern's car, again and again."

The look in Starri's eyes was sad, maybe a bit frightened.

"What's wrong, Starri? You reading my thoughts again?"

"No, it's not that. It's just a feeling. That man was evil and . . ." A tear moved over her cheek. "He'll be back."

It felt as if a blast of cold winter air blew over him. Starri was young, beautiful, a dreamer—and Jackson feared she was right.

He bumped her shoulder lightly. "We'll watch over Zach."

"We will." She whispered her oath. "But I have a feeling if that man comes back, we'll all be hurting."

Jackson felt an invisible cape drift over him. For the first time, he understood his father. He might not be a superhero, or even much of a fighter, but he was a guardian.

Looking down at Starri, he winked, and she laughed. He guessed she'd seen his cape, if only for a moment.

Chapter 26

Friday at Dawn

Zach Holmes rolled onto his back and stared up at the long, thin windows running across the east wall. The glass seemed to bend and open up to heaven's view. He had seen pictures of stars painted on ceilings, but here he had the real thing. After moving his cot to the center of the room, he stared up at the sky. No artist could ever paint anything so beautiful. Zach swore that for the rest of his life he'd put windows on his ceilings.

He'd taken the bedroom at the top of Rusty's house. He'd picked it because anyone entering the home would have to pass through the living area, go down a hall, climb stairs to the second level, walk another hallway, climb another flight, and repeat again to get to the last room Rusty had built in a home that climbed the hill almost to the rim.

Zach had chosen it for safety. A robber would be worn out before he made it up. But after staying a few nights, he knew he'd never move to another room. Every morning he loved watching the sun peek over the rim. He loved watching the clouds drift by, and at night he felt he was sleeping among the stars.

The room was almost bare: a cot, one pillow, two blankets, three stick-on hooks on the back of the door for a closet. He'd made a desk out of two boxes and a long board. But best of all, there was a lock on the door.

Rusty had told him to make a list of what he needed when he'd sent Zach up with all the bathroom essentials and two five-dollar wall clocks from Walmart. Neither had an alarm. That seemed to be Rusty yelling, "Breakfast is almost ready!"

As the sun winked at Zach, he smiled. He'd heard what Starri said about his uncle Vern coming back, but he felt safe here. Vern would have to get past Rusty first, and even crippled up, his big brother would probably take him. If he made it past Rusty, he'd have to search two floors. One had a library of paperback books and manuals on how to build anything from a chicken coop to a rocket. Across the hall was a bedroom without a bed.

Vern would have to climb another set of stairs. Search two more rooms and a bathroom. If he made it to Zach's level, Vern would find the door locked.

His own room with a lock. Perfect.

As he lay on his cot, Zach looked up at the north corner of his bedroom ceiling. A rope looking almost like a decoration hung from a trapdoor. He could climb the rope, open the trap, and climb onto the roof. If he pulled the rope up, no one could follow.

For some reason, Rusty had built an escape hatch, which made Zach wonder if at some time his brother had lived in fear.

For the first time in his life, he felt safe in a house whose owner understood.

"Breakfast in five!" came from below.

Zach jumped up, pulled on a T-shirt and jeans. After a

quick stop to brush his teeth and comb his hair, he was ready for breakfast.

To his surprise, Rusty was standing at the stove cooking eggs.

"No cereal today?" Zach asked.

"Nope. I'm finished with being broken. If you'll drop me off at the hospital, I'll have the doc take this cast off my arm. Then I can wear one of them Velcro bands."

"How you going to get home—hop along with your sliced-up leg leaving a bloody trail, waving at folks with your broken arm?"

"I hadn't thought through that yet. I just know I can't stay in this house another day. I spent most of my time thinking about building another room on."

Zach accepted a plate with half a dozen scrambled eggs piled on bacon. "If you have to build, bro, think about going out, not up. Maybe a sunporch."

"Not a bad idea."

They talked as they ate. Later, when Rusty and Zach stepped outside, Rusty went to the passenger side of the pickup.

"You going to let me drive?"

"You know how. Made it to school and back several times." Rusty slowly climbed in.

"I have and I kept it slow like you told me."

"Then drive."

Zach went well below the speed limit and obeyed every law. Almost to town, he finally thought of a plan. "If you're up to walking a block, you could go over to The Shop. I could drive over there and take you home at noon."

Rusty shrugged. "Sounds good, but wait until I call. I think I'll eat lunch with our lawyer. Then I might go talk to the sheriff. Odds are I'll be tired by the time school's out."

They were both silent for a while. Maybe they both knew trouble was coming but neither one wanted to talk about it.

Finally, Rusty said, "Come summer, I've been thinking that a sunporch might be a good idea. If you want to help with it, I'll make sure you get a starting man's wages. That sound fair?"

"Do I get to keep some of the money?"

"No, Zach, you keep *all* the money you earn. Maybe save up for a car. I'll help you fix it up. It's your money to do what you want."

Zach couldn't talk. He was afraid if he tried, he'd never stop. A paying job. He could save for whatever he wanted. They were in sight of the hospital when he finally found words. "You think I could save up and go to college?"

Rusty laughed. "You can do whatever you want. There is a college in the valley. We'll drive over there and check it out." Both were silent for a few minutes, then Rusty said so low Zach barely heard him, "My little brother, a college man. Imagine that."

Chapter 27

Vern Bonney was so angry he could spit nails. He should have never wasted the gas to drive to Honey Creek. The sheriff kept him all afternoon, asking him questions and subtly threatening what would happen if Vern ever stepped foot in town again or bothered Zach, since he had no legal rights to even see Zachary Holmes.

"Forget the little bastard," Vern mumbled as he walked to his Corvette parked in the trees at an old abandoned roadside rest stop. He'd spent the night drinking alone and cold, then he'd slept in his car until afternoon. "The kid's no good at farming and he eats too much. Let that crippled up half brother take him on. In a month he'll be sorry he even met Zach. The half brother will probably come begging for me to take the brat."

As he pulled out of the rest stop, Vern ran over a few trash cans. His goodbye to a town he never planned to see again.

A few miles down the road, Vern stopped by a run-down

bar out near the truck stop. The bar's name was painted over the door: Outlaw's Watering Hole. That seemed about right for Vern, since he swore he was related to Billy the Kid. The lights were low and smoky. They had free snacks and a two-for-one weeknight special on Coors. He decided it wouldn't hurt to wash out the kid's memory with beer before he drove home.

An hour later, Vern was full of chips and pigs-in-a-blanket and smiling. The bums in the bar knew nothing about the incident at the school, but a few knew Rusty O'Sullivan. They all agreed that he was a good guy.

One man said Rusty kept Brown's Contractors in business.

Another said he wished Rusty would marry his little sister. She was pretty and she claimed he danced with her now and then at the bar, but he never asked her for a date or even walked her out back for a different kind of dancing.

Another whiskey philosopher said Rusty had had a hard childhood. His own mother didn't love him. She disappeared before he was old enough to say "Mama." He didn't think Rusty thought he was good enough for a woman, not even one he could have easily picked up in the bar.

To Vern's surprise, not one man knew where O'Sullivan lived. One said his place might be somewhere along the south rim.

When Vern asked about the kid who lived with Rusty, not one knew about him. Finally, one guy who was napping on the bar raised his head and said his grandson mentioned Rusty's little brother was staying with him. "My grandson complained that the kid got to drive to school, so now my grandson thinks he should."

The drunk took a swallow of beer. "That ain't right. Letting a fourteen-year-old drive. If I see him, I'll run over him just to teach him a lesson."

The friend next to the drunk slammed Grandpa's forehead on the bar and the old guy went back to sleep.

Vern walked out with his last beer tucked in his jacket pocket. He sat in his car to down his drink and tried to remember which way was home. He gripped the steering wheel and closed his eyes. Sometimes he just liked to sit in the Corvette and pretend it was new and he was young again. He told himself he'd fix it up, put in a new windshield, polish it. The Corvette he'd stolen wasn't old; it was a classic. A rich man's car. When he drove it around, he was somebody.

Only tonight he needed to think.

One of the locals had said something about an old man on the other side of the valley dying and leaving money to his scattered sons. A lot of cash. The guy claimed Rusty was getting ready to inherit. Maybe money. Maybe land. Maybe both.

Vern might be drunk, but it didn't take many brain cells to figure out that if Rusty was coming into money, Rusty's brother probably was too. And . . . with Vern being Zach's uncle, he'd need to help the boy. He could hang on to it for Zach. Or invest it after he took out some for the kid's room and board. That sounded like a good idea.

Laughing, he opened the glove box and pulled a bottle of whiskey saved for heavy thinking. He needed to celebrate a bit while he thought about how he could find the kid. It couldn't be hard. Little town. Little valley. Everyone knows everyone.

Half a bottle later, he realized the first step was to stay in town. But he'd need a reason. Sheriff Smith might be young, but he wasn't a fool.

Then he'd have to find out where Rusty lived. The sheriff would know, but he'd never hand over the address. The hospital might know. After all, they fixed Rusty O'Sullivan up.

The hospital was a good place to start. They'd know, but he couldn't just walk in. He had to have a reason.

Vern downed the rest of the whiskey and thought of a plan. Great ideas always floated on hard liquor.

He fumbled for the old bowie knife he kept under the seat. Pulling the blade from the sheath, he opened his car door and stepped out of the car. After all, the last thing he wanted to do was clean up his own blood. And there had to be blood if he planned to get in the hospital this time of night.

One poke. Enough blood to look like an emergency and he'd have the run of the hospital.

He put the tip of the bowie high on his left shoulder, planning to cut an inch. Then he'd yell and someone would come running to take him to the hospital.

Vern's big boot caught on the rocker panel below the door and he fell face-first on the gravel.

All he remembered besides lightning shooting through his shoulder was that blood seemed to be everywhere. Up his nose. In his mouth. On his eyes and face. All over his shirt.

"Damn." He'd overachieved his goal.

About the time he was passing out, someone kicked him to see if he was alive.

A flashlight danced over his face like a stuttering firefly and someone started ordering everyone standing around Vern, "Call 911! A drunk tried to kill himself."

Shadows gathered around the Corvette. Someone said, "He's been stabbed, maybe robbed."

Another argued, "No. The knife is in his hand. He must have stabbed himself."

"I never heard of suicide by knife."

Vern faded into blackness, hoping one of the idiots circling him had remembered to make the call.

In the fog of pain, he heard someone say, "Anyone know him?"

No one answered.

Another said, "Check him in as a John Doe. None of us want to get involved with a guy so dumb he can't even kill himself."

"Right," the first voice agreed. "We found him on a bar parking lot and no one knew who he was. He had a death grip on a bloody bowie knife."

Vern fought to stay conscious while the drunks argued over who would use his phone to make the call.

Finally, they all moved inside to tell the bartender to do his job. After all, it was his lot, so it was his duty.

Vern lay alone, hurting, as blood dripped out of his shoulder.

Chapter 28

Rusty hung up the phone. Starri was the only person who might come over after midnight to watch over Zach. The boy was old enough to stay alone. Probably had been as soon as he could walk, but tonight was different. He'd had a hard week with his uncle making the scene at school, then today he told Rusty that everyone wanted to be his friend and that was about as scary as the uncle.

He complained that he had to talk to people all day.

Before dark, the brothers ate outside and although they mostly spoke about the sunporch they'd build, Rusty had picked up bits of the kid's day. Every teacher had asked how he was feeling. A few of the football players nodded when they passed him in the hall. They were seniors, after all, and couldn't really speak to a sophomore. A girl in his math class told him she almost cried she was so afraid for him.

Some kids had invited him to sit with them at lunch. "And get this, bro, all day people were touching me. Patting me on the back. Shaking my hand. I'm usually invisible and I'm fine with that."

Then, as they finished their hamburgers, Zach fell silent for a moment or two. When he looked up at Rusty, fear seemed to float in his gray eyes that were the same color as his brother's. "Can I stay?"

"Here?" Rusty asked. "In the valley? At the high school?"

"With you. I need to know if I'm just visiting. Can I stay until I grow up? Maybe finish high school. Can I stay here with you?"

Rusty wanted to hug the kid, but he guessed that would probably frighten them both. He stuck out his hand across the picnic table. "You're my brother. You can stay as long as you like. Until you grow up, finish school, maybe get a job you like." Rusty smiled as Zach took his hand in a strong grip. "But if you get married, you'll want to move out. Then I'll help you build your own house."

"Promise, bro?"

"Promise."

Zach picked up the paper from their fries and burgers and grinned. "But I'm telling you right now, I'm never getting married. I'm going to be like you. Only shave now and then, never comb my hair with anything but my fingers, wear anything that looks clean."

"Stop!" Rusty yelled. "You telling me that's what is keeping the women away?"

"Of course it is. Get a clue. Women care about that kind of thing." Zach leaned his head sideways for a better look at his brother. "Who cuts your hair?"

"I do."

Zach stood and reached for the big jar of change he'd been digging lunch money out of every morning. "Tomorrow we'll take this and get you a real haircut and some clothes. Not work clothes. Real clothes with no patches and all the buttons on. I heard a woman on TV say that black hair looks good with black or red."

"I'm not wearing red, kid."

Zach shrugged. "Then black."

"All right. I need to go to town anyway and have the doc check my leg. Those staples she hammered in are itching. But it's Friday night, kid. Let's go wild. You pick the movie and I'll pop the popcorn."

The two brothers smiled. They were setting rules, planning, learning how to talk to one another.

Two hours later, Zach headed to bed as Rusty locked the doors. He never bothered to lock his hideaway home, but he thought it might make the kid feel safer.

An hour after that, when all was quiet above and Rusty was deep into a book, his phone buzzed. He didn't recognize the number but the voice was familiar. One of his nurses. Just hearing her made him a bit homesick for the nurses' dorm.

"Something wrong, Molly?" he asked as he remembered their constant chatter, their laughter, the way they fussed over him, and how good the air smelled after they all got dressed.

Molly told him the sheriff had ordered her to fill Rusty in on a few things. Vern Bonney had apparently been stabbed tonight outside a bar. As soon as he came to, he said he wanted to see his nephew.

"That is not going to happen," Rusty said calmly. "I'll be at the hospital within the hour to talk to both Vern and the sheriff."

Rusty hung up, called Starri, and asked her to keep watch over Zach. By the time she arrived, he had managed to get dressed and had even made a two-second effort to comb his hair.

He filled her in as he put on his coat. "I didn't want Zach to wake up alone. I don't know how long this will take, but Vern may have to die without seeing his nephew."

"I understand. I'll bed down on the couch. Take all the time you need to get rid of that creepy man."

"Thanks. I plan to even if I have to toss him in the bed of the pickup and drive him home. I owe you one, Starri."

She shook her head. "Don't worry about it. Remember when we agreed to be brother and sister? I guess that makes your brother my brother too." Starri whirled around like a little girl. "I've never spent the night in a bachelor pad. Mind if I look in your closets and rearrange your kitchen cabinets?"

"Knock yourself out." He smiled. Right now she looked a very young twenty and he felt a very old thirty-two.

She followed him to the door. "Before Zach, how many people have been in your house?"

"None. It was just a shack when I moved in at fifteen. At eighteen, the land sold for back taxes and my boss, Grady Brown, loaned me enough to buy it. I worked half a year of Saturdays to pay him back. I like fixing it up. It's my cave, my refuge, my sanctuary."

She held the door as he hobbled out. On impulse, he paused and kissed her cheek. He'd never done such a simple gesture, but it felt right.

"Be careful."

Rusty didn't have much of a plan, but maybe he'd think of something on the drive. His left arm was almost worthless and he couldn't walk fast on the wounded leg, but he had to take care of Zach's problem. That's what big brothers do.

Someday he'll be a college boy, Rusty thought. That dream was too big for Rusty, but not for his little brother. Rusty would work weekends to make sure the kid's dream happened.

Thirty minutes later, when he limped into the hospital, Nurse Sloane headed right toward him. She was big enough to knock him down with one blow and bossy as ever. "What do you think you're doing here, Rusty O'Sullivan? You should be off that leg."

"Glad to see you, Sloane." He winked at her. "I've missed all of you."

She didn't even try to act like she didn't know what was going on. "If you're here to see Vern Bonney, he's probably out for the night. The imbecile stabbed himself in the shoulder. The doctor stitched him up. When Vern came in drunk and bleeding all over everything, no one knew his name and he wasn't talking. Half an hour later, some high school kids dropped by to visit one of the wrestlers who got hurt tonight. They all ID'd Vern. I called the sheriff and he said he'd send a deputy over to collect him as soon as things settle down."

"Can I talk to Dr. Ryan, then?" Rusty fought to show no emotion. "There is only one reason Zach's so-called uncle is still hanging around town. He thinks he can get the boy and run. That will only happen if I'm dead."

"Ryan is not here. Dr. Adams is the attending physician tonight. She may be just an intern right now, but she's the best I've ever seen. I think Dr. Adams went to get a few hours' sleep, and I'm not waking her up unless it's an emergency."

Rusty didn't miss the change in tone. In the dorm, Amber Adams was just Amber or Doc, but here on duty, she was Dr. Adams. "Any chance I could talk to her if she's not asleep yet? I won't wake her if she's sleeping."

"Well . . . I saw her go into her office with a tray of four-hour-old food. She's had a hard night. Two deaths already."

"Thanks, Sloane. You're a sweetheart."

"No, I'm not. I'm breaking the rules even telling you where she is, but you might just be someone she would like to see tonight. It's been a hell of a shift. I'll let you know if Vern wakes."

* * *

A few minutes later, Rusty silently opened her office door. The lights were low. The untouched tray of food was on the desk. Her lab coat was hanging on a hook and her ugly shoes were scattered on the floor.

Amber was curled on the overstuffed couch, hugging her bare arms as if she'd fallen asleep freezing.

He pulled off his jacket as rain began to tap on the window. Vern Bonney could wait a few hours.

He covered her with his coat and pulled her onto his chest with his right arm. To his surprise, she didn't wake, she just cuddled into him as she had those nights in the dorm when they were alone.

He banked a few pillows around them and relaxed. Zach was safe tonight. Vern was in no shape to bother anyone, and Rusty was exactly where he wanted to be.

He pushed her short hair off her forehead and kissed her. He'd never loved anyone in his life. If he was honest with himself, he didn't think he had enough love in him to give anyone. But he felt so good holding her. Like a part of him had been missing for years and he'd found it.

He closed his eyes, matched his breathing with hers, and fell asleep.

Heaven wasn't a place to him, it was a person—and somehow this woman he had nothing in common with was his heaven.

The thought came to him that if he could just hold her now and then, just be near her, that would be enough.

Chapter 29

Emma was late visiting Heath. She'd taken another's shift this weekend, more to keep an eye on Heath than any need for overtime pay.

The emergency room had been busy and she hadn't finished her paperwork until after midnight. But she always stopped in to visit with Heath before she headed home. Tomorrow was her only day off this week, but she'd wear her Sunday best in a few hours and come back to visit him.

As always, Ruth was there by his bed, reading. Emma had noticed that she glanced up at her patient every time she turned the page. "See you in thirty, Miss Sumers. I'm hungry tonight."

She was gone before the head nurse could say a word.

Emma moved close to the bed. "Evening." As always, she started with what had happened in the hospital. "You will not believe this, dear, but when I checked on Dr. Adams a few minutes ago, Rusty O'Sullivan was holding her while she slept." After she told the details and said she closed the doctor's door very quietly, Emma apologized for gossiping.

"You can scold me for that. It's a habit I plan to break."

She spread her free hand over his heart. "No word from your daughter. I'm sure she'll be back soon." Emma couldn't tell Heath that Dr. Henton had said Jasmine Rogers Armstrong had called him a few hours after she left Wednesday and told Ryan to call her when the old man died.

A tear ran down Emma's cheek. She straightened like a soldier used to the battle cry. "Wake up, Heath. You have to wake up. For me. I need you to come back. I fear you have no one close to care about you, but many call and ask how you are. You matter to me. I think you always have."

Then, as she did every night, Emma told him about her plans. The future. She had to make him see tomorrow and the next day and the next. "We could go visit Jasmine sometime. Fall might be nice. Maybe we could take in a rodeo at the stockyards in Fort Worth."

She was silent as she closed her eyes and imagined them sitting in the stands. No, that wasn't right, she thought. Heath would insist on box seats down front.

She continued, "I found a pamphlet in the lobby about a cruise of the Mediterranean. Imagine that. I might like to stick my toes in that water. Oh, I almost forgot to tell you that a new barbecue place opened over by the college in Clifton. We could drive over and have dinner, watching the college kids. I don't even know one story about your days at A&M, Heath. I should have asked. Maybe we could eat our barbecue and talk about our college days. That is, if I can get in that big truck of yours; I don't know if you can get in my little car. When we have a date, we may have to eat close enough to walk."

She laughed as if he were joining her with their problem.

Putting her hand in his, she waited for him to move, but not one finger even twitched. "When you get better, promise me you'll hold my hand. I don't care where we go or what we do as long as you're near."

After she ran out of places they might go, she whispered, "Hear me, Heath. You have to hear me."

When Ruth came back, Emma put on her coat and walked out to her tiny car. She could hear a little voice inside her: "*He can't hear you. He's not yours. Even if he wakes up, he won't remember anything you say. You are having a fool's conversation with a man too far gone to hear.*"

For once in her life, Emma told her logical brain to ignore the voice.

Chapter 30

Saturday, Before Sunrise

Rusty woke to his favorite doctor moving her hand down his body. For a moment, he thought she was checking for injuries, then he realized she was caressing him. Gently, boldly. He wasn't sure if it was a lover's touch or she was simply stroking the dorm pet.

In truth, he didn't care.

He didn't move. Holding the doc while she slept was one thing, but this—this was something else. An "If I died and went to heaven" kind of something else.

When her lips brushed over his, Rusty had to react. He took his time, but he kissed her completely. If she planned to take advantage of an injured man, he might as well help.

He didn't plan on stopping until she pulled away. Maybe she sleep-kissed like some people sleepwalk. He didn't care. He'd never felt such passion or hunger.

He knew at some point she'd stop. Then she'd probably slap him.

Maybe she was dreaming and he was her practice dummy. Maybe he was the one dreaming.

Her head dropped to his chest. "Sorry," she mumbled. "You were just here and I couldn't resist. You're a very kissable man."

"Right, I'm irresistible," he answered. Since this had never happened before, he assumed she was delusional.

"Yes, you are," she argued, still sounding half asleep. To prove her point, she kissed him again, launching a full attack on his senses.

He surrendered without a fight. If the world ended right now, at this minute in time, he wouldn't miss it. He was too busy to notice.

A tap on her office door finally pulled them apart. He sat up on the couch, and she scrambled over him and moved to the desk as she pulled down her T-shirt and slapped her hair into place.

He leaned back and studied her while she picked up a book and pretended to be reading. The best few moments of his life were over. A beautiful, smart, sober woman had kissed him like he was worth her attention, and he had no idea how to make it happen again.

"Morning, Dr. Adams," Jackson Landry said as he rattled the door open and walked in, carrying a box that almost reached his chin. "I brought some files my father kept on Jamie Ray. I thought I'd hand them to . . ." Jackson froze halfway to the desk. "What are you doing here, O'Sullivan? You are next on my list to see this morning."

Jackson didn't wait for Rusty to answer; he just launched into what he was working on for Zachary. "I know I can get you custody of your brother. The problem may be getting a restraining order against Vern. I think I can keep him away from the school, but there is no proof that he's mistreating Zach."

The doc had put on her lab coat by the time Jackson set the box down. She didn't bother to talk to him.

Jackson turned back to Rusty. "Most of these files on Jamie Ray are old. I swear Dad saved every paper he typed up."

Rusty frowned as if he thought Jackson would start cross-examining him. Rusty must have figured the best defense was to fire first. "Why are you here, Jackson? No one called you. I thought lawyers kept banker's hours."

Jackson shrugged. "Half my clients are here, so why wouldn't I be here? Besides, some lady named Ruth called me before dawn to tell me Heath Rogers wanted to talk to me. Which is strange because a few days ago his daughter called, wanting power of attorney over him. She said he was in a permanent coma, so there was no reason for her not to take over his businesses."

"Mr. Rogers is awake?" Amber snapped as if interrogating him. "Ruth called you, not me? This makes no sense."

Jackson's shoulders jumped up as if trying to cover his ears. "I don't know what is happening, Doc. You're in charge around here. I'm just here because a client needs me. I brought these files in, thinking someone would get them to Jamie Ray's sons." The lawyer frowned at Rusty. "I have no idea where you hang out, but the hospital is where I usually find you." Jackson looked around. "Don't tell me you're sleeping here?"

Before Rusty could answer, Amber started pacing, obviously working on her own puzzle. "I went off duty at midnight," she announced. "Ruth didn't know I was here." She patted her pockets. "I've lost my phone. I have to have it at all times."

Rusty calmly pulled the cell from between the couch cushions and handed it to her.

A dozen questions came to mind. Jackson picked one. "Why are you here looking like you just woke up?" Jackson studied O'Sullivan and shook his head. "Never mind. I don't want to know."

Amber slipped into her ugly shoes and announced, "Let's go see Mr. Rogers. I had almost given up on him. Everyone in town is going to be thankful that he pulled out of the coma."

Jackson followed her down the hall and Rusty followed him. Two nurses and an aide joined the procession. The town's richest rancher just woke up and everyone wanted to know if he was back.

When they got in the room, all was quiet. Heath Rogers looked like he was sleeping. The doc tapped his arm, called his name, even patted his cheek. No response.

The aide who'd just come on duty said the night nurse reported Mr. Rogers had said he wanted Jackson Landry as plain as day and then drifted back into a coma.

Jackson moved closer and said good morning to the sleeping not-so-beauty. When nothing happened, he spoke louder. "What am I supposed to do, just wait around until he wakes up? I have no idea what he wants me for. Wake up, man, and talk to me."

Rusty finally interrupted before Jackson started shaking the old guy. "Look, Jackson, you're only a block away. Tell the staff to call you when he wakes. And, I'm no lawyer, but if I were you, I'd hold off on that power of attorney the daughter wants. I know Heath Rogers. He's a man who makes up his own mind. If you do something while he's out, you'll probably be his ex-attorney. Since Honey Creek is the county seat, he will not have any trouble finding another one."

"Good point." Jackson smiled. "By the way, did you comb your hair this week?"

The doc stepped between them and took over. "Clear the room. We need to run some tests." Before the two men could get out of the room, Dr. Amber Adams added, "And, Mr. O'Sullivan, don't leave the hospital. I'm not finished examining you."

Jackson could see Rusty was trying his best to look innocent and doing a lousy job of it. The guy looked like week-old leftovers left on the counter, and she was smiling at him like he was as tempting as homemade coconut pie.

They walked halfway down the hall before Rusty looked at Jackson. "You hungry? There's a little room where the staff eats. I can probably get a table there. The menu is pretty much whatever they have left over and the coffee is free."

"You buying?" Jackson wanted to get paid even if it was in pancakes.

"Sure. We can talk there about my absent father. But first we'll need to yell through the pass-through that we need breakfast, and they'll shove something toward us. If someone died or checked out before they ate breakfast, they'll give us their tray free."

Rusty called for two breakfasts and two coffees. A few minutes later came one tray containing two coffees and two sausage biscuits with cheese. Rusty passed the tray back with two dollars on it.

Without any discussion, the two men sat at the table by the window. Both stared out at the empty parking lot while they ate. Neither said a word. It was early and they weren't really friends.

Now and then a nurse would pass by and stop to talk to Rusty. Jackson figured Rusty had something . . . something that was invisible to men but apparently every female saw. Even the old cook leaned down so she could look through the passage to wink at him.

Rusty teased one tall woman that he almost didn't recognize without her towel on. Another short nurse kissed Rusty's cheek and said, "Thanks for the shower." The last one to walk by was shy. She just smiled, handed him a brownie wrapped in plastic, then continued on her way.

Finally, he asked Rusty about Zach.

Rusty said, "Starri is watching over him. The kid thinks she's beautiful but he is a little afraid of her. He says she can read his mind, but I'm guessing it's not that hard to read a teenage boy's thoughts."

"She reads my mind too," Jackson admitted. "I'm fascinated with her, but she's twenty. She's closer to Zach's age than mine."

"You probably should date someone closer to your age, old man. Like one of the nurses or the doctor."

Jackson raised his eyebrow as if expecting a trap. "I would, but she told me she's engaged."

Rusty shook his head. "She told me that, too, but I've never seen a ring and she's never said his name. Don't you think that's a little strange?"

"Not really." Jackson leaned across the table. "No stranger than how she stares at you like you're dessert on her tray. And you don't even comb your hair, and you look like you sleep in your clothes. I swear, you look like a homeless bum half the time."

Rusty plowed his fingers through his tangled black hair. "What is this sudden obsession about my appearance?"

They finished off their biscuits without another word. Finally, Jackson told Rusty he planned to help make sure Zach was safe. "My detective, Wind, did a little digging. The kid has had a hard life. Just the list of schools he's attended was a page long."

Rusty said in almost a whisper, "I let him pick his room. He told me of all the places he'd lived, he'd never had his own room. I hear him turn the lock every night. I don't think he trusts anyone."

When the doc showed up, she ignored Jackson and reminded Rusty he needed to meet her in one of the examining rooms off the lobby in five minutes.

Jackson watched them staring at each other, but he couldn't figure what was going on between them. Probably nothing. They lived in different worlds. She talked all the time in medical terms, and he sounded like he was just learning to put words together.

Jackson laughed out loud. Rusty seemed to be the most popular patient around. The nurses loved him and the doc didn't want him to leave. The guy must be doing something right.

"Too bad Vern Bonney didn't have any of your charm, Rusty," Jackson said to the back of Rusty's head. "Half the school population has called my office offering to testify against Uncle Vern if he ever comes back to town. Even the librarian, who'd been watching from the second-floor window, said she'd thought of running out on the parking lot and clobbering Vern with an atlas."

Rusty faced Jackson. "He is back in town, Jackson. In fact he may never have left. He's here in the hospital right now."

"What? Why didn't I know? Does the sheriff know?"

Rusty stood. "Maybe we need to have another talk with the uncle."

Jackson fired up. "I'll threaten him with charges. He has no right even to see the boy."

"Then we fight," Rusty said low and deadly calm. "My little brother is not going home with Uncle Vern or anyone else unless he wants to."

"What about his mother?"

"Zach says his mom is in for ten to fifteen years. He'll be a man before she's out."

It seemed the staff all stopped and watched the two men headed to the emergency room. Rusty's brace tapped off each step like a time clock.

When they got to the emergency room, a nurse told them Vern had been moved upstairs and the deputy was calling in the new location.

Before they could reach the room on the second floor, a nurse came running out.

Vern Bonney, while in transport from the recovery room to a room, had disappeared.

Chapter 31

Rusty wanted to join the hunt for Vern, but nobody knew where to begin looking. He called Starri and told all he knew. They both agreed that Rusty's place was probably the safest hideout for now. They also thought it might be a good idea if Rusty stayed in town because Vern might be watching him.

"He doesn't know I'm here."

Starri answered, "Where is your pickup?"

"Out front of the hospital." Rusty didn't have to say more. He saw the point. Vern knew the pickup. "You're right, Starri. I'll stay here until they catch him. I might as well let the doc check my leg, but I'm coming your direction as soon as I can be positive I'm not being followed."

Rusty added in a low voice, "Don't make a big deal of this. Zach might decide to run."

"Why would he do that?" Starri asked.

"Because I would if the guy was hunting for me," Rusty

answered as his eyes turned dark with worry. "Keep my brother safe, Starri."

"I will." Starri hung up.

The doctor met Rusty at the admissions desk and he filled her in. While Amber went after charts, an aide who looked like she could still be in high school showed him into an examining room. Before she closed the door the girl said, "Strip and put on a paper gown. Slit goes in back. Might want to put that sheet over your legs."

"I remember," Rusty said as the door closed. "This isn't my first rodeo."

He thought of not undressing. He was fine. Everything hurt, which seemed normal. The break just below his elbow itched more than throbbed. His left leg was useless. If he moved it hurt, but every day he managed to put a little more weight on it. At least he could stand long enough to shower and walk with a crutch taking some of the weight. The wound on his side bothered him more than anything. Every time he moved, pain seemed to rattle around his body. He'd be no help to Zach if he didn't calm down.

"Clear your head," he whispered. "Think of everything that has happened this morning."

He lay down on the examining table and felt like a left-over cadaver. Closing his eyes, he relived the few minutes he'd had with Amber at dawn. She'd kissed him like no one had ever kissed him. It wasn't practiced and planned. It wasn't foreplay for something else about to come. It was a hunger firing up. Raw, unrehearsed, spontaneous. He had no idea what would have happened if they'd had more time, but he was onboard for the ride.

The door opened and closed.

He didn't open his eyes. He knew it was the doc. The sound her shoes made. The smell of the shampoo she used. Even the air changed when she was close.

Without a word she moved her hand over his shoulder to push the paper gown down and began changing the first bandage. She cleaned each wound and applied a salve, then moved to the next bandage. Some were scabbed over. Some were still bleeding on the cotton. All were healing.

It occurred to him that a nurse, or even an aide, could have done what she was doing.

He didn't react to her touch but he felt it all the way to his core. He wasn't a man who was touched by anyone and each slide of her fingers over unbroken skin made him more aware of her.

His body finally tensed when she brushed her hand over his abdomen.

"Easy, Trouble," she whispered. "I'm not going to hurt you."

Rusty almost laughed. He was already bracing for the blow when she left. She might be a few inches from him now but he knew she would walk away any minute. Out of the room. Out of his life. The doc wouldn't even look back when she left and he'd remember the feel of her the rest of his life.

For years, every time he passed the hospital, he'd think of her. He had a feeling he'd reach for her in his sleep. To her, what they had was nothing, a passing flirtation, but to him she was his first taste of caring. He knew that when he danced with women in the bar, he'd compare them to the way she'd felt in his arms. He also knew none would measure up.

She was right beside him now, touching him, but Rusty could feel the pain of her saying goodbye. He was a fool. No one in his life ever stayed around. Why would she be any different?

Now he had a brother who had to come first. There was no time for him and Amber.

The aide came in, talking almost as fast as she was chewing her gum. It took her a few moments to notice he was still and his eyes were closed.

"Is he dead, Dr. Adams?" she whispered. "He looked

tired when he came in. You'd think a man with that many
patches on his body would do nothing but lay around feeling
sickly."

"No, he's not dead. He's just resting. He was watching
over a friend who needed him all night, so I'm guessing he
didn't get much sleep."

The aide sounded near tears. "That friend must be on
hard times, Doc, if he's turning to this guy for help."

Amber's hand moved over Rusty's chest. The paper
gown was gone and a sheet lay across his body just below
his waist. The doc's voice was low as she turned toward the
girl. "I have to go back upstairs. Tell the nurse to let him
sleep for a while. I'll be back to check on him. We're not
busy and he probably could use a nap. I have a feeling he is
going to have a long day."

"Sure. I'll tell her. I like working on Saturday morning.
No one gets beat up in a fight or smashed in a car wreck."

"It's not always like that, but there are calm times. That's
when we clean and stock like soldiers getting ready for the
next battle."

Rusty heard the door open and close. He opened his eyes
and saw the doc leaning against the door.

He sat up and smiled. "Am I going to live, Doc?"

The grin she gave him in response was a bit wicked.

He offered a hand. "Come here. We didn't have time to
say goodbye."

"I was thinking the same thing."

She moved between his knee on one side and the bandage left on the other. The table was tall, making them the
same height. Only a thin sheet was between them as he
pulled her close. This time he took the lead and kissed her
softly, almost as if he were kissing a memory. Both knew
this day might change everything.

Nothing about them fit together in life. They'd known
from the first. He wasn't even sure he could carry on a con-

versation for ten minutes with her, but her body fit his perfectly. She felt so right against his chest.

This time passion came slow; a need to hold her had replaced all else.

She wasn't his. She'd probably never be his, but for a moment they'd touched and as long as he lived, he'd never forget this perfect feeling when, for once, all was right with the world.

He thought of asking if there really was a fiancé waiting back home, wherever home was, but he didn't want to know. Not now.

He wanted a dream to take with him when he walked away.

He deepened his kiss and she moved into him.

Maybe he was dead because nothing on this earth had ever felt so good. For this moment, he was in heaven.

Chapter 32

Sunday Afternoon

Emma walked into Heath Rogers's room in her Sunday best. She straightened and smiled her biggest smile. With each day's passing she doubted her sanity more. She'd never had a man who truly loved her, and this game she was playing with Heath Rogers might be just that, a game. All her life she'd been practical. Done what was right. Done what was expected of her.

For this one time she needed to believe that someone cared for her, listened to her, maybe even loved her. If he died or if he woke up, her fantasy would be over, but maybe she could imagine that once, if only for a blink, it was real.

She couldn't bear to think that she'd lived out her life without filling the hole in her heart, without ever having loved.

She turned toward the window, suddenly angry at herself. She'd lived a good life; she'd taken care of people, even saved lives. She had friends. She'd laughed. There was no reason to feel sorry for herself.

As always when tears threatened to fall, Emma turned to practical things. She greeted Heath.

"Morning, dear. You may not know this of me, but I have four cold-weather suits: one dusty pink, one navy blue, one black—in case needed for a funeral—and one dark red, almost burgundy. All are wool and several years old." She smiled at her ridiculous conversation. "I wear a different suit each Sunday because no one at the First Baptist Church has more than a month's memory. I might go crazy and change the scarves and blouses, but I don't think it matters. No one really notices a lady my age."

She laughed, happy no one was in Heath's room. She set her purse on the chair and went to his side. "Sorry I'm late. I had to stay to clean up the greeting parlor after church."

When she touched him, he moved his hand to cover her cold fingers.

"Emma," he whispered, his eyes barely open. "You're here."

Sunshine came into her cloudy day. "Yes, dear, I'm here." Maybe, just maybe, all wasn't in her imagination.

"I missed you." His words came slow and rough. "I think I missed you even before I called your name in my long sleep."

He's really talking, she thought. For once she wasn't dreaming.

"Do you know what day it is?" The nurse in her began an assessment.

He thought about it for a while and answered, "Sunday. I heard the church bells. I guessed you'd be in the third row." It took a while but he finally seemed to focus. "You wore your pink suit today. That's my favorite. I hope you don't mind me saying that I don't like the black suit. A pretty lady like you should never wear black."

Emma couldn't speak. He'd noticed her. Even kept up with what color she wore. She'd seen him sitting near the back sometimes, but he never stayed around to talk and drink coffee. He never came to anything but the Sunday service, and she wasn't sure he came often.

"Heath?" she whispered. "I'm so glad you woke up."

"I had to. Couldn't let you do all the talking." His laugh was low, almost a rumble in his chest. "I've got things to tell you, so don't you disappear."

"Is that an order, Mr. Rogers?"

"No. It's a request. But I should warn you, if you don't show up, I'll get out of this bed and come looking for you. We're not young and I don't want to waste any more time."

She sat beside him, a little smile on her lips. He was coming back. Talking. Touching her as if they were close friends. Quiet Heath Rogers was even trying to boss her around. She patted his hand. "I'll stay for as long as you want to talk."

He nodded. "If I doze off, I'm not finished; I'm just resting." He wrapped his big, rough hands around her small ones. "I didn't tell you I liked dancing with you that one time, but I'm telling you now that I plan to do it again, if you have no objection."

"I think I'd like that, Heath."

As they passed the day talking about memories of growing up, the staff changed toward her. They saw him reach for her hand. They heard him call her name. They realized Emma wasn't just his nurse—she meant far more.

Some of the staff whispered that they'd known about them for a while. Some said they'd been lovers for years. One aide even claimed they were probably secretly married.

Emma didn't mind the whispers. She'd never been a topic of gossip. She answered no questions. She just smiled.

When he awoke from a nap, he looked for her first. They talked quietly and that night, when they brought his first meal in months, the staff brought Emma broth and Jell-O also. Only Emma's tray had a tiny bud vase with one yellow rose.

Emma thanked the young aide but said the flower wasn't necessary.

The aide who delivered dinner shook her head. "Yes, ma'am, but Mr. Rogers insisted. I would have asked about it but you were talking with the doctor." The aide smiled. "He said his lady should have a yellow rose. I panicked as to where I would find one, then I realized flowers are all over this place."

When the aide left, Emma moved close and kissed Heath's stubbly cheek, then she sat down and waited for him to wake fully so they could have their first meal together.

Chapter 33

Jackson Landry sat across from the sheriff, waiting for Pecos Smith to get off the phone. He'd brought the lawman a dozen doughnuts. His dad used to say if you want something from a civil servant, you'd better bring a gift.

Maybe doughnuts wouldn't be considered a bribe. The dispatcher had eaten half of them, and Jackson doubted he'd get anything out of her besides her phone number. 911.

Finally, the sheriff hung up. "How can I help you, Jackson? You do have an office, right? Seems like you were here drinking my coffee every day last week and now we're starting again today."

Jackson held up his second cup. "I do love your coffee, but I need to talk to you. I think we've got a missing person on our hands, and he's a real bad guy that might cause my clients trouble. We need to nip this in the bud."

Pecos laughed. "Really. 'Nip this in the bud.' No one under sixty says that, and by the way, since when are we a team?"

Jackson groaned. "I'm turning into my father. Which I wouldn't mind in fifty or so years, but I'd like to make thirty before I turn gray and start walking with a cane. Yesterday I walked around the square waving at the people and talking to the trees."

The sheriff laughed. "Did he always worry about his clients?"

"Yes, he did. Now for as long as I've been a lawyer, I've taken over the worrying. Which is less than six months. I'm pulling out my hair over the what-ifs."

"Slow down, Jackson. Which client are you talking about? The one in a coma or the one bandaged up? The teen runaway or the happy couple I had to put in jail last week so they wouldn't kill each other? You've got more clients, lawyer, than you can handle."

"Maybe you should speed up, Sheriff. It all started with Jamie Ray. Some people might be loose lipped, but old Jamie Ray Morrell was loose with another body part. You'd think he would have known better."

"Jackson, stop talking like your dad or I'll have to lock up my service weapon to keep from shooting you."

Jackson decided he'd stop talking to stay alive.

Pecos yawned and looked like he'd lost his train of thought. "We're a pitiful pair. I'm tired and you're crazy. My baby girl isn't sleeping nights and she wakes her big sister up so my wife and I both have to get up. I'm counting my night's sleep in minutes, not hours. You wouldn't believe what a three-year-old wants to talk about in the middle of the night. When I tried to tell her that unicorns aren't real, she started crying and my wife got mad at me.

"When we were first married, I was perfect, but I slip a little with each kid. By the time the fifth comes along, I'll be brain dead."

Jackson smiled as the sheriff answered another call. Everyone knew the sheriff was happily married. Pecos just needed a little sleep to remember it.

When Pecos hung up, all he said was, "It's Monday. What can I say?" After a bite of doughnut, he leaned back. "So, you think you have a missing person. Just to make it clear, you're not the one missing?"

Jackson wasn't in any mood to laugh at the sheriff's dumb joke. "You remember that guy who claimed he was Rusty O'Sullivan's brother's common-law uncle? He made a scene at the high school. You weren't there, but I handled it."

Pecos looked blank. He must have gotten tangled up on "Rusty O'Sullivan's brother's uncle."

"The man at the high school!" Jackson shouted. "Pecos, you should take a sick day, lock yourself in one of the cells and sleep."

"I'll wake up after a few pots of coffee." He pulled out a folder as if staring at it would at least keep his eyes open. "Vern Bonney. I saw his rap sheet and you're right; he's bad. He came to town to beat up his fourteen-year-old nephew and drag him home.

"I remember. The kid we held here so Rusty O'Sullivan could talk to him was not going back with his uncle. I would have never booked a kid for stealing food. I did hear you stood up to Uncle Vern, Jackson."

"Me and half the student body. When your deputies pulled up, Vern couldn't get out of there fast enough. If Vern Bonney finds out Zach may come into money, I'll bet he'll come back."

"Yeah, I heard about his disappearing act at the hospital. I'm worried about that too. Everyone is talking about what Jamie Ray left his sons. I told all my deputies to keep an eye out for Vern. If he shows up, it won't be a warm welcome."

Jackson finally had Pecos's full attention. "My detective, Wind, has a friend checking on him down south where he lives. The friend reported that he hasn't seen Vern in days. Where would he go after he left the hospital? It's been two days and I'm afraid the snake of a man is holed up, planning how to get to Zach.

"Maybe his junker of an old Corvette broke down before he got back to his farm. I don't really care where he is as long as he's not in the valley."

Pecos raised his head. "Did you say Corvette? What color?"

"Dirty red, with more rust than paint."

The sheriff grabbed his hat. "Come on, Jackson. I think I know where that car is."

Jackson had to run to keep up with the lawman.

"Outlaw's Watering Hole is about two miles south. Vern was picked up from the parking lot there after he stabbed himself. And that's where the owner called in, saying he had an abandoned old Corvette in the lot."

As they drove, the sheriff said this one bar contributed to half the patients in the emergency room most Saturday nights. When the bartender rang last call, it was fighting time. Most customers were too drunk to remember who hit them or to file charges.

As the patrol car swung into the gravel parking lot, Jackson saw the red Corvette parked near the back. A slow rain started about the time the men climbed out, but the water didn't improve the look of the Corvette.

"That's his car," Jackson said. "I remember the cracked windshield and that dent in the bumper. Thought it looked like the car was grinning. So, if the vehicle is here, where is Vern?"

Pecos motioned with his head and they went inside.

At nine o'clock in the morning, no customers were in the bar. A young bartender was stocking. "Don't open till two," he said before he faced the men.

Pecos didn't waste time. He started asking questions.

The young bartender/janitor said he had no idea whose car was parked out near the back. Lots of drunks get too plastered to drive home and the next morning they forget where they left their car. He did remember the night bartender saying something about Friday night being wild.

Some guy stabbed himself. It took the ambulance thirty minutes to come because they were on another call. The bartender swore the drunk was dead. Blood was everywhere, so the other drunks let him lie half in and half out of the old car. Said one of the bikers stepped in a puddle of blood and cussed the dead guy out, then slugged him for ruining his new boots.

As they walked away, Jackson vowed never, ever to go in Outlaws again.

"Should we check out the hospital to see if he came back?" Pecos asked.

"Or the funeral home."

Before they got their safety belts buckled, an emergency 911 call came in from the Patterson Ranch. Fred Patterson was yelling so loud over the dispatcher Pecos probably could have heard the man if the sheriff just rolled down his window.

About the time Pecos said, "I'm on my way," Jackson's cell rang. Miss Heather, his always calm secretary, patched a call from Susie Patterson to Jackson's cell. The not-so-happy wife in the recently jailed duo was talking so fast Jackson didn't understand a word.

Finally, she stopped to breathe and Jackson ordered her to stop firing. "I'm on my way and I've got the sheriff. Whoever is still shooting will be going to jail."

Both the radio and Jackson's cell went dead.

"Good job, lawyer. They must have stopped." Pecos hit ninety when he passed the city limits sign.

Jackson feared it was more likely their last two shots had hit their marks. They could both be dead.

The thought crossed his mind that neither one probably had a will. Like everyone, even the lawyer thought he'd prepare his final wishes later.

Worry doubled. They could still be shooting when they pulled up in the cruiser and a stray bullet might hit him. He'd be dead with not one file closed.

Between guns and knife fights and wild rides downhill in a storm, being a lawyer seemed more dangerous than he thought it would be.

If he lived through this day, Jackson decided he'd go over to Starri's house and sit on her porch and watch the sun set. She'd calm him, or a heart attack might be coming on any minute. He had enough adrenaline to launch a rocket to the moon.

Chapter 34

Monday Afternoon

Zach figured he was caught in an alternate universe. School had never been like this. Thursday his uncle had embarrassed him in front of the whole school, and now he felt like he'd finally found where he belonged. No one picked on him. A few of the football players teased him about LouAnn standing up for him, and everyone laughed at how Zach's redheaded gladiator was a foot shorter than he was.

For the first time, Zach had his group to sit with at lunch. They talked of games he'd never heard of and books he planned to read. He even had lunch money.

· And best of all, he had time to just think because he didn't have to worry about what might happen after school. He was doing his homework for the first time ever. Most kids griped about the load, but Zach was staying awake in class. The librarian had turned into his fairy godmother. She fluttered around him, finding books she was sure he'd love. She even let him check out books without a lecture about what would happen if he didn't bring them back.

When he walked down the school hallway Monday morning with his new backpack on one shoulder, he decided Vern wasn't his uncle anymore. He never had been. There is no such thing as a common-law uncle.

Zach had real family now. Three big brothers. Rusty was great and the other two would be too. One had gone to college and another was in the Army on a mission. Zach didn't know much, but he knew it must be important. He'd watched enough movies to know there was no such thing as a "secret" mission; they always had "top secret" missions.

As he headed to his last class, LouAnn popped out of nowhere, which made him jump. He shortened his steps so they could walk together. She talked. He listened.

Finally, he got in a question. "You still got that big rock?"

"I do. My mother says I'll probably need it when I marry." Three steps later she asked, "You still growing?"

"I don't know. My brother says I'm taller than he was at my age, so I'll probably be taller than him and he's six feet."

"Ohhh," she moaned as if disappointed.

"What's wrong?"

"You will be tall. When you get older, I'll be too short for you."

It took him half the length of the hallway to understand what she was saying. She liked him. A girl really liked him. For a moment he tried to think what was wrong with her. It must be something. Brain hemorrhages. Early, early Alzheimer's. Maybe she was going blind. She was dying and wanted to be nice to him. No, none of those were true. Somehow, she just liked him.

He looked at her. Cute as she could be. Brave. A bit crazy. Perfect. "Maybe you'll grow. Until then, I can lean down so we can be eye to eye when we talk."

She shook her head. "No. I don't think I'll grow any higher. Mom says once I got my period, I'm full grown."

Turning into the classroom, she left him standing in the

doorway like a human turnstile. When he finally got to Lou-Ann, he whispered, "What is a period?"

"If you don't know, I'm not telling you. Ask your brother."

Zach worried about it until he made it home. Then he asked his phone and was more confused. When Rusty got home, Zach asked his brother, then saw something like panic in the big, strong man.

"Get in the truck. I know who to ask." Rusty whispered as if they were talking about a state secret.

Twenty minutes later, he knocked on the nurses' dorm door. Sloane, the bossy one, was the only nurse home. After she lectured Rusty about keeping his wounds clean and making sure he kept moving his leg until it hurt, she was ready to hear what they needed.

Rusty hesitated but Zach jumped in. "My brother drove over here so you'd tell me what a girl's period is." Zach lowered his voice. "You might want to talk loud, 'cause I'm not too sure my big brother knows either."

She marched them into the kitchen, sat them down, and explained everything. Zach asked a few questions but Rusty was silent. He did nod now and then like pieces of a puzzle were finally fitting together.

Sloane ended her lecture by saying that Zach should remember to be extra nice to girls just in case it's their time of month.

"It happens every month," Zach pointed out. "How will I know when it's coming?"

"They might act different. Sad, or they might cry, or act like they are tired."

The kid took in the advice and asked, "Maybe I'll just ask them?"

Sloane tapped him on the head. "If you do that, they'll kill you. It's a known fact that women who murder usually do so during their period."

Zach walked out feeling more confused than when he came in.

Rusty thanked Sloane but she just huffed. "I swear men don't know anything. I'm convinced women discovered fire, invented the wheel, learned to grow their food, and a thousand more things while they were having babies to continue the species and cooking supper for the community."

Rusty smiled as he kissed her on the cheek. "Thanks, anyway."

"Anytime." She straightened and looked him in the eye. "He's a good kid, your little brother. It won't be long until you two are back for the child-birthing talk."

Zach heard Rusty say, "He is a good kid. I'll pick a few books up so we won't be bothering you too often."

Twenty feet later, they turned into the hospital lobby and started dropping quarters into an old candy machine so they could have dessert for supper.

Zach was having fun, but Rusty was watching the hallway, probably hoping to see Amber. He said the doc wouldn't go home until later but he claimed he needed to see her. Zach didn't know why. He'd had all he wanted to hear about periods. In fact, he'd like to go back to thinking periods were dots.

Chapter 35

Monday at Dusk

Jackson had no idea how long it took Pecos to find the Patterson Ranch. They had taken so many dirt roads he thought they had to be in Oklahoma by now. He was too worried about his clients being dead to think about dropping breadcrumbs so he'd find his way back.

If they shot each other, it was all his fault. He wasn't a marriage counselor. In truth, he was barely a lawyer. For a moment, Jackson was angry at Fred and Susie for hiring him. If he'd had any sense, he would have suggested a separation.

When the sheriff's cruiser finally pulled up to the Pattersons' ranch house, it looked abandoned. One window taped up. Two steps broken. Five years ago, Fred had inherited the land as far as Jackson could see, but the place looked like it was rotting. Old farm equipment had been left out and tall weeds had grown knee high around them. The big house needed painting and the corral was empty.

The sheriff honked a few times.

Silence except the faraway sound of gunfire.

When Pecos got out and pounded on the ranch house door, only a housekeeper was there to answer. She said the Pattersons had been out by the shooting range all morning.

She huffed and added, "If them two aren't working themselves into an early grave or trying to kill each other."

"Mind telling us where that'd be, ma'am?" Pecos asked politely.

Company obviously irritated the housekeeper. "Do I look like I'd know, or even care? Try following the noise."

On their way driving out from the ranch house, the cruiser passed a pickup pulling away from what looked like a bunkhouse. The sheriff pulled up close to the driver's window and waved the cowboy over. "Hey, mister, you know where the Pattersons are?"

"Nope. Don't know. Don't care. Fred fired all the hands at dawn. I took time to feed the stock. I heard Susie fired the housekeeper but wanted her to finish up cleaning first. I tell you, Sheriff, some days it's like the Alamo around here. The only thing them two have in common is shooting and yelling at each other. Both were national champions by the time they were out of high school. Fred's old man kept the ranch going, but Fred doesn't have the brains God gave rabbits." He barked a laugh and added, "Or the sperm. Five years and not one bunny."

The pickup was gone before the sheriff could ask any more questions.

Pecos pulled up to the barn door. "You think you can talk some sense into them, lawyer?"

"I doubt it." Jackson shrugged. "But I could try. We just stumbled over two reasons they're mad. The ranch is falling apart and at least one of the Pattersons wants kids."

A dozen rounds shattered the silence.

The sheriff shook his head. "This could be dangerous. I'm leaving you here for safety. If I'm not back or haven't called in ten minutes, dial 911 and tell the station I need backup."

Gunfire sounded like faraway thunder, so Jackson opened the car door and followed the sheriff's plan of staying behind. He hadn't been a lawyer long enough to die in the line of duty.

Another plan hit Jackson before he could step away from the cruiser. "I got another idea. I'll call Susie and you have your office call Fred. Tell whoever answers the phone to order Fred to come into the station and press charges against his wife for attempted murder. I'll tell Susie we'll meet her at the barn and I'll have papers for her to sign. I'll tell her the first one to file will be the innocent one in the court's eye.

"Once she's here, you can cuff her and take her in, and call the deputy at the office to arrest Fred when he gets there.

"Since they both called in a crime against the other, they'll each think the other is going to jail, so the talking one won't think he or she is in trouble. If they both turn in the other, I'll have divorce papers ready. They'll never have to see each other again. Of course, one of the Pattersons might be serving two to life if there's any bullet holes in a spouse."

"Sounds like a plan." Pecos lifted his radio as Jackson walked away to make his call to Susie.

One fact bothered Jackson, though: How could two national marksmen fire for an hour and not hit each other?

While they waited, Pecos stage-whispered, "Fine plan, Jackson. Hope it works."

"I had to think of something. I didn't like the idea of you getting in the cross fire."

Five minutes later, Susie Patterson came flying toward them in a dusty old Land Rover. She slammed on the brakes so hard she made her own tornado. When she jumped out, she was yelling and cussing and telling Jackson she wanted Fred sent away for attempted murder.

"The idiot I married shot my hat off my head!"

"Were you hurt?" Jackson shouted back.

"No, but he was working his way down."

Pecos put his arm around her as if in sympathy and had handcuffs on her before she noticed. She screamed louder when he shoved her into the backseat of the cruiser. The back windows were closed, but Pecos cracked the front window a few inches as if he were adjusting the volume to bearable.

They parked the car by the barn and walked fifty feet to the house's porch. The men who came to save the day sat down to wait out the hollering and were surprised when the housekeeper brought out iced tea and ginger cookies.

The plate of cookies was gone and Jackson was on his third glass of tea before Susie finally stopped.

Pecos walked over to his car and opened the back door. "We can go into town if you'll turn the volume down. If not, the housekeeper offered to cook us supper, but you'll have to wait here."

Susie glared at them both but didn't say a single word on the way to Honey Creek.

Chapter 36

Jackson felt like he'd spent the entire day in the sheriff's office. Susie had no problem telling the sheriff that Fred was trying to kill her. She signed the divorce papers the minute the sheriff handed them to her.

Fred did the same.

When the couple passed in the hallway neither said a word. Neither one was carrying a bullet hole or had even a scratch on them that Jackson could see. He doubted the charges would stick, but he guessed they'd managed to finally kill the marriage.

The realization that something that must have started out beautiful could die such a terrible death seemed to make the whole office sad. Jackson was sure he heard the dispatcher crying.

Not a sound came from the three jail cells.

While Jackson was finishing up the divorce papers, he saw Rusty walk into the sheriff's office. He must have seen Jackson's truck parked out front of the station and thought he'd stop by to hand back the box of papers about Jamie Ray. With a crutch under one arm and the box cradled beneath the other, Rusty didn't seem very steady. Jackson hurried to help even though he looked as bad as his friend did.

Rusty probably didn't want the file of his dead dad any more than Jackson did.

Jackson must have looked so tired Rusty took a minute to ask, "You all right?"

Jackson shrugged. "I wish you had Starri with you. I could use a little comfort. That girl can cheer me up just smiling at me. I promised myself if I made it through this day I'd go over and sit on her porch until the Earth slows down."

Rusty stared at Jackson for a moment then said, "I'm stopping for pizza, then heading home. Starri is there watching TV with Zach. They're watching a Harry Potter marathon. You're welcome to supper."

"Sounds like heaven."

Rusty raised an eyebrow and, as if testing new waters, said, "Happy to have you join us?"

"I don't know if I can remember where you live."

Rusty smiled. "Maybe it's time you tried. Just go to the bridge and follow the road. When the road ends, you're at my house."

When Jackson still hesitated, Rusty added, "I'll even buy an extra pizza. It's the least I can do for the man who saved my life."

Jackson shook his head. "We'll call it even. I've had one hell of a day. You're saving my sanity tonight."

When they made it to Rusty's house, Starri hugged Rusty for bringing pizza and Jackson because she said he looked like he needed one.

They all crowded onto the couch after eating and watched the movie. Even the puppy wiggled between Rusty and Zach.

Starri leaned close to Jackson as he snored through the movie. All was calm.

Jackson barely heard Rusty telling everyone to leave Jackson right where he was.

"I've got to go into work for a few hours tomorrow. I'll make sure he wakes up," Rusty said quietly as he layered a few blankets over Jackson. Zach said he'd walk Starri out to her car.

The last words Jackson heard were Zach talking about the movie and Starri laughing. For a moment, he wished he was the one walking Starri out, but then he remembered that he was too old for her.

Nine years between them, Jackson almost said aloud. Too many. Yet, he was drawn to her. Without thinking too much about it, he vowed he'd look out for her. In a strange way, she wasn't just reading his thoughts, she was climbing into his heart.

Chapter 37

Tuesday at Sunrise

Emma Sumers sat on Heath's bed. Two trays were on the portable table—one turned toward Heath and the other turned toward her. They were both smiling as they had another meal together. His eyes were wide open and clear. The cowboy was back.

He ate slowly as if relearning to move his limbs. She did the same because she didn't want to finish before he did.

The aides and nurses who had sat with him for almost three months and monitored everything were gone. Emma told him the day caretakers were shift workers who each worked a few days a week, but Ruth was with him at night.

"I know," he said. "I sometimes heard her talking to you." He smiled. "When it got very quiet around here, she'd read a chapter from her romance to me." He winked at Emma. "I have to say it was entertaining. If I ever get out of this place, I wouldn't mind reading to you. If you invite me, of course."

Emma laughed. "I don't know. Would I have to cook you dinner first?"

"Of course." Slowly, his smile faded. "Emma, we've wasted so much time. From now on let's promise to always be honest with each other. I don't want to leave things unsaid so I'll start first. Emma, I want you in my life."

She blushed. "I'd like that."

"Ruth is a nice lady, but one night when the lights went off for a few minutes, she held my hand and told me not to worry." Heath was silent a minute and said, "That was nice of her, but even in the dark I knew it wasn't your hand. I worried about you."

When Emma looked up she saw the depth in his eyes. He was staring. Really seeing her as if he never wanted to forget her face.

"I'll have to thank her again. I know Ruth works trying to pay off her mortgage, but a 'thank you' will still feel good."

He set down his spoon. Half of his oatmeal was uneaten, but she knew he wouldn't eat more. It would take time to recover.

"I always knew when you came in my room every morning. You opened the blinds. I think of you as my sunshine."

"I feel like we became friends while you were sleeping."

In response, he covered her hand as she had covered his for so many nights.

"Now, I have to leave and you have to go to therapy." She stood and straightened like the soldier she was.

Emma left his room. After therapy she checked on him and found him asleep. In the afternoon, Jackson Landry, the young lawyer, was sitting with him when she passed by. The lawyer was working, using his briefcase resting on his legs as a desk.

The hospital stayed busy until after dark. She stopped in to check on Heath and pull the blinds so car lights wouldn't flash across his walls. For a moment, she allowed herself to sit close. She loved sitting on his bed with her leg pressing slightly against his side.

She could feel his warmth, and for the first time he rested his hand along her thigh and pulled her closer. His words were barely a whisper. "I know this is not the place, but I want you closer to me. Do you understand? I'm not a man who knows the right words. I'm not flirting. I'm stating a fact."

His hand moved along her leg as he wrinkled her white uniform.

If he'd been any other man in the world, she would have put him in his place, or jumped back, or even run. But this was Heath. An honest man.

"I have to tell you how I feel, Emma. I've spent too many years hesitating. I want you beside me for however many years we have left."

"You're just thankful to be alive."

His hand moved over her leg. "I've been with Ruth every night for months and I don't feel that way about her. It's you. You were in my dreams long before I had the heart attack. Half the time I came to the board meeting just to see you. Once in an elevator I almost pulled you to me. The hunger was so strong to feel you in my arms. So, Emma, tell me if there is any way you return my affection? If you don't want this between us, I'll back away and never mention it again. I want it all. I want you against me every day I have left."

No man had ever spoken to her like this. She was a woman that men were polite to, if they even saw her at all. She was short, bossy, and always professional. Her hair was mousy brown with gray showing.

Emma straightened as if testifying. "I feel the same, Heath. I feel like something is missing when I'm not near you."

She leaned closer and kissed him. "You do know I'd have to jump to kiss you if you are standing."

He smiled. "Then I guess we'll have to lie down whenever you kiss me."

Emma blushed but didn't turn away.

Just a few more minutes before the hospital would be busy. She needed sleep and he'd start a routine of becoming stronger.

When she pulled his blanket over his shoulder, he whispered, "Emma?"

"I'm here, dear."

His fingers reached out for her hand.

Leaning toward him, she rested her head next to his shoulder and closed her tired eyes.

The nurse woke her when she came to check his vitals. Emma apologized for being in the way.

The nurse said softly, "I understand. I'd probably do the same thing if my man was in the hospital. Now, go home, get some sleep. We'll watch over your cowboy."

Her man. Emma thought about correcting the duty nurse, but decided against it.

Chapter 38

Friday Night

Rusty felt like it had been forever since he'd seen Amber. Every day he tried to do more and slowly he was growing stronger. He moved about the house with more confidence. He worked a few hours at The Shop. Tried to stay awake until supper. It had been five days without seeing his doc. Most of the pain from the wreck was gone, but now he felt like a hole was growing in his heart. How could he miss someone so much when he hadn't known her even a month?

He walked out of his office and into the huge workshop. Fighting against limping, he stepped under the large overhead door big enough to drive a one-ton truck through. The night air was cool and fresh. He decided to stroll along the creek that gave Honey Creek its name.

He loved moving about when the town was sleeping. Though he'd never belong among people, he liked watching, trying to figure them out. Amber Adams had become his favorite to think about. One moment she was ordering him around and the next she was touching him with a tenderness he'd never felt.

His muscles were stiff tonight but half a block later he could feel them beginning to ease up.

He'd never lived in town, but it seemed everywhere in the valley, if you listened, you could hear the gentle sound of water: the Brazos River raging sometimes and splashing around bends, and the streams breaking off in spots making creeks. Old-timers said that if you lived in the valley all your life, you could feel the river and streams flowing through your veins.

Rusty liked to believe that was true.

When he was a boy, he'd found the sounds among people frightening. The rattle of the coal train that passed through without stopping. The rush of a car engine. Lawn mowers coughing when they started. People yelling. The screech of tires or the blast of a truck's horn. Now and then he heard music floating on the air. Laughter sometimes moved in the wind, but so did the whispers of unknown cries.

The only sound he truly loved was the rustle of the water as it journeyed on. Once he'd thought he'd be like that when he grew up. Free. Not tied to anyone or any place. But now his world had changed.

He had a brother. The boy mattered to him. They had similar backgrounds. No father. Absent mothers. Grew up belonging nowhere. But now they had each other and Zach was growing better every day. Someday soon they'd stand as equals. Rusty wanted things for his brother. A stable home. A peaceful place to live.

Rusty made a mental list as he limped past the sheriff's station, then the coffee shop. The front of the shop, which faced the town square, was all polished and bright, but at the back door a fat cat chased mice near the dumpster.

Another block and he was on a quiet street. Jackson's office was there, but he wasn't working tonight. Starri, Jackson, and Zach were spending the evening at Jackson's ranch house. A cookout and another Harry Potter movie. Rusty had thought of joining them. He'd been invited, but it was time he went back to work. His arm was only a bother and his stitches were closing. Soon his side and his leg would only be scars.

Mr. Brown had called him almost every day since the accident. Little jobs were piling up and a few big jobs needed bids turned in. Rusty hadn't noticed it, but over the years his boss had leaned on him more and more.

Rusty turned toward the lights of the hospital and whispered, "Chalk it up to Brown to be another person I care about." First Starri and her aunt; then Jackson and Ryan, who'd ridden to save him; then the nurses and, of course, his doctor. Most of all, Zach. At the rate Rusty was making friends, he'd have a long list by Christmas.

He ached to go in the hospital's lobby and see if Amber Adams was still on duty, but he didn't want to bother her. He might have held her all night, but over coffee he'd be hard-pressed to keep a conversation going.

Crossing the parking lot, he noticed an empty bay where the ambulance usually waited. Someone else was having a bad time tonight. Maybe a car wreck, maybe a heart attack. Maybe a baby before the parents could make the drive to Honey Creek.

One last glance at the hospital windows, then Rusty started back to his mountain of paperwork and bids to finish. Walking in the shadows toward the stream, his thoughts were on Amber. He knew the feel of her body against him sleeping, but she wasn't his.

Another hour of work and he'd head home. He couldn't see the river but he could hear it just beyond a line of trees fifty feet away. The slow sound of the water moving near calmed him.

He concentrated on waiting around near the hospital. His thoughts were on what was inside. She was near but he didn't know if she'd welcome him dropping by. Not knowing how she felt toward him was enough to make him hesitate. The rumble of faraway thunder reminded him to move on.

On the hospital grounds the grass was wet and slippery from recent rain. For the first time he wished he'd brought his crutch or even the cane that kept rolling around the bed of the pickup. He'd traveled too far tonight. The way back wouldn't be without pain.

He glanced toward the lights of town, thinking the streets would be easier to travel than the riverbank. Maybe he'd see a deputy patrolling on Main Street and catch a ride.

Suddenly he saw something moving in the night like a ghost. As he moved closer he made out a white lab coat blowing in the wind. Someone was standing outside the garage bay. Her face was to the building, but her light blond hair shone.

He had no doubt who it was. He forgot the pain in his leg.

"Amber?" he said when he was five feet away. "Doc? It's me. Are you all right?"

As she turned, he saw sadness and exhaustion in her eyes, then a moment later she was running toward him.

He wrapped her in his arms and held tight as she cried.

Rusty didn't say a word. He just stood there. He'd never seen her like this. Something had shattered his warrior.

Footsteps came running toward them from inside. "Dr. Adams, are you all right?"

Slowly, Amber straightened. "I am. Thank you, Miss Sumers. Sometimes it just gets to me."

The little woman with gray-touched brown hair and kind eyes answered, "It gets to us all. Go home. Dr. Henton is on the night shift tonight and Admissions only has one patient waiting. If we need you, Dr. Adams, I'll call you." The head nurse looked at Rusty. "Mr. O'Sullivan, good to see you getting around. Now, if you'll loosen that hold on the doctor a bit, you should be able to talk her into going to get something to eat. I believe she hasn't had lunch or dinner."

For once the doc didn't argue when someone told her

what to do. Rusty put his arm around her shoulder, and they walked toward the parking lot.

"You don't have to . . ." she began.

"Yes, I do. When I was in the hospital, Sumers bossed not just the staff, but me too. I was more than half afraid of her with her sweet manner and gray hair. I got the feeling her spine was made of solid steel. If she tells me to feed you, I'll go find a place."

Amber circled his waist with her arm. "How about the coffee shop down the block? They've got sandwiches and desserts."

He reached her car and he opened the driver's door. "Anywhere but here," he said as he helped her in. "You're driving. Not enough room for my leg to bend in your car."

As she started the car, he climbed in on the passenger side and stretched his arm across the front seat to touch her hair. The knowledge that he could touch her so easily made him feel half drunk. She'd run to him. She'd pressed so close to him he had felt her breathing.

In the shadows he rubbed his leg, trying to push the throbbing away so he could think about just being with her.

"Are you in pain?" she asked as she reached over and brushed his jeans layered over bandages.

"A little, but it will pass."

"That settles it. We're going to the drive-through."

"Not exactly fine dining, sweetheart."

"Where do you eat out when you've worked late at the shop?"

"Usually a little place over by the rodeo grounds that can't make up its mind what it is. They serve great tacos and chili burritos with guacamole on top. On weekends they sometimes have a three-piece band and everyone dances around the waiters delivering food."

"That where you take your dates?"

"I don't date."

"Ever?"

"Ever." He forced himself to look at her. Every time he saw her, he feared it might be the last time. If so, he wanted to be honest. "My first girlfriend made a fool of me. I made up my mind I'd rather be alone than be made fun of."

"Will you tell me about it?"

"No. I'd have to know you better." The chances of that were slim unless he wrecked another car.

A few minutes later, she turned into a dirt parking lot next to the rodeo grounds. "This has got to be the place."

"Take off your lab coat, sweetheart."

She laughed. "Doesn't that come after you buy me dinner?"

Rusty was glad it was dark because he had no doubt that he was blushing. "No, no. I mean you'll stand out in that coat. Folks will start lining up to tell you their aches and pains." A slow smile moved over his lips. "So, just for reference, if I pay for dinner your clothes come off?"

She laughed as if he were joking. While he was trying to decide if he should ask again, she stepped out of the car, pulled off her lab coat, and grabbed a baggy sweater from the backseat.

Ten minutes later, he'd ordered a platter and two beers. The band started playing so loud he would have had to yell to say anything to her, but it didn't matter, he couldn't think of anything to say.

They ate in silence as they watched the dancers. Finally, she leaned close and asked, "What are you thinking, Trouble?"

He answered honestly, "I'm thinking that I'd like to sleep with you tonight."

"Sleep, or just sleep?"

He wanted to stand up, pull her against him, and dance, but he couldn't dance with one leg. Leaning so close his lips brushed her ear, he answered, "I don't care. I just want you with me."

"Let's get out of here," she answered. "Maybe what we need is just sleep."

Rusty wasn't sure if that was a yes, or a no, or even a maybe. He barely noticed that most of the bar crowd was watching them. When he pulled her close and kissed her on her cheek, even the band stopped playing for a moment.

He guessed that everyone was thinking that O'Sullivan finally found a lady he liked. Several regulars grinned at him and Rusty guessed it was time to go.

Then they were almost running to her car as rain began to pour. She was plastered to his side as if acting like a human crutch. He didn't care about the pain. She was close.

Both were wet by the time they climbed into her car. She jerked off her wet sweater and turned up the car's heater. When he pulled her toward him, there was no gentle courting. His kiss came hard and full out.

She giggled for a moment and joined in. His injuries were forgotten and the cast on one arm didn't matter. She seemed to need him as dearly as he did her. The smell of her blended with the rain. The taste of her. The feel of her.

When she finally came up for air, both were breathing hard. "Where did you learn to kiss like that?"

"Pansy Johnson. Eighth grade. I think she was on a mission to teach every boy in her class to kiss. She said I was a fast learner, but we still practiced for a while. Our senior year, she gave more advanced lessons in sex ed. But I didn't sign up for her instructions."

He stared at Amber for a moment, loving how her lips were swollen, her hair a mess, and her cheeks red. Digging his fingers in her curls, he pulled her slowly to him. This time he kissed her tenderly and deep. When he finally moved to tasting her throat, she whispered, "I . . . I . . . I've never been kissed like . . ."

"Hush, Doc," he whispered into her ear. "We're just getting started."

The rain pounding outside isolated them from the world. Their kisses seemed to ride on waves, pure passion one moment and then settling into complete tenderness.

As she rested her cheek on his chest for a while, he took in all the emotions flowing over him. Boldly he ran his hand over her as if just touching her was a treasure.

One of their cell phones pinged.

"It must be the hospital." She pulled away a few inches that might as well have been a mile.

He saw it in her eyes. She felt the loss as dearly as he did.

"Not the hospital," she said as she stared at a dark screen.

"It's mine. Zach, texting," he whispered.

"What does he say?"

One word whispered over Rusty's whole body. "*Geronimo.*"

Chapter 39

The roar of a poorly tuned engine sounded out near the turnoff of the Landry Ranch. Jackson silenced the Harry Potter movie, glanced at his houseguest, and whispered, "Vanish, Zach."

It might be someone pulling into the entrance to check a map, or check a tire. Or it might be trouble slowly heading toward Jackson's home.

The visitor stopped out of the porchlight's glow. He didn't turn off the engine, but Jackson heard him step out onto the gravel. Whoever was coming didn't plan to stay long.

The pup of a dog shot off the couch and hit the screen door like a bucking bull coming out of the gate. He was barking and running into the night.

Three heartbeats later, the pup yelped and all was silent except for a hard kind of laughter.

Jackson remained frozen. Waiting for another clue.

One second. Two. Three.

He could hear country music coming from the kitchen along with the smell of popcorn.

Four, five, six.

The music was turned up but he could sense someone moving around outside.

Jackson could hear Starri sliding over the tile floor as if waltzing with an invisible partner. For a moment, he relaxed. Zach was hiding and Starri was dancing, but Jackson stood frozen, waiting to hear danger closing in.

Seven, eight, nine.

He thought he heard movement at the side of the house. Focusing on the bare windows, he stared into the night.

One minute, two before he saw a shadow moving among the brush near the house. A form, rushing in the night. A man carrying something. No, a man pushing something. Another person was locked in the shadow's arms and fighting to get free.

In one fluid movement, Jackson lifted down the old Springfield rifle that his father had kept over the fireplace mantel all Jackson's life. The story was that his great-grandfather carried it through WWI, then disassembled it and sent it home one piece at a time. Jackson had watched his dad clean the weapon once a year but they never fired it. The rifle had stood ready for a hundred years.

When he glanced back, no Zach. Jackson heard nothing but the music coming from the kitchen. For a moment, Jackson couldn't allow himself to think what he knew was true. The shadow was dragging either Starri or Zach away.

Tonight, it was time to defend his home. He prayed he didn't have to fire, but he'd do what he had to do. Chaos had ridden in on bald tires.

If Starri was still in the kitchen. She had his phone. With luck, she'd hidden somewhere. Jackson would have to walk out alone.

Like an old-time sheriff, he stepped out on the long porch

lined with white rockers and raised the butt of the rifle to his shoulder.

An old Corvette was thirty feet away, half-hidden in the line of twenty-foot-high evergreens that ran both sides of the lane from the county road to the yard. For a few minutes, all was silent as if the evening was holding its breath.

The heavyset man shoved something into the back of the car and beat it down out of Jackson's sight. Then he slammed the door and slowly walked around to the driver's side in full sight of Jackson. He stood tall, even smiling as if he knew he'd already won the fight.

"I came to get my kin, lawyer. It wasn't long until some-one figured out John Doe was me. That young sheriff told me to leave town and never even drive through again. But what he didn't know is I ain't leaving without what's mine."

"You are not welcome here, Vern Bonney. Get off my land."

"I ain't leaving without Zach and you can't stop me from taking him. His mother said I could keep him until she got back. You got no right, even if you are a lawyer, to take him away from me and give him to someone else." Vern laughed. "I'm the law tonight. I'm making the rules, and I say the boy is going back where he belongs. I've made a few friends in this town. If you make this hard, I'll simply cut them in on Zach's inheritance."

Jackson stood his ground. "How'd you find me?"

"Wasn't hard. I just asked. Folks are real friendly." Vern laughed.

"You'd best leave. I've already called the law. Sheriff Smith is flying full throttle toward us right now."

"No. You're bluffing. I left my car back a ways and made sure the kid was in the house, then I pulled up closer so I wouldn't have to drag the kid far if he puts up a fight. I was right outside your window watching you for a while. You gave your phone to the girl so she could call her auntie. I could hear her talking in the kitchen when I slipped around the back."

An evil laugh floated on the night reminding Jackson of a horror movie.

"You are not so smart, lawyer. All I had to do was slip in the back door. It wasn't even locked. I tossed a blanket over her head and I got both her and your phone. Once I tied her up and told her I wouldn't kill you if she kept quiet, I haven't heard much out of her."

Vern barked a laugh as he leaned against his car and crossed both his arms and legs. "I did have to hit her up beside the head several times, just so she'd believe me. Then I had to hit her again for making too much noise crying. The blanket was over her head. It was like hitting a punching bag. She made these little sounds, half screaming, half crying."

Jackson stiffened. Never in his life had he felt such anger. He steadied the rifle and sighted on Vern's chest. He'd shot a deer when he was twelve and cried that night, but if Vern didn't back down Jackson would not cry tonight.

"Let her go, then leave my land while you're still standing."

Vern laughed as if they were playing a game. "I ain't here to hurt her. She's tied up tight in the back of my car. If you fire that gun, you might just hit her. I think she can breathe just fine under that blanket, but you might want to make up your mind about making the boy come out."

"He's not going with you."

Snickering as if he thought Jackson was kidding, Vern added, "Once Zach and me are heading home, we'll toss her out on a back road. If she's got any sense, she'll untie herself by dawn. Which reminds me: Tell Zach to hurry up. We got a long ride home."

"I don't know where he is. He probably heard that junker of a car you drive and took off. He could be halfway to town by now; it's only a few miles."

"Like hell! He was sitting on your couch ten minutes ago. What'd you do to him?"

"He's gone. Even if you bullied him into leaving with you, he'd just run away again. He's not an animal you can keep."

Vern's anger built in heavy breathing as he stepped nearer, almost in the edge of the porchlight. The light flashed on the blade of a hunting knife.

"Anyone ever tell you not to bring a knife to a gunfight, Vern?" Jackson sighted on the knife. He could hit the man's hand and end this argument.

"I'm not going to fight you, Jackson, but if Zach doesn't come out by the time I count to three, I plan to push the blade into that blanket in the back of my car. It'll be interesting what I stab. An arm maybe, or an eye, or deep into her chest." He stepped back to his car in deep shadows.

With the car between Jackson and him a shot might hit Starri, or if Jackson missed, Vern could get in a few stabs.

"One! Two!" Vern bellowed as he leaned into the car and grabbed the top of the blanket as if showing off a trophy.

"Wait!" Zach shouted from the doorway. "I'll go with you. Don't hurt Starri."

An evil laugh started, then died suddenly as Vern's scream blended with a solid thud. Then another. And another. A silhouette seemed to rise up from the trees.

Vern was yelling, "Stop!" but the tall, thin outline didn't slow down.

With a hard *slam*, something hit the hood of the Corvette. Vern's scream seemed to echo across the entire valley as the stranger picked Vern up and slammed him down again.

The big knife Vern had used to threaten Jackson now lay ten feet in front of the car, shining in the porchlight.

The pup lay a few feet away. Still. Bleeding.

Suddenly, all went silent except for Starri's crying.

Jackson, his hands still holding at the ready, stepped off the porch as the stranger moved around the car.

Zach saw his brother a second before Jackson did. The boy flew off the porch running.

A white cast on one arm reflected the light.

Zach ran into Rusty so hard they both almost tumbled. Jackson swore they were both laughing and crying at the same time.

Jackson rushed toward the Corvette and shouted, "Where did you come from, Rusty?"

"I brought him," Dr. Adams said calmly as she stepped from the shadows and looked at the kid. "Zach, you think you could turn loose of your brother for me to see if he's dripping blood?"

Jackson knew Rusty was in good hands. As he ran toward Starri the doc asked, "How is Vern?"

"I can hear him cussing and I don't care how he is." Jackson was at Starri's side.

"He'll have to wait his turn," Amber said. "The sheriff should be pulling up soon. We called and told him to meet us here."

Jackson didn't answer the doc. He was too busy untying Starri and pulling off the blanket.

Vern had lied. She *was* hurt. Her face was bruised and bloody. The intruder had hit her hard, and several times.

Chapter 40

Nurse Emma Sumers was just leaving Heath Rogers's room for the night when she saw lights flashing as three vehicles raced toward the entrance of the hospital.

Adrenaline rushed through her, and Emma's tired muscles went into action. She took the stairs and entered the back of the emergency area. "All hands on deck! We've got three cars about to rush the emergency entrance."

As she shouted order after order, she realized an ambulance was not with them. If it had been, the driver would have called in.

By the time she hit the side door of the lobby, nurses were headed out and men were running in. Emma took it all in with a flash.

Rusty was limping with one arm around Dr. Adams for balance. The cast on his forearm was shattered and dangling. His face was pale with pain as he tried not to put any weight on his leg. The first nurse pushing a wheelchair took over Rusty while the doc shouted facts.

The lawyer who always visited Heath carried a woman wrapped in a muddy blanket. "She's hurt!" he roared as if anyone might miss the bruises on her face and blood dripping from her nose and one ear.

"Starri?" Emma's voice came low and caring, showing none of the shock she felt. "You're safe. We'll take care of you." After years of emergency room patients, Emma knew all the signs of trauma due to a beating. The bruises that matched a fist. The fear in her eyes. And the way she held on to Jackson, her lifeline.

A nurse offered a wheelchair but Jackson didn't stop. He rushed straight into the emergency room with Emma right behind him.

Dr. Ryan Henton, already in scrubs, hit the swing doors with both hands. Since Dr. Adams was with Rusty, he moved to the girl in Jackson's arms.

"It's Starri," Jackson said as if his friend might not recognize her.

For once Ryan's professional, almost cold, exterior cracked. "Starri? Someone hurt Starri?" The possibility that anyone would hit such a gentle soul rattled the doctor.

Everyone in the bay saw the anger in his eyes, but when Dr. Ryan turned to her, he cupped her face. She didn't look at him.

"Starri, we've got you." He turned to Jackson. "Lay her down in the third bay. Nurse Sumers, will you clean her up?" It was an order, not a question. Ryan let go of her face. "We got you, honey. You're safe now."

"Can Jackson . . ." she whispered.

Ryan didn't wait to hear more. "He's going to stay with you, Starri, for as long as you need him."

She relaxed a little and let go of Jackson's shirt and took his hand.

Emma smiled. The lawyer was bracing himself to stay and stand strong no matter how much blood.

When the doctor met Emma's stare, they both saw worry

in each other's eyes. They were dealing with more than physical injuries and right now Jackson was the medicine she needed close.

Once Emma washed the girl's face, she made a slight movement of her head to Jackson, who was standing on the other side of the bed. He turned his back while Emma slipped off Starri's clothes and put on her gown. All the while Starri kept a white-knuckled grip on his hand. Emma said what she had to say to Jackson as he turned back. "If you faint, we'll finish taking care of her before we pick you up, understand?"

Ryan turned to his friend. "Jack, you up for staying with her?"

"I'm not going anywhere." Jackson nodded once as if accepting an assignment. "I should tell you, there is one more car coming in. Sheriff's bringing the man who caused this: Vern Bonney. You can't miss him. Pecos already has him handcuffed."

Ryan nodded once. "We'll fix him up and then he'll be the sheriff's problem. No matter what he did, we'll treat him the same. And Jack, don't say a word to him. This is a hospital, not a courtroom."

Jackson looked like he might explode, but he nodded. "I'll not leave Starri with the man who hurt her near, and there will be no scene. She's my priority."

Ryan glanced at his friend as he worked. "So it's like that, is it?"

"It is."

Emma saw all the anger go out of the lawyer. He was a man who just figured out he cared.

She had been on duty all day, but she wouldn't be leaving until dawn. She smiled amid all the chaos and blood. She cared about these people. They were her family.

A few minutes later, when Vern Bonney was rolled in on a gurney, a deputy walked beside him.

The room grew silent for a few heartbeats, then all the staff did what they'd trained to do. They went to work.

Chapter 41

Saturday, 2:00 a.m.

An hour after Vern Bonney was admitted, the sheriff, Pecos Smith, stepped out of the hospital lobby to make a private call. A chilly silence greeted him in the darkness. He figured it was a fifty/fifty chance Kerrie, his wife, was awake with one, maybe both, of his daughters. They'd bought a little house after the first baby was born, and the house was perfect, but now, with two, the home seemed to be closing in.

He needed to hear her voice.

She answered on the first ring. She was awake.

"Hi, beautiful. How are my girls?" Pecos loved talking to her when she sounded sleepy. They'd been friends first but Pecos had loved her all his life. Everyone in Honey Creek knew the sheriff's heart beat just for his Kerrie.

"They're fine. Sleeping. When you called saying it was going to be a hell of a Friday night, I called Mom. She said she'd sleep over and take every other shift with the baby. Any chance you'll be in before dawn?"

"Not much, but I'll be wishing I was. I love climbing into bed when you're all warm and wanting to snuggle."

Her voice shifted to velvet. "And I love waking up with my man in bed. I can't sleep peacefully without the sound of you breathing beside me."

He could hear her burrowing into the covers. "I love you, you know."

She sounded half asleep. "I know."

A muffled laugh came from the darkness by the building's corner.

"See you soon," Pecos said into the phone, then dropped it in his pocket.

He took one step into the night and saw an outline of the kid who'd ridden in with Jackson and Starri. Rusty's little brother. Pecos remembered him having a smart mouth, a boy trying to be a man. Zachary Holmes, the fourteen-year-old who Vern had come after tonight.

Pecos kept his voice conversational. "What are you doing out here, Zach?"

The kid shot a laugh. "Listening to you talk sappy to your wife. How'd you get a beautiful woman like her to marry you? I saw you guys at the bakery when my brother and me went in to buy his crew doughnuts."

"I mean, what are you doing outside, Zach? Your brother is inside getting put back together again. They'd let you in if you wanted to go."

"My uncle is in there, too, and I never want to be near him again. I heard him yelling death threats to everyone except me as your deputy rolled him in. He wants to keep me alive so he can work me to death. But I'm never going back. Thanks to Jackson, I got three big brothers."

Pecos leaned against the building. "It's cold out here. How about we go in and have a cup of coffee? I'll stay right by your side. I might even tell you how to marry a beautiful woman."

"I can't go in. I'm not hurt and the lady at the front desk said I couldn't bring my pup in. I figure I'm safe enough waiting here. My brother ordered me to stay close and Jackson said he'd call when they knew whether or not Rusty rebroke his arm. I'll wait here until he calls.

"This is about as close as I can get with the dog and I'm not letting go of him. He's no more than a pup but he went after Vern." Zach patted the dog beside him. "He's hurt, Sheriff, and the nurse said they don't treat dogs. I don't know anywhere to take him."

Pecos knelt, flicked on his flashlight and saw blood on the half-grown puppy.

"I don't like that he's bleeding, but I'm not leaving. My brother and Starri are hurt all because of me."

Pecos looked toward the town square as he pulled out his phone. Ten seconds later, he said, "Evening, Nate. This is Pecos. You guys busy tonight?"

The answer came loud and fast. "What do you need, Sheriff? We're all in for the night, I'm guessing. No fires to put out and, surprisingly, no wrecks."

"I've got an injured dog outside the lobby of the hospital that was involved in an attempted kidnapping. He's a hero, but the hospital won't let him in. You think William MacLaine could walk over and patch him up? I've heard he helps out the vet at the animal shelter."

"Hell, Sheriff, MacLaine volunteers every place in town, but he saves Friday for the firehouse. We order out pizza and he always takes the leftovers home. Claims he loves pizza for breakfast. Wait a minute, I'll ask him."

Pecos could hear Nate shouting, "William, you still awake?"

There was a moment of silence, followed by a brief back-and-forth, then the fireman returned to the sheriff. "He said he'll meet you at the ambulance bay out back of the hospital. There's a storage room there with good light. He's packing a bag right now. Said he'd meet you in five minutes."

"Thanks."

"Glad to help," Nate answered. "Old William's been telling Vietnam stories for over an hour. If he hadn't been in that fight, we might not have won that war."

Pecos grinned even if the youngest recruit couldn't see him. "Nate, I'll let you in on a fact. We didn't win."

"We didn't? No one ever told me that."

"Another news flash: the South lost the Civil War, and all the heroes at the Alamo died."

"Thanks for the history lesson, Sheriff. History was always my napping class. Lucky me, I don't have to know history to be a fireman."

Pecos made a mental note to dig out his college history book and take it to Nate as he followed Zach around to the back of the hospital. Zach wouldn't let him carry the dog. That seemed to be his job.

Once inside the bay, Pecos pulled a few towels and spread them out on a worktable. When Zach laid the dog down, the pup licked his hand. Pecos didn't want to tell Zach that if the dog couldn't hold his head up, he might have lost too much blood to survive.

When a man in his seventies hurried in with a backpack that looked to be half his weight, Pecos greeted him and told William the facts.

The old soldier listened as he began gently patting the pup. When the dog accepted him, Will pulled out a needle and gave the pup a shot in the muscle on his shoulder.

"He your dog, kid?" MacLaine asked.

"Yes. He's mine and my brother's. Is he going to be all right?"

"I'll do all I can. I'm going to clean the wound, sew it up, and wrap it. That's all I can do."

Pecos noticed tears were running unchecked down Zach's face.

William's hand shook a bit as he pulled out his kit. "Tell

the truth, I could use some help, Zach. You think you're up to it?"

"I'll try." The kid's eyes were saucer size.

Will shook his head. "Ain't no trying. You got to do it. I'll walk you through each step. Pup may whine, but he's not in any pain. He knows you. You start by talking to him in a low voice. Let him know you're with him."

Pecos knew he was watching a miracle. Not from the dog, or the old man, but from the kid. Zach did everything the old soldier told him to do.

When they were finished, Will helped Zach lift the dog into a box. Pecos saw no signs of a shaking hand. What he did see was pride in the kid.

Will invited the dog and Zach to spend the night with the firemen. "We got a big room upstairs lined with bunks. Some of the guys stay up and play cards. Some sleep. But a few are always on duty by the phone. You and the pup will be safe upstairs with a dozen firemen watching over you like guardian angels."

Pecos promised he'd check on Starri and Rusty and text the kid. He'd also let Rusty know where his little brother was. "There's probably no safer place except the jail."

"I'll stay with Mr. William. I've got questions."

He watched them walk slowly to the town square, heading to the fire station just beyond. He heard Zach ask how the old guy learned all this doctoring stuff and William said he was a medic. Until Will's voice faded, Pecos heard war stories on the wind.

Pecos made a round in the emergency room. Starri had been moved upstairs and Emma told him that the lawyer said he'd stay with her.

When Pecos found Rusty, the guy was arguing that he had to leave and find his little brother.

Once the sheriff let him know Zach was safe, Rusty settled and admitted the second floor of the fire station would be perfect for the boy and the dog.

Vern was still in the emergency room, cussing as loud as he could. Since no other patients were in the big room paneled off by curtains, and he'd refused to take any of the painkillers, he was strapped to the bed and left to yell. Once Pecos told him he could leave anytime but he'd only be going to jail, Vern decided he'd sleep right where he was.

When he left, a deputy stayed by Vern's side, and Pecos headed home smiling. He hadn't told Zach how he got such a beautiful wife. She was also kind, and smart, and loving.

How could he tell how he did it?

Pecos had no idea.

Chapter 42

Rusty lay back and closed his eyes. The bright lights of the emergency room made it impossible to sleep. The memory of this night would never leave him. Getting the text from Zach and knowing he was in trouble had felt like a blow to his chest.

Amber circled by his tiny curtained room to ask again if he wanted a room upstairs. Three times he'd told her no.

The doc had finally agreed that she'd drive him wherever he needed to go as soon as she finished up.

Their third trip tonight. First, they'd driven doing ninety to get to Jackson's ranch after Zach's text. The second was slower, to the hospital with Rusty bleeding, and now she'd offered one more ride where he could sleep in peace.

Flashes of the night raced through his mind. He'd climbed out of her car the moment he saw Jackson standing on his porch with a rifle. Rusty had started limping his way through the trees until he was closer to the scene unfolding. He remembered every part now in the chaos of the emergency room. When he heard Vern detailing what he planned to do to Starri, Rusty had forgotten his pain and run full out.

Five feet from Vern's car, Rusty stepped out of the tree line and roared as he stormed into the uncle.

Vern was so shocked, he didn't have time to block. Rusty hit him hard, breaking the cast on his own arm. Then he'd lifted Vern up and slammed the guy on the roof of the old Corvette.

The uncle had shouted for Jackson to help him.

Instead, Jackson lowered his rifle and watched. Rusty wasn't hitting Vern. He was simply picking the screaming man up and letting him fall into the badly dented roof of the car.

Thirty seconds later, Rusty heard one of the sheriff's cruisers turn onto Jackson's land. With lights flashing across the lane and sirens on high, the sheriff slid to a stop beside the Corvette.

Rusty was a bit fuzzy about what happened next. The sheriff yelled for him to drop Vern. When he did, the sheriff took over. Amber ran past him toward Starri, still wrapped in the muddy blanket, half lying on the ground and half still in the car. Everyone could hear her crying.

The doctor stood in the center and yelled roll call. As each one answered, they calmed and went to work.

Amber announced they were all heading to the hospital.

Jackson ran from the porch and gently lifted Starri. Blood seemed to be everywhere.

Amber looked over Jackson's shoulder and pushed the blanket away from her face. "How fast can you get her to the hospital?"

"Five minutes." He held Starri close to his heart and headed toward his pickup.

"I'll get Rusty in my car and race you." Amber yelled but Jackson was on a mission and didn't look back.

The sheriff was left to take the bleeding uncle, who seemed to think that Pecos had come to save him until the sheriff locked the cuffs on. Once Vern was in the backseat of the cruiser with a deputy reading Vern his Miranda rights, Pecos helped to buckle up the injured.

"Try not to bleed all over my car," Pecos snarled as he slammed the door.

Rusty caught the sheriff's order on the wind as he buckled in and smiled for a moment.

As soon as Starri was in Jackson's pickup, they all headed out. Her crying seemed to echo in the slow rain as they turned onto the county road and headed toward Honey Creek.

Amber faced Rusty and whispered, "I'm staying right with you. I need to see how many bones you rebroke." She moved under his arm for support as she glanced at Zach. "I'll need you, too, kid. Your brother's too heavy to handle."

The boy was a great help, but as soon as Rusty was in the doc's car, Zach ran back to get the dog.

"He's hurt, Doc. I'll find someone to help him. I can't leave him. He'll die." Zach jumped in her backseat with the pup, who was whining.

As Amber backed down the lane, she whispered, "If it's bad, the sheriff may have to put him down."

"No! That ain't happening!" Zach sounded like he was fighting tears as he wrapped his jacket around the dog. "He ran straight toward my uncle and into the blade of Uncle Vern's knife. He was trying to protect us and that makes him part of the family."

"Then he's going," Rusty said.

At the hospital, things got fuzzy again for Rusty. The doc shot something in his good arm and then went to work on the broken one. All the while she was griping at him. "What kind of an idiot runs into a fight with a broken arm and only one leg to stand on?

"You may have erased all the healing.

"I swear you must have a death wish.

"You could have slipped in that rain and broken a hip, or a shoulder, or your back, and I'm the one who'd have to put you back together."

It seemed to make her even madder when he agreed with her, so Rusty closed his eyes all the way to the emergency bay and pretended to be dead.

Half an hour later when she finally settled a bit she told him his leg was fine but the arm would have to be reset.

When Rusty opened one eye, she still looked angry. He almost laughed. She cared. A beautiful, bright woman cared about him.

When she circled by the emergency room all was quiet. She asked him one more time if he'd go upstairs. When he didn't answer, she added, "All right, my broken superman, would you let me take you somewhere else?"

Rusty thought about it and decided to meet her halfway. With his luck lately, if he didn't get out of her emergency room, she'd record her objections and put it on replay.

"I have to stay close. I know where we can sleep in peace. The guy who owns the fishing cabins between the Brazos and the town is closed for the season, but I know where the key is to the back cabin. If I stay near, I can be only a few blocks away if anyone needs me."

She pulled up a wheelchair and this time he took the ride to the outside door. There he stood and insisted on walking.

"If I can lean on you, I'll make it. The wheelchair would be useless in the mud near the cabin, and your car would just get stuck."

She put his arm over her shoulder and her arm around his waist. He'd managed to get his clothes earlier, but neither had a jacket.

He hurt so badly, Rusty figured it couldn't be worse.

When they opened the cabin door five minutes later, he stumbled in. Rusty felt like he was sleepwalking. The rain had beaten him down.

She pulled the covers back and helped him pull off his boot and climb in. Then she leaned on her knees at the bed's edge and removed his bloody shirt. "Be careful. Don't move around too much."

The fresh cast on his forearm felt tight, but he was too tired or drugged up to care. He reached for her but she straightened.

"Stay with me until I warm up," he whispered.

Surprisingly, she didn't say a word. She dropped her ugly shoes, slid off her lab jacket, then the bottom of her stained scrubs. Next came the top, leaving only a T-shirt, panties, and black socks that were pulled up to her knees.

He could barely see the hint of a smile as she clicked off the bedside lamp and climbed in beside him. She had to be as tired as he was. Maybe she'd decided to nap before heading home.

"Good night, Doc," he whispered.

"Good night, Trouble," she answered.

By the time he warmed, they were both asleep.

Sometime in the middle of the night, he pulled her close and she cuddled into his side. For a moment he almost laughed when he thought that they were two people who didn't go together at all unless they were asleep.

Chapter 43

Saturday, 4:00 a.m.

Jackson closed the hospital blinds and turned the over-stuffed recliner to face Starri so he could watch her and he'd be the first one she saw when she woke up.

He knew it would be dawn in a few hours. Light would wake her, or maybe the noise. He hated that her dreaming would end.

He'd asked Starri last night if he should call Ona-May. She'd said no because her aunt had been up two days with a neighbor. The old nurse had climbed into her bed as Starri left for Jackson's place. Her last words before she closed her eyes were, "Don't wake me till the Lord's Second Coming."

Jackson didn't make the call. Later this morning would be soon enough, but he hoped the world didn't end; he had a score to settle with Vern. And he had to make sure the kid was safe while Rusty was in the hospital. And ensure Starri got the best care.

"Hell," Jackson whispered, "I'm becoming a den mother."

He glanced at Starri, hoping she hadn't heard what he

said. She was the kind of woman who made a guy be a better man. Only it would be hard to be a better man whenever he'd never had time to be wild and crazy.

Jackson had been his parents' world. They'd always told him how proud of him they were and he never wanted to disappoint them. And now, after they'd gone, he hadn't had time to go nuts or "sow some wild oats," as his grandfather used to say. If anyone still said that kind of thing. Wild and wicked, in Granddad's day, was called Friday night now.

But tonight, even though they were just friends, he never wanted to see sorrow in Starri's eyes because of him.

She looked so young and so battered tonight. When he realized that the four bruises in a row on her cheek were left by Vern's knuckles, Jackson had to grip the chair's arms to keep from running back to the emergency room and clobbering Vern while he was tied to the bed.

One of Starri's eyes was swollen closed and the other had a ring of red marks that were slowly turning darker. Her lip was split, and her arms were lined with dark marks where he'd grabbed her.

If Vern died tonight, Jackson wouldn't care. He might never be able to kill a man, but he could wish Vern dead. He couldn't go to jail for that.

"No," Jackson said aloud. "I don't wish him dead. I hope he lives a long, miserable life out on his little farm with no one to talk to, or anyone to work the land, or even bury him. Let him rot." He leaned back. "I don't care. He hurt my Starri."

Vern had probably been beefy when he was younger but now, moving into his late forties or early fifties, he'd become flabby. If Vern pressed charges on Rusty O'Sullivan, Jackson would be O'Sullivan's lawyer.

If tonight's crimes went to court, it would be a circus. Pecos had had one of his deputies take pictures of Starri's injuries. One look at the bruises on her face and the jury would throw the book at Vern.

Jackson took her hand. "I'm so sorry, Starri." Cupping her hand in both of his, he leaned over and kissed her palm. "If I'd acted faster . . . If I'd shot him in the leg . . . If I'd demanded he . . . If I hadn't hesitated . . . Somehow this was all my fault."

He lowered his face atop her fingers as he fought back tears.

"Jackson, am I really your Starri?" Her voice was low and slow as if she was still half asleep.

"Of course you are, honey," he said, trying to smile. "You always will be."

"Do you love me? Because I love you." Her whispered words sounded almost childlike, as if she was trying out the words for the first time.

He kissed her fingers. How could anyone not love Starri? There was something magical about her. An angel on earth.

"Of course I love you. I think you're perfect."

She smiled on the one side of her mouth not swollen and closed her eyes. She might be drifting to sleep but he kept talking.

"Starri, if you were a few years older I'd make you my girl. I'd carry you around on a pillow. I'd even write a song about you. 'Course, after I sang it once you'd probably beg me to never do that again. I'd spend my life just looking at you." He was laying it on strong, but he wanted her to know how special she was to him.

Her fingers relaxed in his hand and he guessed she was falling asleep. "If I wasn't too old for you, we'd probably get married. We'd live out on the ranch and ride horses every evening. I'd go to work in town but every night we'd sit out on the porch and talk while we watched the stars come out. I'd kiss you every morning and whisper that I love you. We'd . . ."

Jackson slowly closed his eyes, thinking about what it

would be like to build a life. For the first time, he realized he wanted his parents' happiness. Being a big city lawyer wouldn't make him happy, but living here in Honey Creek just might.

"If you were only older," he said once more before he drifted off.

Chapter 44

As the full moon shone through the cabin's big window, Rusty woke to realize Amber was curled around him again. One of her long legs lay atop his good leg. Her arm rested on his chest with her fingers spread out over his heart.

The old cabin bedframe creaked as he moved, rolling toward her. His skin was dark from working shirtless and hers seemed white as snow in the moonlight.

She adjusted and lifted her other arm over his shoulder so their chests touched. Which he wouldn't have reacted to except with no lab coat or scrubs and no bra, he came fully awake to the fact that she felt a great deal different. Her breasts weren't big like the nurse named Paige, who always wore a towel in the nurses' dorm. Amber's were small and perfectly formed. With the thin T-shirt over them, she seemed to be giving him a hint of how soft they might be.

He started at her elbow, which was almost touching his ear, and moved along her arm, then her shoulder and down along her side.

Her skin was silk. The tight T-shirt didn't reach her panties. Right there below her waist he spread out his hand on bare skin. He realized paradise was a few inches in both directions but he couldn't move.

He'd held a few women while dancing, even kissed several when he was more drunk than sober, but he'd never gone all the way. Not since he was eighteen. Not since he'd sworn off women completely.

Nowadays no one seemed to make it to twenty without having several partners. Some even claimed to have bedded a hundred or more. But he wasn't interested in the girls in the bar. They were usually loud and aggressive. And the liquor on their breath pushed him away.

The rest of his life was void of females. The few women who worked in Brown's office were rounded into middle age. A few of the barmaids were his age and a hard kind of pretty, but none interested him. Once in a while he saw a woman in a store or at the coffee shop, but she was either married or she wanted to tell anyone who would listen why she was no longer married.

Rusty had been living alone several miles from town before he was fifteen. That first year, he'd ridden the school bus to and from school, but he'd been too scared to talk to girls. A few times a week he'd skip lunch and go across the street to buy groceries. Mostly junk food. When he stayed in the cafeteria, he ate alone.

That first year after his grandparents ran away, he'd sold off the farm equipment for half of what it was worth to the farmer a mile down the road. For the great price, the farmer offered to help Rusty get an old truck running. By sixteen, he was teaching himself to drive in the worthless fields.

Before he turned seventeen, he was down to eating one meal a day when he saw a "Help Wanted" card on the grocer's community bulletin board. He quit school and went to work at Brown's Contractors.

He thought he was lucky to survive. Until now. Until he'd realized all he didn't know and hadn't experienced. He never had those awkward years to learn to talk to girls. How to ask a girl out. How to move through the bases slowly. He'd never said he liked a girl, much less loved one.

He'd collected a hundred manuals and books on how to build everything, but none told him how to construct a relationship.

At eighteen, he found bar meals were cheap. He was big and solid from work, but inside he was still a boy. Now, lying beside Amber, he wished he knew how to please her. How to make love to her.

His first attempt at eighteen had been a disaster. The woman had given the entire bar all the details of what *didn't* happen in the storage room. It seemed a year before the joking stopped, and by then he swore he'd never try again.

Amber rolled a few inches away and stretched. "You asleep, Trouble?"

Rusty pulled her back to him. "Why do you call me Trouble?"

"Because you're dangerous. I knew it the moment I saw those eyes—bedroom eyes. I figure you were one of those guys who sleeps with a different partner every night and leaves a trail of broken hearts."

"You're wrong, Doc."

"You know, I'm starting to believe you. I've been next to you almost naked and you haven't made a move. The nurses said you were a gentleman while you were in the dorm. I see how women look at you and I see you don't even notice. How about we tell each other the truth? Are you even attracted to me?"

"I am. I thought that was obvious. Sometimes I can't even think when you're near." He brushed a kiss across her cheek. "My turn to ask a question. Do you really have a fiancé?"

"It's safer if I do. I still get hit on, but most men will take 'no' for an answer if they think there is a man somewhere waiting for me."

"Do you have a fiancé, Amber? Yes or no."

"Does it matter?"

"No, I still want to be close to you, but the truth is important to me."

She huffed and folded her arms. He didn't remove his hand from her waist. She didn't move away. "No. I'm not engaged, though I have been half a dozen times. Men seem to fall in love with me fast, and just as fast they fall out. I'm not an easy woman to love. I was spoiled by both my divorced parents. Until college, I got everything I wanted, then I had to fight to get into med school. Medicine will always come first with me. Lovers will have to wait their turns."

"Any other thorns you want to show me?"

"Hundreds."

"I'm not scared of you, Amber, and your thorns don't worry me." He whispered, "I feel like we've talked enough. Any chance you'd stop talking and just cuddle up and sleep?" He wanted so much more, but he had to do it right. With his luck this might be his only chance to even get a taste of loving.

"That's all you want to do? Cuddle. I'm a banquet and all you want are the crackers."

"No. When I make love to you, I'd like to have two arms and legs. No patches. I've got to do this slow. When, or maybe if, I make love to you it has to be just right."

"You're kidding? Fast and awkward is fine with me."

"No, I'm not kidding. For once in your life, you're going to take it slow."

"What is wrong with you? No one takes it slow these days. You're the first man I've even thought about sleeping with since I got to town and you want to take your time. You do know I'm only in town for a year, and half of that is over."

"We're going to do everything right. Get to know each other. One step at a time."

"And what if I don't like this plan? How about I go through all the steps while I'm taking my clothes off?"

"Then I'll respectfully walk away. I want to experience every step and polish all to perfection before we move on."

She laughed. "Really? I swear, you sound like you've never had sex."

"I haven't and when I do, I want it to be fireworks."

She was so still he thought she'd stopped breathing. He pulled her closer and waited for her to say something. She might tell him she didn't believe him. Or simply call him a liar.

Finally, her body relaxed against him. He felt one tear fall on his shoulder. Her words came in a whisper. "I've had a lot of sex, but I've never made love."

"I guess that makes us both virgins." He pushed another tear off her cheek. "I want to know you so well that I can read your emotions in your eyes. I need to feel every part of you. Not just your body but your thoughts, your dreams, and what you need."

He drifted toward sleep. She hadn't said yes, but she hadn't said no either.

They weren't kids in the backseat of a car. He'd grown up always getting hand-me-down clothes and toys and even books, but this one thing had to be real.

His breathing was starting to slow when Amber hit the side of his pillow hard, waking him fully.

"I can't do this. I can't. I won't. It is now or never with me. I don't know what game you're playing."

He settled back into his now lumpy pillow. "Sure you can, sweetheart."

When she raised her fist, he caught it in mid-flight toward his pillow. Without a word he tucked her hand between them and closed his eyes.

"Something's wrong with us, Rusty. Men are the aggressors."

He moved his fingers over her almost white hair in the moonlight. "I figure you've got enough gladiator in you for both of us."

She huffed a few times, then laid her head on his chest and whispered, "This conversation is not over."

He kissed her curls and answered, "I have no doubt."

Chapter 45

Zach asked if he could leave his pup at the firehouse while he walked over to the hospital to see his brother and his friends.

The men all nodded, then went about their duties.

He ate more breakfast muffins after taking the dog out the back door for a walk. Then he offered to help polish one of the trucks. When he finally asked William what he was watching, the old volunteer, who'd been sleeping in front of the TV since dawn, woke up and tried to figure out what was bothering the kid.

William put his glasses on and asked, "What's troubling you, soldier?"

It occurred to Zach that William might not know what year it was. But he asked anyway, "You want to walk with me across the town square to the hospital? I wouldn't mind a little company."

William sat up, leaned close to Zach. "You scared, boy? That ain't nothing to be embarrassed about. Any good man with a brain knows to think what might happen. That is what keeps you alive in war. And you were in a battle last night. I didn't have to ask any questions to know your dog suffered a knife wound." He took a long breath and began another story. "I remember I faced some bullies in an alley in Galveston when I was about your age. They were just looking to fight. Three of them and one of me and nowhere to run. No moon or streetlight. All I could see was dark forms closing in around me."

"What did you do?"

"I got beat up."

Zach jumped off the couch. "That's a terrible story. That doesn't make me feel any better."

A few of the firemen gathered to follow the argument.

William grinned. "No, I was lucky. I made up my mind that night that I didn't ever want to repeat that mistake. So, I decided to learn to defend myself. Those lessons have saved my life a few times since. Learning a little is miles away from not knowing nothing."

"Can you show me?"

"No, not until you'll agree to follow three rules. One, never start a fight. Two, try to walk away if you can. And three, if you have to fight, end the fight so you both know it's over."

All at once the firemen were showing Zach what they knew. One of the in-training firemen showed him a karate move. Another demonstrated how to block a hit. The middle-aged fireman who usually only talked to complain about his wife said when outnumbered that playing dead always worked.

Several of the men took Zach outside to practice. William told them it was easier to fall on grass than concrete.

Zach suspected the old man just wanted to continue his nap. Zach knew William was a wealth of knowledge, but sometimes it wasn't easy to shake it out of the guy.

By the time the boys were finished practicing, supper was ready. Since his brother had called almost every hour to check on him, Zach knew Rusty was busy and probably hurting.

It occurred to Zach that Rusty might be hesitant to go home.

Chapter 46

Sunday Morning

Emma Sumers went to church like she did every Sunday, but she couldn't remember the hymns and she couldn't follow the preacher's sermon. She was too lost in thinking about what she was going to do as soon as church was over.

It had been over a week since Heath Rogers squeezed her hand. Seven days since he'd called her name as if he had to see her. She'd spent all her free time in his room. Before his heart attack he'd been quiet, but she felt as if she knew him. He was a good man. A rancher who'd built his fortune without help of family. A man who cared about people.

Yet in the months he was in the coma he'd changed. He was still a man of few words, but somehow all the dreams Emma had imagined between them had come true while he was sleeping.

He cared about her. He drew her out of her shyness by asking questions. By calling her name every time he woke, she knew she was needed. No, not just that. She was important to him. So important he reached for her hand every time she neared.

On the third day after he woke up, he'd asked if she'd come close enough for him to kiss her. The next day, she walked the length of the hallway by his side. Before climbing back into bed, he'd leaned down and hugged her. The touching, the hello and goodbye kisses, their holding hands were now routine.

The people circling by his room also seemed never ending. The lawyer, the foreman from his ranch, the housekeeper, even a banker stopped by daily. But about the time she finished her shift, all his visitors would vanish and they'd spend the evening together.

When she finally left, Emma had the strangest feeling she was leaving something behind.

On Friday, he told her he loved her and asked if she'd think about marrying him.

When she came in Saturday morning, he met her with his workday clothes on. Emma couldn't stop smiling. She'd forgotten how tall he was and how handsome in his Western clothes. Pearl buttons, Western-cut white shirt. Handmade boots by Lucchese. Jeans with a crease.

She couldn't help herself. She had to circle him.

"You making sure I can still dress myself?"

"No, dear, I was making sure you didn't have your spurs on. I remember once you were called in for an emergency board meeting and I could hear the jingle of them as you stormed in."

He reached for his hat. "And I remember you ordered me to take them off. I laughed for two days, thinking how your eyes fired. No one had told me what to do in years, but I didn't mind if you felt the need. I think that was the moment I fell in love with you."

Emma straightened to her full height, almost to his shoulder. "Oh, now you're in love with me, Mr. Rogers?"

Heath didn't even blink before he said, "You know I am. You were the only person I wanted to see when I woke up after my long nap. You are the one I want to talk to and touch whenever we get close. I may not talk much, but I need to tell you, Miss Emma Sumers, that you are the one person I want to see when I wake up every day for the rest of my life."

He reached for her hand and slipped it in the bend of his arm. "Let's take the air. I need to get out of this place and see the sun and the clouds. I need to hear the river and feel the wind."

They took it easy and walked outside. When they stopped to rest on a bench on the town square, he told her the doctor said he could go home tomorrow.

"I want you to come with me."

"Of course. I can take a leave. You'll need care for a while."

He took her hand. "I don't need a nurse, Emma. I need you as my wife. Jackson has all the paperwork ready. I want to take you home."

Emma panicked. She couldn't just leave her job. She had a house. She hadn't even seen his place. She'd never lived outside of town.

They sat without talking for a while. Finally, he said, "What do you want, Emma? You know I can give you anything, dear. I could buy a place in town if that's what is bothering you." He smiled that kind smile at her. "I've had months to think and I've figured out all I need is you by my side. In a few months, we could travel, maybe go to New York City. I've always wanted to go there."

She couldn't give him an answer. There were a hundred things to consider. Things were happening too fast. She'd always lived alone or been a caretaker. The strong Heath was coming back. All signals were pointing to a full recovery—but what if something happened?

At midnight, she drove to her tiny home, thinking about what it would be like to move. She'd have to decide what to take if she moved in with him.

As she unlocked her door and stepped inside, that feeling of missing something came over her again. A sense of having lost something.

She checked to make sure she had her keys. Her purse. Her bag with her lunch box and a change of clothes, her umbrella. The book she always carried but never had time to read.

For a moment she felt she might be the one lost. She couldn't remember what she could have forgotten.

Then it hit her. It was Heath. He was her home. She wanted to be with her cowboy.

Nothing else mattered. Not her job or her house or the town. She dropped everything on the kitchen table and picked up her cell.

Heath answered on the first ring. "You all right, Emma?"

For a moment she couldn't breathe, then she jumped into life. "I *will* marry you. Any time, any place."

There was a long silence, then he said simply, "Wear your pink suit tomorrow. And after church, come straight here if you can. Don't stay to clean up the parlor. We've got things to say to each other."

"I will."

She didn't sleep. At dawn she dressed in her pink suit. Her body might be in church, but her mind was lost in the unknown. Her only hope was that when church was over she could go to Heath and he'd talk to her.

Everything would be all right as soon as he was holding her hand.

Chapter 47

Sunday, Noon

Rusty O'Sullivan woke to church bells ringing across the valley.

Amber must have opened the window sometime during the night. For a few minutes he just listened. The little cabin at the edge of town was usually silent inside, not even the air moved, but outside the creek played a gentle melody. The cabin had been nestled among the trees so long it seemed a part of nature. He could hear birds and the splashing of fish now and then. Peaceful sounds floating through the air. It might not beat the quiet of the country, but still the bells seemed to set a tranquil tone.

Amber was close; he could feel the beautiful doctor's warmth.

He wondered what it would be like to live in town. Seeing people every time he stepped out his door. In the country, time seemed to pass with the sun and the seasons. Here, the world was marked in days of the week. Monday work started, Taco Tuesday, Friday nights out, Sunday church.

Amber rolled closer. Her body warm and relaxed against him as if they were one, not two very different people. His doc was sound asleep. Her presence was a strong pull for him to stay in town as long as she was here. In truth he didn't want to leave this bed or this cabin. They could stay until starvation set in.

He kissed the tip of her nose and she batted him away.

Rusty laughed and kissed her on the lips lightly.

She mumbled, "I've been known to kill people who wake me up." She rolled over and pushed her back against his chest, having no clue what a gift she was giving him.

"I have no doubt." He realized he'd just repeated the last thing he'd said to her before he fell asleep.

After wiggling for a while, she turned back to face him. "I've been thinking about this insane game you want to play—you know, 'one step at a time.' I'll go along with the premise on one condition."

"Just one?"

"Well, maybe two. Who knows, I may think up all kinds of rules myself. Like, can I date someone else while we're taking it slow?"

"No."

She pouted for a few moments, then said, "All right. No other men. It shouldn't be that hard. There is not one man I've met that I'd want to even shake hands with. Since you are the only one I'm hot for, I'll go along. But, there are two things that have to change."

"Fair enough."

"Number one of my rules: No matter how long we play the game of step-by-step, it ends when I leave."

"I agree. I don't plan to ever leave this valley, and I'd slow you down in your career if I asked you to stay. But we'll have a memory to keep."

She calmed. "Second: As we go through the steps of loving, I get to name the other steps. I have to assume at some point you'll not know what to do. I'll have to become the coach."

He put his hand on her waist where bare skin showed. "I think sleeping together should count as one step. We know our bodies mold together. I like sleeping next to you. On some level, I am obviously attracted." He laughed. "Make that every level."

"Me too."

He leaned back and studied the ceiling to keep from staring at her bare midriff. An inch of the bottom of her breast was peeking out. Apparently she was going to give him a heart attack for thinking up this game.

Without looking at her, he began. "Tonight, we have a date. A real date. Dress up. I pick you up. We go out to eat. Maybe cuddle in a booth. I've always wanted to do that."

"Sounds perfect. Just me and you. Everyone who sees us will have no doubt we're on a date. I plan to be touching you every chance I get." She thought for a moment and said, "I might wear something sexy."

"Everything you wear is sexy." He scratched his head, feeling like he needed all his brain cells working if he planned to keep up with her.

"Okay, how about I *don't* wear something? It'll be something you can't see, but you'll have to guess what I forgot to put on."

This game was turning into torture.

He kissed her for a while, then she pulled away. As she slipped into her wrinkled scrubs, he watched.

"I've got a light shift this afternoon. Pick me up at seven. What about Zach?"

"I'll pick him up at the fire station and take him home. Starri's already told me tonight is the last night of their Harry Potter marathon, and Zach said it won't be over until after midnight. I don't think either one wants to be around people."

As she slipped on her ugly shoes, the sexy woman he'd slept with turned back into a doctor. She was halfway through her talk before he could adjust to the difference.

"With that horrible so-called uncle in jail, Zach is safe, and watching movies will help him relax. The sooner he gets back to normal, the better he'll be."

Rusty doubted Zach had ever known normal but the doc, a child who'd been spoiled by her parents, wouldn't understand that.

"I'm guessing the pup will be with the kid tonight too." The dog they called Duck slept at the bottom of Zach's bed at the firehouse Friday night, then Zach had asked if he could spend his Saturday there with some old guy named Will. Claimed he had more questions to ask.

Jackson said he'd take Zach home to pick up clothes if he needed anything. He also planned to drive out and get Starri something to wear when the hospital released her later today.

"Jackson texted to tell me Starri was going home. He said he isn't letting her out of his sight until the bruises are gone. I'm guessing since there is no room at her auntie's place for Jackson, they'll all be heading to Jackson's ranch or my place. Zach will welcome their company. Zach will be closer to school Monday after watching movies half the night." He grinned. "With Zach safe, I won't have to worry about getting home early or at all."

"So," Amber headed toward the cabin door, "we'll have a date and then I'll have all night to turn you into the best lover in the world."

"Slow, remember?" His gaze never left hers. With her as a lover he had no doubt he'd die in bed.

"Believe me, waiting until after dinner is going slow to me."

"We'll talk about it when I pick you up." In his mind he'd thought the "just dating" period might last a few months.

After holding her all night, he'd moved the finish line to a few weeks. But now, with her smile and the lift of one eyebrow, he was probably counting in days, or even hours.

She blew him a kiss but her eyes promised so much more. Then she turned to the door. "I'll walk back to the hospital. See you at seven."

She disappeared in a blink, leaving only the chill.

He closed his eyes, not wanting to see the empty room. Deep down he knew that would be the way she'd go when she finally left him. Fast. Without a word. Without looking back.

Only problem would be, she'd take his heart with her.

Chapter 48

Emma gripped her bouquet in her hand as they stood in the tiny chapel on the first floor of the hospital. It was the one room in the building she rarely entered. Loved ones went there to pray and sometimes went back to cry.

A small crowd waited just outside the door. Two lawyers, one from Honey Creek and another who taught at Clifton College. Both doctors wearing scrubs along with every nurse not on duty. The county judge. The sheriff and a half dozen old cowboys that Emma hadn't had time to check for spurs.

"I can't do this," Emma whispered in the silence. Her words seemed to echo off the walls.

Heath pulled her to the nearest pew. For a moment, he just held her, then he shifted and faced her. "Do you love me, Emma?"

He waited until she looked up at him. "I do. But you don't know me. I can be stubborn. Set in my ways. You've lived a full life. You've been married before. You have a daughter who will probably hate me. She barely spoke to me the one time I saw her. I don't know anything about living on a ranch. I—"

"Stop." The order was low and kind, but an order.

She continued, "And I don't take orders. I have my own mind. I like everything discussed and agreed on."

He laughed. "All right. No more orders. But, Emma, I do know you. I know you have three younger sisters and all three swear they'll never live in Texas. One, Sadie, has been married five times. She only has one son and complains about bringing one more man into this world.

"Your two other sisters take cruises together every spring but never have time to come home to Honey Creek. But they call, always complaining that there are too many foreigners in Europe. Both live in Georgia. You have no living aunts or uncles. The first car you bought was . . ."

Emma giggled. "You do know me, Heath."

He continued, "I know how you handle your nurses—with kindness. If they make a mistake, you call it 'our problem' and help them solve it." Heath put his arm around her. "I know what you like to eat—nothing fried, a salad for lunch with no cucumbers. I know you do laundry on Friday while watching all the *Jeopardy* shows you've taped the week before."

He leaned closer and whispered, "You feel like you got left out on love. You always thought it wouldn't come."

"How do you know—"

"Emma, I've been listening to you for months. I remember your childhood worries. I know what you're afraid of, and one is that you might make a mistake. I think you may have hesitated about every step you've taken in life. It's not just what you told me, it's me watching you all our lives. For once in your life, jump, Emma. I won't let you fall."

Tears were drifting down her cheeks.

"Look at me, Emma."

"An order?"

"No. A request."

When she looked up, he said again, "Do you love me? We can stop this right now if you say no, but if it's yes we're getting married."

Heath took her hand and leaned back. "I'll sit here until you give me an answer. Take all the time you need."

"Would you mind asking the question again, dear?"

"Not at all. I'll ask every day as long as you don't say no." He winked. "Miss Emma, will you go home with me? Will you put up with me? Will you marry me? Will you sleep beside me every night? Will you say yes to giving up waiting to live?"

She closed her fingers around his big, rough hand. "I think I've always loved you, Heath. But a rancher won't be easy to live with. You order people around all day."

The rancher grinned. "Couldn't be much tougher than living with a head nurse."

At that moment, Jackson Landry swung the doors open. "It's time to get this wedding started."

The judge took his place and everyone else stood around the couple. Apparently these witnesses thought they were part of the wedding party.

When the judge ended with "God bless this marriage," all the cowboys and nurses yelled, "Amen!"

Emma turned and told them all to lower the volume. This was a hospital.

Heath didn't say a word. He just leaned down and kissed his bride the way he'd been wanting to kiss her for years.

The crowd all yelled again.

Before Emma could scold them, Heath kissed his bride again as if they were in love for the first time.

As they walked down the aisle, she held tightly to her

husband. Deep inside, she didn't believe one part of this marriage was real. It was just a dream. She'd wake up and go to work and now and then think about what a grand dream she'd had. The only part of this that was real was the fact that she'd always loved Heath. He'd always been quiet and kind.

Part of her knew she'd never belong in his world and he certainly didn't belong in hers.

When she helped him into the wheelchair, he swung his arm around her waist and settled her on his lap. One of the cowboys stepped behind them and began pushing them outside at far too fast a speed.

Heath was laughing, while Emma was letting out little screams.

As soon as they were settled in the backseat of the biggest pickup Emma had ever seen, she spread a blanket over both of them. The day might be cloudy with a promise of rain, but Emma couldn't stop smiling.

After a few moments of silence, Heath said, "I tried to get a limo but they couldn't get one in time. The boys thought of getting one of the buggies fixed all fancy, but we'd get wet."

The day had been like riding an avalanche.

Resting her head on his shoulder, she whispered, "Is this real?"

"It's all real, dear. Jackson made sure of that. My cook even made a wedding cake. I figure that's as real as it gets. If you look around, you'll see a dozen cars following us."

She turned back into the nurse. "Now, don't overdo, Heath. You just got out of the hospital."

"I'll take it easy. Cook's got a light supper waiting, then we'll cut the cake. After that, I'd like to dance a few times with my wife." He grinned. "Then I thought we'd run everyone off and go to bed early."

Emma gazed at him, seeing this one man at different

stages in his life. She didn't know why, but she'd always been drawn to him. The boy too shy to talk. The young man full of dreams. The widower lost in a world he didn't understand. The strong rancher stepping up to help when the town needed him. The wise man he'd aged into. And now, her husband.

She'd loved them all.

Chapter 49

Rusty O'Sullivan watched Dr. Amber Adams walk out of the hospital. He'd never seen her in a dress. For a moment, he just stared. Her hair was combed back, showing off dangling earrings tapping along a beautiful neck. Her full skirt went almost to her knees and he couldn't believe it, but she was wearing boots. Red boots. Cowboy boots.

"Here comes my date," he said out loud to himself. "*My* date."

She opened the passenger side of his pickup before he thought to jump out and open the door.

He wouldn't have cared if she'd walked out in her lab coat, but he was appreciating the view. For a moment, he wished he'd taken her to Dallas and made reservations at some fancy restaurant. Or maybe brought her flowers.

"You clean up mighty good, Mr. O'Sullivan." She leaned over and kissed him lightly on the lips.

Rusty wanted to ask her to go back in the lobby and come

out again. He was doing everything wrong. "I should have walked you out. I should have opened your door. I should have complimented you."

"And what might that compliment be?"

"I'd say you look beautiful. You always do."

"If you think I look good in scrubs, you're either blind or easy to please."

This wasn't going where he wanted it to. He'd been thinking about her all day.

He tried to start over. "I'm not easy to please, Doc, but I'm irresistible and very kissable."

Without giving her time to say anything, he cupped his hand behind her head and pulled her closer.

By the time he finished kissing her, Rusty saw the sparks in her eyes. One kiss and she was speechless.

He kissed her again.

The second time he pulled away she managed to say, "Date's over. Let's go back to the cabin."

"No way. I'm starving. I want to sit in a booth with you with the lights low and talk while we eat, then I want to dance with you. A slow one may be all I'm up to tonight. Then we'll drive around the town square a few times and maybe drive over to Eagle's Peak and watch the stars."

"You're a romantic. How is it that no girl has snatched you up?"

Rusty stared at her for a while and finally said, "I was waiting for you."

An hour later, when they finally walked into the café/ bar, every head turned. More than the fact that Rusty's hair was a mess or that the doc's lips were slightly swollen, what everyone saw were two people who only saw each other.

They ordered meals that they barely picked at and drinks they never finished. They sat in a corner booth with their bodies touching as they whispered. Though atop the table all was proper, below, he never stopped brushing his leg against hers. When a slow song started, he limped slightly as he led her to the center of the tiny dance floor and swayed to the music. Rusty barely noticed that everyone stood back, just stopping to watch them.

The music slowed and she whispered, "Again."

He pulled her closer and they slow-danced to two more songs. Though he knew how to dance, all he wanted to do was hold her. They barely moved to the music.

When they left the café, they drove around and around the square, talking about nothing and everything. She told stories of her childhood and he talked of funny things that happened on the last job. They discovered they both loved books and watching old movies.

By the time they reached Eagle's Peak, neither bothered to look at the stars. He felt half drunk on her nearness. She never stopped touching him and every time she kissed him, they went deeper into passion.

As they drove the winding road back to Honey Creek, both were silent. Words didn't seem to matter. When he pulled beneath the trees, all was in shadows crossing over midnight. It seemed they were both invisible to the world.

For a while they both sat still, holding hands.

Finally, she said, "You should know that this is the best date I've ever had. I went into it as a challenge. Part of me didn't believe you. Part thought you were too broken to care about anyone, not interested, or worse, you were just feeding me a line. But I was wrong." She kissed him lightly and moved a few inches away. "I'm calling this game off. I don't want to play. We can go as slow as you want. I'm not going to rush what's between us."

"I was never playing a game, Amber." He opened the door. "You want to come inside and cuddle?"

"You're a strange man, Rusty O'Sullivan. I've never met a man like you. Why is it so important to take your time?"

"I want to enjoy every step." He held her against his chest for a while and then, more to himself than her, he said, "Because I love you, sweetheart."

Chapter 50

Monday Night

As they stepped into the cabin, Amber just stared at the man before her. His cast still shone in the moonlight. He was still bruised. He limped to the bed and she realized he'd been right.

He was irresistible. As were the low glow in the fireplace, the smell of pine trees, and the whispers of the water twenty feet from the cabin. She felt she was more in a dream than reality.

She tugged her boots off and sat down on the bed beside his good leg. "I can't stay long. I need to be at the hospital by six. Right now, I'd rather cuddle with you than sleep. I don't want our date to end."

"Any chance you'd take that dress off?" he asked as he unbuttoned his shirt.

"You made it pretty clear you weren't planning to make love to me tonight. So, why take it off? It's already wrinkled."

"I'd like to touch your skin. I can't get enough of the feel of you. When you're the doc, you've got this invisible shell around you, but when you're in my arms you're velvet."

"If you want it off, you'll have to take it off."

Even in the shadows she could see him smile. He rolled on his side, almost touching her. Slowly, one button at a time, he undressed her. Beneath the dress was a thin lace camisole he could easily see through and panties made of the same material.

"I must have forgotten my bra," she whispered.

"I noticed that while we were dancing." He gently pushed her back. "Now, relax. Don't move. I want to learn the feel of you."

She closed her eyes as he moved his hand over the silk of her skin as if she was fragile as winter's first snowflake.

He took his time with feather-light touches. Slow, tender, and loving brushes. Now and then he'd slow his hand and lean over to kiss her lightly. Every time he pulled away she couldn't help but make a little sound of protest. He'd laugh and kiss her once more, deeper, longer, then return to moving his hands over every part of her body.

She thought of reminding him that no matter what he did or said now, she would still be leaving in six months. She had goals. Mountains to climb.

But somehow the words didn't come. She could give her speech tomorrow. His hand had moved to her legs and she couldn't interrupt.

An hour later, when she was floating on a calm, loving feeling, half awake and half asleep, he stopped and pulled her gently against him. With his arms around her, against his chest, he drifted into sleep.

Peace, she thought. She'd found total peace in his arms.

Chapter 51

Tuesday Morning

Jackson was thinking he was going to have a nice, normal day for once. Vern was in jail and probably would be for years. Rusty was recovering and becoming a friend, even though he still didn't want anything from old Jamie Ray's estate.

Zach was back in school, making friends. The firemen told him to call as soon as he got out for the day and they'd pick him up. Evidently, one of the firefighters was teaching him karate.

Since Rusty had gone out on the town last night, he'd asked if Zach could stay over one more night. Jackson said he'd make sure the boy got to school. They were eating dinner with Starri at Ona-May's. Rusty was invited, too, but no one had seen him since he left the house yesterday. He claimed he had a date Monday and was strong enough to drive.

Zach and Jackson thought about filing a missing person

report on him, but Rusty called in a little after six to say he was sleeping over at a friend's house.

Jackson leaned back in his chair and decided things were settling. He was even looking forward to rewriting the cat lady's will.

As he looked over to the window with his father's ashtray on the windowsill, Jackson realized he'd thought of the chair in the office as his chair now. His office. His chair. His view of the town square.

He went to the window and looked out. People were moving around. Walking. Driving.

This was his town. He'd become one of the guardians of Honey Creek.

He had a feeling his parents had known that all along. Their son belonged here in this valley.

A noise rattled from the back hallway. Jackson suddenly went on full alert. After what had happened last week, he was always on edge. His mind raced. No one used the back stairs. Only one storage room filled with files was beyond his office. He must have left the office back door open when he'd carried Jamie Ray's files out to take to Rusty.

Jackson looked around. It was early. Miss Heather wasn't in yet. The office back door had been open all night. Anyone could have come up the back staircase and now be hiding in the office.

A thud came from the storage room. Jackson picked up an old umbrella from the hat rack. Slowly, he advanced. What if someone had surprised Miss Heather when she came in early for a change? They might have tied her up, gagged her so she wouldn't interfere with killing the lawyer.

Wait a minute, Jackson almost said out loud. "I'm the only lawyer in the office."

Another thud sounded. He took a step backward and raised the umbrella higher. Flight was an option.

But no, he couldn't run. Miss Heather might be in the

storage closet with someone who wanted to kill him. But the only person Jackson could think of who would want him dead was Vern, and he'd been shipped to the county jail.

Jackson moved forward again, umbrella high.

He was almost to the storage room door when the door handle rattled.

There was no time to jump back and run. The door opened.

Jackson's heart jumped up to his tonsils.

Everything happened at once. Jackson swung his flimsy weapon. Miss Heather screamed. And Wind Culstee raised his hand and caught the umbrella as if it was no more than a string on a balloon.

Jackson froze and stared at one place in this mixed-up scene. Miss Heather's blouse was unbuttoned so low her bra showed.

Jackson felt he was trapped in one of those escape rooms and they forgot to leave the clues. "What's going on?" he asked with more confusion than anger.

"Nothing!" Wind shouted. "Thanks to you, kid."

Finally, Jackson's scared little-boy brain woke up and his adult brain kicked in. "I'm sorry I interrupted. I didn't see a thing. I didn't hear anything. Nothing. Hell, you two weren't in the storage room."

Miss Heather's eyes were closed as she leaned against the big man's chest.

The investigator was staring like he was trying to decide whether to kill Jackson or just knock him into tomorrow.

Jackson jerked the umbrella out of Wind's hand and turned toward the door. "I think I'll go have coffee. Might stay to eat breakfast, or maybe lunch."

He didn't turn around as he reached the front office door. "I'll take the umbrella. You never know, it might rain."

As he stepped over the threshold, Jackson broke into a run. He was halfway to the café before he slowed and looked at the cloudless sky and started laughing. "I love this town."

If anyone on the street thought it strange that the new lawyer was talking to himself and carrying an umbrella, they didn't mention it.

That night at dinner with Starri, Zach, and Ona-May, Jackson told the PG-rated version of what had happened. Everyone laughed and Ona-May said everyone in the valley knew Wind loved Miss Heather but she thought he lived too wild a life for her. So, they just had a closet affair.

An hour later, while Zach tried to explain the difference between *Star Wars* and *Star Trek* to Aunt Ona-May and the old lady tried to explain what Wind and Miss Heather were doing in the storage closet to Zach, Jackson and Starri walked out on the porch.

He put his arm around her shoulders to keep her warm. "It's been a crazy day," he said. "I know I'm too old for you, but just because it's been a wild day, would you mind kissing me just one time?"

She stood on her tiptoes and gave him a polite kiss.

He thanked her, turned away with a smile, and went back inside. For a moment, he remained still as he heard Starri murmuring something.

He leaned closer and pressed his forehead against the doorframe as she made a promise.

"When I plant the strawberries along the lane this spring, we'll do this again, my clueless lawyer. I'll be twenty-one then," she whispered. "And when we kiss, you won't be able to turn away. It's written in the stars. I'm already in your heart, Jackson Landry, you just don't know it yet."

Jackson smiled. He was a young girl's dream. He'd never thought that possible. He knew her fantasy would never happen. She would forget his name and that she'd ever kissed him.

Wouldn't she . . . ?

Chapter 52

Emma watched Heath push his breakfast around on his plate. His color was good and he was gaining weight, but her husband of three days was frowning.

She poured him more orange juice that she doubted he'd drink. One glass was his limit of vitamin C. Emma didn't worry about or push the orange juice as she set a shot glass full of pills in front of him.

He downed them like they were a handful of peanuts and stared at her. "You going in to the hospital today?"

"It's time. We can't stay on a honeymoon forever, but don't you try to do too much. And don't you dare climb on a horse while I'm gone. If you don't take a nap after lunch, at least sit down and watch the news or work at your desk. And no shot of whiskey at five. I told the cook to make you a healthy shake. That is all you need until dinner. And, Heath, don't you—"

"Hold up there, Emma," Heath interrupted. "How come

you get to boss me around but I can't boss you around? I want to be married to you, Emma, not be one of your patients."

She moved closer and smiled that smile that always made him grin. "I promise once you're well, I won't be bossy."

"I have no confidence in that theory."

She picked up the keys to the sky-blue SUV he'd bought her. Four-wheel drive. Equipped with everything he could order. One more way to show his love.

"I'm sorry the hospital is so busy. They are trying to hire someone so I can cut my hours." She started to leave, then stopped right in front of him and folded her arms. "No, that is not right. I'm not sorry. I love you, Heath Allen Rogers, and I want you to live a long, long time. If that means ordering you around, then that's just the way things are between us."

She hated seeing anger in this kind man's eyes.

"I'll make you a deal. I'll boss you around all day and get you well as fast as I can, but at night, you're the boss. We play by your rules at sunset."

Anger disappeared from his eyes. "You mean that? You'd sleep nude, my shy Emma."

"I will." She giggled, loving this game. "But when you're well, we flip. I get to rule the nights every other month. You'll have to wear pajamas. You'll be the boss in the day and I set the boundaries at night."

"You'll have to learn to ride a horse. We'll go for a ride before sunset when we're home. I plan to take you on a date often to show off my beautiful bride. And when I'm in charge of days, we're going to Dallas and I'm buying you a dozen new dresses just to confuse the Methodists on Sundays."

She kissed him lightly on the lips. "That is, if you have enough energy running around the city all day."

"I'm worried about the nights with you in charge. We are

still counting our marriage in hours and you're wanting to try something new. I had no idea you were such a wild woman, my love. What will we do when I run out of ideas?"

She giggled. "I guess we will have to start over."

He pulled her onto his lap. "I see myself taking naps when you're in charge of nights."

She saw his frown change to promises. What had started as an argument now ended as a challenge.

She tugged away. "Follow my rules all day. I should be home before dark." She picked up her bag. "Then you'll take the lead."

As she rushed out, yelling that she loved this man so dearly, she noticed he grabbed his orange juice and downed the glass.

Life with Heath might not last fifty years like newlyweds hoped, but they'd pack as much love in as they could.

Chapter 53

Thursday, 8:30 a.m.

Jackson unlocked his office and stepped in slowly. He was turning into an old man before he was thirty. One surprise two days ago and he was jumpy. Every closed door might be a surprise.

But all was quiet. No thuds from the closet. He moved to his desk.

One more step and he dropped his briefcase. A shadow was sitting in the windowsill. For a blink, Jackson thought his father was back.

Just before he screamed and ran, he recognized the uniform that wasn't a uniform.

A Texas Ranger.

Jackson took a deep breath. "How did you get in here, Ranger Daily? Surprised to see you again so soon."

"I came up the back stairs. Everyone knows your dad always kept that way to the office unlocked."

"I'll change that habit. Thanks for reminding me." Jackson tried to smile. "Want to tell me why you're out here?"

"I thought I'd help you with one of your clients. Wanna pay your dad back for a favor, I guess."

"Which one of my clients?" Jackson thought it probably wasn't the cat lady.

"Jamie Ray Morrell. I heard the two offspring you've found don't want anything to do with his estate. But the captain should know he died."

Jackson moved closer. "You know where one of the two missing sons is?"

"I do, but you got it wrong, Jackson. Captain Andy Delane is a woman. I'm here to tell you to forget about her. If you go looking for her, you may wake up dead. She's deep undercover on a mission. I'll get a message to her, and if she cares about her no-good daddy, she'll contact you." Ranger Daily stood, and vanished out the back door so fast Jackson didn't have time to think of a question.

The ranger disappeared, probably because he didn't want to answer any questions.

Jackson sat down in his office chair and let his forehead slam against the desk a few times. Then he announced to no one, "Another one that isn't in the law books. I should have skipped law school and just started practicing law."

The phone rang, pulling him back to reality. "Hello, Nut House Law Firm."

The sheriff, Pecos Smith, laughed. "You heard already?"

"Heard what?" Jackson picked up his pen. He'd better write everything down since his mind died days ago. Sex in the closet. A girl thinks she's in love with him. A doctor who loves a man who never talks.

Pecos laughed again. "The Pattersons just left for their second honeymoon. I heard they were stopped at the airport for trying to take firearms aboard. I thought, as their lawyer, you'd like to know."

Forehead hit the desk one more time.

Chapter 54

Friday Night

"You've got a call on three, Dr. Adams."

"Can you take a message?"

"Sorry, caller said he'd hold until you pick up."

Amber grabbed the phone, pushed three, and said, "Dr. Adams."

A familiar voice said, "How about a date?"

She smiled. "I don't get off until ten, Rusty. It'll be too late."

"I'll wait for you forever, sweetheart."

Just hearing his voice made her want him next to her. Their night together in the cabin had been paradise. "I'm leaving in six months, Rusty."

"We'll see. Give me six months to change your mind."

She knew she should cut and run from this man, but she couldn't. He'd already stolen her heart.

* * *

Eight hours later Rusty dropped Zach off at Ona-May's cabin at the bend in the road where the pavement turned to dirt. Jackson was already there to pick up Zach to go to the high school football game.

Starri rushed from the barn to wave them goodbye.

When Rusty saw Jackson's eyes as Starri jumped on the porch, Rusty made a diagnosis. The lawyer was falling hard for Starri.

Rusty watched as Jackson and Zach climbed into Jackson's old pickup, and the lawyer turned as if needing one last glance at Starri. Rusty had the same symptoms. The doc didn't fit with him, and Starri lived in a different world than Jackson, but somehow they blended. Perfect harmony.

If a lawyer and a strawberry farmer matched, so might a builder and a doctor.

As Rusty watched his little brother drive away, the sun spread over the scar he'd left when his old Ford Fairlane rolled down the hill. That night he thought he was dying, but it turned out to be the beginning of living.

In the last sparkle of sunshine he saw something strange. Starri must have planted her strawberries inside the earth's scar he'd made, and one bright strawberry shone bright in winter's twilight.

Starri walked up behind Rusty as silent as a breeze.

When he turned and smiled at her, he pointed at the spot of red nestled atop the green leaves.

She whispered as she had when she'd held his head weeks ago when Rusty thought he was dying. "That little plant may be fragile, but it holds green all winter and the one strawberry will die, fall into the dirt you plowed up and, come spring, a new plant will grow from its seeds."

He grinned. "My family is growing too. I've got my little brother to watch over now, and Jackson told me this morning that I've got a sister . . . but no one, not even the Texas Rangers, knows where she is. I've lived half my life thinking I was alone and now my kin are growing as fast as your wild strawberries."

Starri laughed. "I'm so happy for you. And then there's the two of us."

He held her close. "Yes, we're family, too . . . not by blood, but by choice."

Don't miss the next Someday Valley novel from
New York Times bestselling author Jodi Thomas,

THE WILD LAVENDER BOOKSHOP

Chapter 1

Noah Lane O'Brien stepped out of his bookshop into a beautiful dawn on the main street of Honey Creek and began dusting off the tiny tables and chairs for the morning coffee drinkers.

He gazed at the town square lined in huge old elms covered in autumn leaves. The big county courthouse watched over the park set in the center of town. Half a dozen stores faced the square. An ice cream parlor, a used furniture store, a café, a great bakery that sweetened the dawn air, and a flower shop that had accidentally given Noah the idea for the name of his bookshop.

There was a two-pump gas station run by two brothers which never closed. The repair shop next door to Noah was run by a farmer who only worked when he wanted to.

The last fourth of the square was plain. No signs or colorful windows. A young lawyer's office and a life insurance salesman's office squeezed between the fire station and the bank. Three years ago, Noah O'Brien had driven into Honey Creek, Texas, and decided it was Heaven. He'd been pushed by his parents since he came out of the womb. He'd learned to read by the age of five, played every sport offered at school, made straight As, gotten into the best colleges, worked to climb the ladder of success.

He'd played their game until on his thirty-third birthday he shattered, or in his parents' words, went crazy. He packed his car, sold his house, emptied all accounts, quit his IT job, and ran away from his life. Then he drove until he found where he wanted to live.

For three years he'd read every book he found interesting, and sold a few in the shop. He made good coffee for a buck a cup and sold sweets he bought from the bakery a block over.

But his favorite thing he loved to do in this little town was to listen to the locals' conversations. They talked of the family problems they never seemed to resolve, and life goals they'd never work toward, and the life adventures they'd never take.

Most of all, Noah loved the conversations that began with "if only I could . . ."

Every night he'd climb to the roof of his apartment above the bookshop and write the conversations down.

Some days, he'd whisper to himself, what if I write about a town where people actually lived their words?

The question he'd try to figure out would be, "Would they be happy?"

Chapter 2

Ben Griffin locked his repair shop on Main and headed out before his two daughters showed up to take him to lunch. Whenever they wanted money, or needed anything from him, they always fed him.

"Morning, Bear," Noah from the bookshop said as he walked toward his shop entrance with a tray of empty coffee cups. "You headed out for an early lunch?"

Ben growled at the question, but he managed a one-sided smile. "Nope. I've got to go pick up a broken refrigerator. May take a while. I'll try to fix it out at the farm so I won't have to haul it in. If anyone needs me have them leave a note and I'll call them when I can."

"Will do, Bear," Noah said as he turned into the bookshop.

Ben frowned at the young man's back. Someday he'd tell Noah to stop calling him Bear. That had been his nickname when he was a mechanic in the army. Ben figured he'd go back to his rightful name once he mustered out, but somehow Bear stuck.

He growled again. That first year he'd lost his real name and his wife. Oh, she didn't die, she just ran back to Europe and never came back.

Noah O'Brien, who moved in three years ago, was renting both the bookstore and the apartment above from Ben. Nice guy but they had nothing in common. Ben was in his fifties, served eight years in the army then came home, and Noah had run away from home somewhere up north. He might be in his early thirties and talk a bit funny but to Ben he was still wet behind the ears.

Between Ben's farm and the repair shop, he worked every single day, whereas Noah spent his time reading books.

Noah stuck his head out of his doorway. "If anyone asks where you are, what should I tell them, Bear?"

Ben fought down a grin. "I'll be out at Holly Rim."

Noah said what everyone said, "Holly Rim. Don't get lost."

For once Ben had told the truth. He rushed to his pickup. Ben didn't want to talk to anyone. He drove ten miles over the speed limit to get to one of the oldest homesteads in the county.

Deep in the rocky hills that formed the east rim of the valley lay a rugged plot of land that one family had owned since the first settlers came to this part of Texas. A legend was told by the Apache, who traveled through the valley from their winter campsite to their summer hunting grounds. They swore sorrow walked among the uneven paths and thorny holly that grew as tall as trees on the east rim. Rain washed away paths and the winds cut more trails as if to confuse strangers.

Several tried to climb to the rim in the early days, but few did today.

Ben knew the legend well. His people had settled just below the wild land near the ridge. All below Holly Rim was farm land. All that was above was wild. And standing in between the two was one lonely house.

Ben suddenly smiled. One house half a mile from his farm. One house. One woman. Eliza.

His Eliza.

Visit our website at
KensingtonBooks.com
to sign up for our newsletters, read
more from your favorite authors, see
books by series, view reading group
guides, and more!

Become a Part of Our
Between the Chapters Book Club
Community and Join the Conversation

Submit your book review for a chance to win exclusive
Between the Chapters swag you can't get anywhere else!
https://www.kensingtonbooks.com/pages/review/